KEEP ON PADDLING

TRUE ADVENTURES IN THE BOUNDARY WATERS WILDERNESS

ROY CERNY

 www.trafford.com

North America & international
toll-free: 1 888 232 4444 (USA & Canada)
phone: 250 383 6864 ♦ fax: 812 355 4082

CONTENTS

1	BSA	1
2	Greenhorn	5
3	Charlies Mine	9
4	Ten Feet Tall	15
5	The Night Paddle	18
6	Summer Of The Flies	23
7	Yum, Yum, And Eat-Em-Up	26
8	A Boatload Of Fish	29
9	The Day The Dam Burst	32
10	Spotted Dog, Bulgur, Packsack Stew And Other Gormet Delights	35
11	I'm Not Lost . . . Just Confused	39
12	The Loch Agnes Monster	42
13	The Bare	46
14	Minor Miracles	50
15	The Perfect Crew	55
16	The Tough Trip	59
17	Bad Air	63
18	Nutz	68
19	The Island Of Rodentia	72
20	Bugs	76
21	Fishing Is A Blast	80
22	Bullwinkle	85
23	The Cougar	90
24	Canis Lupis	93
25	The Cathedral	96
26	The Bad Choice	100
27	The Leviathan	103
28	Her First Trip	107

29   Overconfident 110
30   The Storm 113
31   Crack Fish 116
32   Ferguson 120
33   The Bear Caper 123
34   The Crash 126
35   Moto-Ski 129
36   Up Wildgoose Creek With A Paddle 135
37   Jasper Lake Ducks 139
38   The Big Fight 143
39   The Mouse That Poured 148
40   Back Aches And The Brown Trout 152
41   Fascinated By Maps 157
42   Kashapiwi 160
43   Lepidoptera 164
44   Fast Cars And Hot Women 167
45   Old Town 171
46   Diamond Willow 175
47   Randy 179
48   Cold, Wet Summer 183
49   The Gigantic Fish 186
50   The Bulgur Brigade 190
51   The Grandkids Great Adventure 194
52   The Second First Trip But Not The Last 198

DEDICATION

I would like to thank all the Northern Tier Canoe Base staff that have served with me over the years and who have served as an audience as I told these stories. Thanks to my wife Midge, my son Matt and all my friends and family who gave me encouragement and constructive criticism as I penned these tales. I want to say how much your contributions have helped me. To those who have gone on to the great beyond, I wish you could share in my joy in seeing my first book in print.

PROLOGUE

Never having written a book before, I have discovered that it is a lot of hard work. You stare at the blank page and wait for the words to come out of your head. Sometimes they spill out so fast that you can't keep up typing them, but at other times you just struggle figuring out how to say it in just the right way. After the words are down you have to read them with the eye of a novice and you realize you need a glossary of terms. Then you need to edit and often reword what you wrote. Spellings and punctuation errors have to be corrected. Then you have others test read the stories and you quiz them to see if they get the same picture you are trying to convey. Then, speaking of pictures you ask yourself . . . should I include some sketches to try to match up to the stories? And what about a title and a cover design? I had a lot of help and encouragement from Midge, my wife, Matt, my son, and from numerous friends that I asked to read and critique what I wrote. I have included names of many friends in my stories to make the tales more personal and I hope I have shown them in a good light and made them smile.

1

BSA

I joined when I was 13. The new Boy Scout Troop 160 was organized at my church and my brother Paul and I, and a number of our friends thought it would be fun. We met every Monday night in the church basement. Our scoutmaster, Claude Gulbranson and his two assistants were new at the scouting game and we all learned together. We went camping nearly every month and took part in all the council camps and activities. Summer camp back then cost 10 dollars for a week at Lake Shetek in Minnesota. Paul and I mowed lawns, shoveled snow and sold doo-dahs door to door. We collected pop bottles and saved from our paper route. That first summer in 1956 was great fun. Paul and I were both second class scouts and our only disappointment was that we didn't get to canoe because we had not yet learned to swim. The next summer we had both learned to swim and we got to go canoeing for the first time. It was like magic. The light craft could go anywhere there were a few inches of water and could be turned on a dime. They could race past the slower rowboats and provided hours of great fun.

Paul and I determined to build our own watercraft. In one of the Boys Life magazines we found the plans for a kayak. Dad had always let us putter around his workshop but this time we took it over for a few weeks as we assembled our craft from scrounged scrap wood and a big piece of canvas we had bought from an upholstery shop. We must have put six coats of paint on the canvas before all the pinholes were sealed. Soon it was finished and ready for a test launch. The kayak was lighter than any canoe mainly because it had no planking . . . only canvas stretched over stringers that were fastened to bulkheads. It was light, fast and fragile. We tested it in several local lakes and the Big Sioux River that ran through our hometown, Sioux Falls South Dakota.

A few years later we built a canoe. Again it was made out of junk wood . . . an old elm plank that we cut up into stringers and a big packing crate that had very thin lumber on its sides. It weighed a ton and after it was fiber-glassed, it weighed even more but it looked cool and it floated. We had great fun with it and took in on many camping trips.

We graduated to a more rugged camp after a few summers. Our Sioux council* had purchased land near Yankton on the Missouri River. Behind Gavin's Point dam the backed up Lewis and Clark Lake had formed a nice inlet. The camp was named Lewis and Clark for the early 1800 explorers that had paddled up it on their way across the continent. It boasted cactus and possibly rattlesnakes. We were constantly looking for new adventures and the next year, 1959, our council was putting together a canoe trip to the boundary waters. The Scout canoe base at Moose Lake*, 22 miles east of Ely, Minnesota, was operated by Region 10 at the time. The base was called the Charles L. Sommers Wilderness Canoe Base*. Our group was a provisional crew* meaning any scouts in our council could sign up for the trip.

My best friend Ordell Steen and I as well as a couple of the dads and several other scouts from our troop and other troops in and around Sioux Falls that met the 14 year old age requirement signed up to go. At that time it cost $32.50 for the 10 day trip. I had to work extra hard to earn that much because I was also signed up to go to bible camp as well as the usual one week stay at the council scout camp. It was a summer that I wasn't home much. Three weeks before the awaited trip I spent a week at bible camp at Lake Shetek. I came home with a bad cut from a swimming accident and had six stitches across the underside arch of my right foot. I couldn't seem to stay off of it and soon had the stitches torn out and developed a bad infection. Dad took me to the doc who told me to stay off it and wrap it with hot wet towels for several days or I was going to lose my foot. I was less worried about my foot than maybe missing my upcoming canoe trip so I followed his advice and soon healed up.

Finally the day came to leave on the trip. We piled into an old Jackrabbit bus that had been hired to take us to Ely and we were off. We were looking forward to the adventure with as much excitement as opening presents on Christmas morning. We camped at the air base in Duluth that night and pulled into Ely the next morning. I was already impressed with the pine trees and all the rock formations that were so different than my native South Dakota prairie. It was as if we were in a foreign land. At Winton 2 miles east of Ely, the road turned to gravel for 20 miles. It got narrower the closer we got to the base. The base had only moved to their leased 25 acre site 15 years previous and was really on the edge of the wilderness. It boasted a brand new dining hall that year. The guides quarters had burned down that summer and the guides had lost most of their personal gear. Jim Thomas was introduced to us as our guide. It was going to be his last trip that summer so he wanted to make it a good one. We planned to travel the western half of Hunters Island* in the Quetico*. Because we had never been on a canoe trip through the base before, we were called grubs* or grubbies. I was appointed to be the camp cook . . . one of two jobs that didn't rotate on the work schedule. My friend Mike Neuroth was chosen to be quartermaster, the only other job that was permanent. The other kids took turns being fireman, washing dishes, and digging the latrines.

We learned in quick lessons how to paddle and what to do if our canoe swamped. We spent several hours packing our food into cloth bags from the bulk food bins. Plastic bags had not yet made an appearance on the camping scene. We packed our kettle packs and rolled up the 25 pound wall tents* that we would be taking on our trip. We had a campfire in the lodge where we watched a movie about the wilderness and listened to more instruction from the guides on camping and fishing. That night we could hardly sleep because of the anticipation.

If canoe tripping was a woman I fell for her at first sight. I loved every minute of it. The portaging was hard but the scenery was breathtaking to me. This was not the dry Dakota prairie. This was God's country.

Our guide was great. Even when the weather was bad he looked at the bright side of everything. As I heard the stories about the miners and the loggers and the early Voyageurs I was sure that this was a special place that I definitely had to come back to. I was in love!

Upon returning home the canoe trip was all I could talk about. I grew up a lot on that first trip both physically and mentally. I went a boy and came back a stronger, well tanned young man. I didn't get to go back to the base until five years later but then I spent five summers guiding scouts just as my guide had done for us. After I got married I worked three more years as maintenance director of the base. Those experiences have had a huge influence on my life and even now many years later, I still take trips to the "Bound"*and revel in every minute I am there. I suspect if I could remember all the friends, family, coworkers, employees, youth groups, grand kids, and church members I have taken into the woods since my guiding days that it might number over 200 people. I hope some of the magic of the woods has rubbed off on them.

2

GREENHORN

I took my first canoe trip in August of 1959. It was a busy summer as I had already spent a week at bible camp and a week at the council scout camp at Lake Shetek, Mn. But the canoe trip was a magical time and I was so taken by the lake country that I hoped some day to return. In the spring of my third year in college I found myself without employment for the upcoming summer. I thought about what I would like to do and remembered fondly the eight day trip I had taken five years previously. I paid a visit to the Sioux Council* Scout office in my hometown of Sioux Falls, South Dakota and asked about working at Sommers Canoe Base* as it was called then. The base was operated by Region 10* of the BSA*. Back then there was not yet a nationally operated high adventure base. There were canoe bases also operated by Region 7 in Wisconsin as well as Region 1 in Maine. The base in Northern Minnesota was the oldest, having been started in 1928 and operated out of Winton, a small town four miles outside of Ely. The base located to its present site in the winter of 1945 after several Finnish log cabin builders constructed the main lodge and the directors' cabin over the winter. The base continued to grow and when I took my first trip in 1959 had just constructed a new dining hall. The other buildings at the base included the Bean Bay Post, a sauna*, and a guides quarters that also served as equipment storage. The whole base was located on

25 acres of land that the base had on a 99 year lease from the forest service. The property abutted the BWCA* and was the last privately owned parcel of land on the Moose Lake road.

The base director, Cliff Hanson, contacted me shortly after I had written my letter expressing interest in employment at the base. He hired me to be a guide on the spot, not because I was especially qualified but because the base was very short staffed for the summer. He told me to report to the base on June 1 for a week of training.

I drove up to the base in my old '50 ford and dutifully reported in. The base was much the same as I remembered it from '59. I was issued equipment to be used for the summer and subjected to a couple days of training. I learned more from talking to other experienced guides than I did from the informal training program. After more of the staff showed up we were broken up into crews and sent out with an experienced guide for our break in guide trip*. I must not have done too well since I didn't get a very good recommendation from Butch Dieslin our crew leader. As I recall he mentioned that he didn't think I was strong enough to portage a canoe. I was hired anyway and within a couple of days after the training trip I was assigned my first crew. They were from LaSalle, Illinois and there were 12 of them . . . 13 counting me. That meant taking five canoes and three tents. Any time the number of crew members is not divisible evenly by three, portaging* becomes more difficult because of the extra canoe that is needed.

We planned a trip that followed the route of my first canoe trip in 1959, at least up to Sturgeon Lake where we would double back Southeast, and return through Kashapiwi Lake. It was a fairly ambitious trip especially for a brand new guide but I didn't know any better. The trip started out OK but I struggled a bit on the portages as I hadn't built up my upper body strength to be able to flip a canoe easily. Soon my skills improved as well as my ability to read a map and compass.

The guide typically does most of the work of setting up camp, fire building and cooking the first couple of days and spends considerable effort in training the scouts how to do everything correctly and safely. As they learn the skills the guide becomes less of a doer and more of an observer and a resource person. When I guided my goal was by trips end the crew wouldn't need me anymore and when the trip was over their confidence level would be high enough for them to come back and take a trip on their own. On this, my very first trip, I was learning along with the scouts. I learned patience and how to answer questions like "How deep is it here?" or "How long is the next portage?" I learned the best ways to show the scouts how to roll the tents and how to keep their gear dry.

When we arrived at the big beach on Sturgeon on the evening of the third day we discovered that we had left one of the tents at the previous campsite. I learned then how important it is to take a last minute check and to make sure that everyone keeps the same gear in their canoe the whole trip. One of the strongest scout paddlers went with me and we headed back to get the missing tent. It would have come out of my pay that back then was only $35 a week. We had battled a terrific headwind going down Sturgeon so I figured the trip back would go fast. It did. But our empty canoe shipped so much water that it swamped before we could get to the far end of the lake. We both got wet but paddled to shore and doggedly dumped the water and continued on. We found our missing tent right in the middle of the campsite where we had left it. We grabbed it and turned around to head back to Sturgeon Lake. We got back to our camp at 1:00 in the morning but I had learned a valuable lesson. I never lost a tent in the next five years of guiding.

The crew had a great time even though I took them across Yum-Yum portage that ranks high on the difficulty scale. It was then that I thought that the guides could sure use a main resource map that we could all mark portages and campsites on for future reference. When I got back to the base that became one of my projects and it was so well received that even outfitters from town came out to use it for reference for trips.

After doing OK on my first trip I went on to take trips to Powell Lake, to the Height of Land Portage, and to Cirrus Lake. I stretched how far crews could go in eight days to the limit. Maybe I was still smarting from my bad recommendation from my first guide trip and felt I had to prove my worth. As I gained experience canoe tripping became just plain fun. It is the only job I have ever had that was such great fun and adventure that I would have paid money to work at the Scout base. I liked it so much that I guided for five years and then when I got married I worked three more years as the maintenance director for the base. I am so thankful that I was given the opportunity to work at so rewarding a job.

3

CHARLIES MINE

Life at the Scout Canoe Base was never boring. Most of the staff members hired each summer worked as guides or as they call them now—interpreters. The summer began with a few days of training interrupted frequently with work projects such as unloading the 25 tons of food it took to operate the base through a summer of scouts. One summer the food semi truck came early in the evening and got stuck on the muddy road up to the dining hall. All the staff had to form a line and unload all the items by hand passing them from person to person, several hundred feet, all the way up the hill to the kitchen. It took several hours and of course it was raining the whole time.

A gentle soul named Henry Bradlich was in charge of work details and projects for the guide staff for several summers. His responsibility was to keep us working and to keep the base in good shape during the hectic summer. We got one day off between trips to do our laundry, write letters and keep our gear and canoes in good shape. If we had more than a day between trips then it was understood that we belonged to Henry.

Some projects bordered on the mundane. Raking the road was a good example. If Henry or others couldn't dream up some good projects, there was always the rutted old gravel road to level out. The base operated on a shoestring budget and had little in the way of equipment so everything was done by hand. Some projects required all hands on deck and the announcement would be made at breakfast or lunch in the dining hall. We had to eat and that was the surest time to have a captive audience. The guide chief might get up and say "right after lunch drop what you are doing and we will all work together to portage all the canoes from the winter storage area down to the waterfront. All 300 of them!" Now that was a project. Or perhaps the maintenance director would announce that "I have just completed five new cabin tent platforms and they need to be moved from the workshop area out to tent city in the woods." Dutifully 25 or 30 guys would trudge out and surround the tent frame and floor and all would grab hold. On the count of three all would lift up the several hundred pound structure and we would march away with it often carrying it several hundred yards to its new designated location in the woods. Getting around the trees took some doing.

During my first summer, the base was installing a state of the art sewer system with piping, a lift station, a big aerator and a settling pond. That gave Henry lots of projects to put us on. We buried pipe under trails when it was too rocky to do it any other way. We had to cut all the trees down where the pond was to be behind the dam. It was tough to run the chain saw out of the canoe as the water was already backing up behind the dam. At least one chain saw went in the drink and got ruined. One especially detestable job was to wash down the aerator that we affectionately labeled "Charlie's Ago-go." Washing it down was supposed to keep the smell of the sewage from becoming overpowering but we never noticed that it made much difference. Studying the nasty water bubbling in the aerator you could often tell what had been served in the dining hall the previous day. We called corn "tracers" because the kernels weren't digestible and showed up in the waste later. Soon the pond developed a layer of green scum called duck weed and it was determined by the powers that be, that it was blocking the sunlight from doing its job on the sewage and needed to be removed. When chemicals were unable to kill it, another means of removal had to be found. We rigged up seines that we dragged between canoes and began harvesting the foul stuff. Soon we had tons of it piled up 6 ft high on one side of the pond. The stuff grew so fast if we cleared the surface of the pond it would be scummed over by the next morning. We made snowballs out of the stuff and had a big fight one afternoon. We were all splattered with the green goo and soon headed for the showers to clean up.

One summer it was determined that as a camp we needed to have a nurse. Most if not all of the staff at that time were guys so having a female staff member sounded pretty appealing. We decided she should have her own cabin and infirmary. We began a marathon session of construction that went on day and night for four days. The completed project wasn't much bigger than a yard shed with a wing on it but it sufficed. By the time the nurse came I was out on the trail and I don't remember ever getting to meet her. If I did her looks must not have made much of an impression.

As the base operation grew in size it was decided that the small parking lot needed to be expanded so gravel was brought in and the swampy end was filled. A number of large trees were cut down but the stumps were in the way. Ron Walls procured some dynamite and caps and we rigged for blasting. The cars were moved back as far as possible and the stumps were buried in old tires. The sticks were set and we all hovered behind the old '49 Ford dump truck as the wires were touched to the battery terminals. The stumps were blasted out in an afternoon but not without landing a few chunks of roots and rocks on cars.

The base went from pumping drinking water directly out of Moose Lake to running it into redwood water tanks for storage. A few years later the tanks were replaced by a railroad tank car set on the highest rock that served as a water tower. Then we began to chlorinate the water. It was my job to change the chlorine tank that summer and I dreaded it because I had almost knocked myself out with a blast of the gas through a leaky fitting. The next summer the base decided to quit pumping out of the lake and instead drill a well to supply the tank. A drilling rig came out and bored through the Ely greenstone for about a week. I don't know why they drilled it behind the dining hall but maybe somebody witched* it there. At 480 ft deep and two dump trucks full of powdered Ely greenstone later, they pulled the drill and dropped in a pump. They got some water but the pump would run it dry after only 10 minutes of pumping. You had to wait for a half hour for the well to fill again. They decided to try to blast the casing open to fracture the rock to increase the flow. The drillers hung 300 lbs of dynamite down the hole and set it off at 7:00 the next morning. It was about a six on the Richter scale and the column of water that shot into the air must have gone up a couple of miles because it rained for about five minutes after the blast. It worked and the base had a water source that was pollution safe.

Another favorite project that Henry put staff to work on over the course of several years, was hand digging a basement under the dining hall. We called it Charlies' Mine. The dining hall was built in 1959 and was constructed on pillars of concrete block to avoid having to excavate or fill for a level floor. One end sat on the ground and the other was airborne about nine feet. It was a ready-made storage area. The high end was walled off and a small concrete floor was poured. As storage area needs increased more soil was dug out and more area was walled off and more concrete floor was poured. Eventually a giant hog-back of bedrock was hit and no more could be dug out. It took the staff about 10 years to dig it all out. Henry was a stickler for making sure no one was ever loafing on his projects and it became a game to see what we could get away with.

One particularly warm and humid day about six of us had volunteered to dig in the mine. We knew where to go to stay cool. We had shovels and a wheelbarrow but also had ideas of lounging around in the cool basement. We posted a watchman to warn us of Henry if he came to check on us and we loafed in the cool basement telling stories about our trips. When our watchman warned us of Henrys immanent approach, we all jumped up and madly began shoveling dirt to each other in a circle and into the wheelbarrow and then out again to the first man in the circle. Henry stuck his head in and saw we were all busy and left us alone for a couple of hours until he noticed that none of the dirt was coming out of the mine. I think he moved us to cleaning the latrines where the results of our work were more evident.

Remodeling the sauna* was another challenging project. The sauna had to be fired up every other day for the incoming crews and the work we planned had to be finished in time for the new arrivals so we had only one day. The sauna was wood fired from outside the building and the guides typically over-fired it so the temperature was hovering near 200 degrees. When the rocks were doused with water it would flash to steam so fast it would make your ears pop with the increase in pressure. After a summer of this the old stovepipe was burnt thin from being heated red-hot so often. We thought it would be neat if we took a sauna while we worked. So we fired up the stove and stripped down to wearing only nail aprons and began working putting up new wall panels. As we multitasked we had all worked up a good sweat in the 180 degree heat. With all the hammering we were doing on the walls, the old stovepipes finally gave up the ghost and came apart, filling the sauna with smoke as they fell in ruin to the floor. We had to flee the premises wearing only our nail aprons and douse the fire from the outside so the building wouldn't burn down. Eventually we completed the project but had enough sense not to fire it up again while we worked.

One summer it was decided to varnish the outsides of all the buildings. Back then all exterior surfaces got a coat of what we called log cabin syrup every four or five years. It had been long overdue so the varnish was ordered in a couple big 50 gallon barrels that had spigots on them. Pails were rounded up and brushes were passed out and for two months the priority project was refinishing the exteriors of all the buildings. Wasp and hornet nests and hanging bats all had to be removed for us to do our work. Ladders were in short supply so work was not always done safely. One guide put his short ladder on top of a barrel to extend its reach. When everything tipped over and the varnish bucket dumped its load in his hair, beard and down in his boots he was a sorry sight. He looked even sorrier later when he had to shave his beard and his hair to get the varnish off.

After coming off the trail one summer, I noticed a big pile of gravel behind the lodge and I knew another project was a foot. Sure enough, a crew was formed and we were ordered to move the 20 yard load of gravel 100 yards down the hill to the waterfront because a new canoe landing was to be built. We looked at the two sorry wheelbarrows they gave us and decided there must be a better way. We took my 49 Willys CJ2A jeep and fashioned a wood box behind the seats. With a little modification of the trail we thought the jeep could serve as a powered wheelbarrow. The brakes were not the greatest and one turn involved backing down a part of the trail. It was a bit scary especially when the front end came off the ground when I tried to back down the slope. A bunch of the guides jumped on the hood to keep the jeep upright and after many loads we managed to move all that gravel down the hill in one afternoon. Necessity is the mother of invention.

In spite of all the mundane tasks and seemingly idiotic projects I would not trade my experiences working with the staff at the base for anything. We built character and made friendships that have lasted a lifetime. And yes, we accomplished a lot to be proud of.

4

TEN FEET TALL

It was early June in the summer of 1967 when we were undergoing our guide training week at the Sommers Canoe Base*. We had all braved the cold water and practiced swamping* our canoes in the lake and paddling them back in. We had been issued our kettle pack* gear and each of us had put the finishing touches on the logos on our paddles and fixed up our Selega* canoes with fresh paint and varnish and in some cases fiberglass patches. The older more experienced guides enjoyed sharing tales of the past summers canoe trips with the newest guides just hired that summer. Sharing experiences was important in the learning process. The highlight of training week was the guide trip*.

The 60 or so guides hired each year would be divided up into groups of 6-10 with an older experienced guide appointed as the leader. The groups all tried to outdo each other in the length and difficulty of the training trips that would go out for 5 days after the initial training week. The trips were like an intensive boot camp for guides. The camaraderie developed during the trips was unlike anything you could imagine. The guides taught each other by example and sometimes you had to place a lot of trust in your fellow guides to get you out of a tough or dangerous spot. The trips were intensive in physical and mental training that the staff would need to handle the scout groups that would soon be coming to the base to start their canoe trips. The base put over 3000 scouts on the trail each summer and the guide was responsible to make each crews' trip as memorable as possible. The guides had to show the scouts how to cook, navigate, paddle, and stay safe. They had to share stories about the voyageurs, the Indians, the loggers, the explorers that all had an impact on the area. They had to show them how to fish, how to recognize plants and animals in the area, and how to take care of themselves in the woods. They taught them how to be courteous to others and to leave no trace of their presence in the woods.

Each guide would develop his own persona. The guides grew beards and let their hair grow long so they would look like mountain men. It was a time of butches, buzz cuts and flat tops so the guides did indeed stand out in a crowd. The outfits the guides wore on the trail were as individual as their personalities. Some wore cutoffs, some wore lederhosen*, others dressed as voyageurs* complete with knitted hats and colorful sashes. One guide wore a tuxedo and a top hat and insisted on being called the Bourgeois*. I wore a leather fringed deer hide war shirt decorated with rattlesnake rattles and leather breeches. Hats and headbands came in every style and color. We each were memorable in our own way. We were colorful, brash, and each of us enjoyed immensely the role we played.

I took my first canoe trip when I was 16 in 1959 and I still remember Jim Thomas who was my guide. He was everything I described above and more. He was big and tall and wore a black Stetson. He could carry a pack and a canoe and never rested on portages. He could cook up a seven-course supper in the rain standing in front of the fire in his underwear singing joyfully some silly ballad. He could find his way with only a compass and map through fog so thick you couldn't even see the bowman in your canoe a few feet away. He knew how to tie the canoes together to make a catamaran* and to rig a sail out of the dining fly so we could sail 20 miles up Lake Agnes running before the wind in only two hours. He knew where the fish were and what to use to catch them and showed us how to fillet them. He showed us moose* tracks and deer droppings and pointed out the nesting bald eagles and the heron rookeries*. He could do no wrong in our eyes. He was TEN

FEET TALL! Yes, I'll never forget him. He took me on the trail as a boy but brought me back a man.

Sigurd Olson* spoke to our group of guides in mid June when we had all returned from our guide training trips. He was old and frail and trembled badly from Parkinsons disease, but he used the words "ten feet tall" to describe how we were regarded by the scouts we served. I never have forgotten what he said. I can name only a few of the hundreds of scouts that I have introduced into the boundary waters over the years, but I know they all remember me. I hope I was ten feet tall in their eyes and lived up to their expectations. I am thankful that I had the opportunity to turn them into men.

5

THE NIGHT PADDLE

I was 21 years old and working as a guide for Sommer's* Boy Scout Canoe Base out of Moose Lake*. This Boy Scout base is still in operation but is now called Northern Tier High Adventure Base*. Each summer over 3000 boy scouts are introduced to the BWCAW (Boundary Waters Canoe Area Wilderness) on the U.S. side and Quetico* wilderness on the Canadian side, by the dedicated personnel of this unique camp.

Each of us that worked at the canoe base developed our own mountain man or voyageur* persona. I wore my blond sun bleached hair quite long and had a goatee and big handlebar mustache. I wore a deerskin shirt adorned with rattlesnake rattles and a pair of leather breeches. I had a homemade knife with a deer antler handle on my belt. Some of the staff thought I looked like General Custer. It was fun to be in character for the scouts who held you in awe.

Crews of scouts came to the base from every state in the nation and usually arrived with limited canoeing skills and little expertise in how to camp and travel in this unique environment.

On this particular adventure, I had a crew from Texas who had never been to a place like the Boundary Waters.

The wind had started to come up, and we battled a nasty chop paddling our way north through Moose, Newfound and Sucker Lakes. Two hours later, we reached the Canadian customs and ranger station* at Prairie Portage*. At the rangers station the scouts were issued their fishing licenses and were eager to paddle on into Canada. This was the first time for most of them to set foot or paddle into a foreign country. After going through customs, we embarked out into Bayley Bay of Basswood Lake. First I had the crew put on their life jackets as the rollers* coming in from the north were up to three-feet high, even though the wind was only moderate. Eight miles of open water let the wind build the waves up to a pretty good height. The shallow bay turned the whitecaps into tsunami-like waves as they rolled in from the big lake.

The scouts were sorely tested as making forward progress in the big waves became exhausting hard work. After 45 minutes of riding bucking canoes with much frantic bailing of splashed-in water, the crew found quieter water near the far shore where we portaged two smaller lakes named Burke and Sunday. There we sought shelter from the increasing wind along the protected north shoreline.

Next we came to the three-quarter mile long rocky portage* into Meadows Lake. It was a bit tough for the green crew, but they made it in fine shape. The paddle through Meadows Lake is a mere 200 yards before you have to face another three-quarter mile portage into Canadian Lake Agnes. The scouts, though tired, made the rocky hike, and soon assembled at the far end of the portage trail in the late afternoon. The view looking north up the long, narrow lake showed huge whitecaps as far as the eye could see.

I had suspected we were going to have a rough time paddling due north up lake Agnes because of the wind funneling down the lake, and I was right. Canadian Agnes is nearly 20 miles long, and it lay parallel to the wind. The waves hitting us in the face at the end of the portage were immense; it was apparent we were going nowhere . . . We were wind-bound.

Our intent had been to camp a good distance up Agnes that night but instead we were stuck at the end of the last Meadows portage facing impossible traveling conditions. Our only option was to hole up for the rest of the afternoon and hope the wind would abate in the early evening. There was no campsite at the end of the portage so we still needed to travel a ways up the lake to find a spot or else roll our sleeping bags out on the trail for the night. There was no room for tents. I told the crew members to find a comfy spot in the moss back in the woods, out of the wind, and take a nap. The scout who was serving as cook, the advisor, and I started a small fire, put the coffee pot on and began cooking an early supper.

I hugged my warm mug of coffee trying to absorb its heat to ward off the chill. I snuggled up to the base of a large birch tree next to the adult crew advisor and related stories about other trips I'd led that had gotten into trouble with the wind or had other problems.

There was the time on Lac La Croix when the wind was so strong it had blown my map case out of the canoe, and because we were broadside to the waves, it was too dangerous to try to recover it. We were forced to wait out the gale and paddle across Lac La Croix and Crooked Lakes late into the night, negotiating a path through dozens of islands in the dark. Because the night was overcast with clouds we had no moon or stars to guide us. Finding our way had been a real challenge. We'd felt a little like Navy Seals sneaking between battleships as the dark hulks of islands passed by on either side. We took the Bottle Portage in the dark, holding flashlights in one hand to help guide the way across the portage. Later, back on the water again, we scraped a few rocks and collided with a low spit of an island as we'd gingerly threaded our canoes through the difficult passage in the inky blackness. We had finally called a halt to progress in the wee hours of the morning on a point campsite in Thursday bay of Crooked Lake.

On another trip in the northeast corner of the Quetico*, our planned route into the upper part of the Wawiag River passed through an area a tornado had ravaged. We were unable to find the portage trail, so our path through the tangled downed trees took nearly eight hours and we got seriously behind schedule. When we finally reached the river the next day, it was mid-afternoon and the crew opted to keep going to try reaching Kawnipi Lake to set up camp.

Night paddling a river has its own set of challenges: you won't get lost but the river can seem never-ending with all its bends and wiggles. We crashed into a couple of sandbars and islets as we doggedly kept on paddling that dark, cloudy night. Then we ran headlong into a gigantic 100-foot white pine that had fallen across the river, totally blocking progress. Following the light from our flashlights we pulled over the trunk and debris-laden branches and kept on going. We called a halt at the seven-foot waterfall a few miles from the mouth of the river and rolled out our sleeping bags right on the portage trail at about 1:00 in the morning. At dawn we were awakened by a moose walking right through our scattered sleeping bangs and down the trail, deftly avoiding stepping on any of us.

"We won't run into anything like these difficulties when we take off up the lake" I said encouragingly to the adult leader as I slugged down the last of my coffee and stirred the pot of stew. An hour or so later we interrupted the snoring crew with "Time to eat!" Everyone was stiff, sore and a bit cranky from the hard paddling earlier, but the warm supper helped the boys feel better. I explained we would "night paddle" after dark when the wind almost always dies down. Already the giant whitecaps had diminished in size, and the wind of the day was abating.

"How can we do that? We can't see nuthin' and we'll get lost" the boys questioned.

"I've been up this lake enough times that I don't even need the map; besides it will be a great adventure . . . you'll see," I assured them. Gradually the wind died down and by 9:00 PM it became dead calm.

"We're off," I said, and we loaded the canoes, extinguished our fire and set out paddling north.

Night paddling is an adventure in itself as the darkness, the quiet, and the calm air, fine tunes the other senses to cope with the lack of vision. Map reading becomes an interpretation of the hills on the distant tree line faintly outlined against the stars. The night sky offers a panorama of sights not seen while one is asleep in the tent. Sounds of owls catching prey and of wolves howling in the distance are the things of memory—often missed when turning in early for bed.

The scouts had come to the wilderness from a large city bathed in lights at night, and they were awestruck by how dark it was and by the myriad of stars they could see. The Milky Way with its hazy band spanning across the night sky was clearly visible. Occasionally a meteor fell, leaving a streaking trail of dying sparks. The scouts were awestruck into silence as they beheld the sights, some really seeing the stars for the first time. The crew paddled their canoes behind my canoe like little ducklings following a hen mallard, and the small wakes of the canoes angled off toward the shores a mile distant on each side.

We paddled slowly and quietly each lost in our thoughts. We needed to take in the wonder of the moment as the starlight flickered on the fading wakes. The lake had become smooth as glass; so calm the stars were clearly reflected in the water. I could see the upside down big dipper and the North Star in the black glassy mirrored surface ahead of us. Acquiring their night vision over time, the scouts were surprised by how well they could see in the starlight that night. The horizon and tree lines were clearly visible against the night sky.

A couple of hours and six or seven miles up the lake, as midnight approached, a magical eerie greenish glow slowly appeared in the black northern sky. The Aurora Borealis*, or northern lights, began to put on a show. Coming from Texas, none of the scouts had ever seen this north-country phenomenon. They stared, mouths agape and eyes wide, as the display began. We called a halt to paddling for a time as the lights danced in curtains of pinks and pale greens and beams of white with rippling, waving wisps of color covering the whole northern vista ahead of us.

It was so bright we could read our watches! The amazing display captivated its audience, and all thoughts of paddling vanished as the awestruck crew gaped at this Technicolor panorama that nature had to offer. Only after several hours did we move on, to find a place to camp in the dark, that magical night. I dare say each scout would recall and retell the story of that magic night paddle for the rest of their lives.

6

SUMMER OF THE FLIES

Gypsy moths are an insect plague that attacks birch and poplar forests on a cyclical basis. It's the caterpillars that do the damage. At the beginning of one particular canoeing season, it became apparent that this was going to be a bad year for them. They were everywhere. Their caterpillars would drop into your coffee in the morning. They would crawl into your hair and into your sleeping bags. Their squashed bodies would stain your clothes. The Fernberg road*, out to the canoe base from Ely, had so many caterpillars on the road surface it became greasy with their squashed bodies. I think the highway department must have at least considered sanding the roadway to prevent car accidents. The worms denuded the hardwood forest of its leaves. On hot days the trees no longer provided shade as their greenery was eaten up. You could almost hear the ugly green worms chewing on the leaves and bits of greenery floated down like snowflakes beneath badly infested trees. Crossing portages made one think of October after the leaves had fallen and the trunks and branches of trees stood naked in the sun. In spite of the worms the trees seldom died from outbreaks of the worms. I am sure their growth must have been stunted and the tree growth rings would probably attest to those years of bad infestations.

I don't believe scientists have ever come up with a good way to control the moth infestations but they keep trying. As this was an especially bad year for the moths on the Quetico* side of the BWCAW*, the Canadians thought they would try desperate measures to control the pests. They had discovered a fly that laid its eggs on the backs of the caterpillars and as the eggs hatched the fly larvae burrowed in making a meal of the worms and killed them. They opined that this would then kill off all the caterpillars and thus eliminate the infestation without having to resort to environmentally unfriendly chemicals to reduce the numbers. Aha . . . a natural predator to take care of the problem.

In their wisdom they captured and raised millions of the flies which they then released over the park by airplane drops. As they had anticipated, the flies had the desired effect on the moth larvae population and the plague of the gypsy moths began to subside.

But alas, when man tinkers with nature sometimes the results are not exactly what were expected. Yes, the worms were dying but the fly larvae were now hatching. The millions of flies released laid billions of eggs, which now became billions more flies who in turn laid trillions of eggs and the fly population increased logarithmically by the day. The scientists didn't do the math.

Canoeing that summer required the addition of another piece of equipment . . . the flyswatter. Every guide had one dangling from his belt. It wasn't that the flies sucked blood or bit you. They didn't do anything. But their sheer numbers would nearly drive you nuts. Now we had flies in our coffee in the morning and fly stains on our clothes. They would buzz around your head like a cloud of hungry mosquitoes not requiring anything of you but to be noticed. If you caught a fish and wanted to fillet it you had to assign one scout to fan away the flies so you could see what you were doing. They landed in your food when you ate and were in your face all the time. Conversation and story telling became an exercise of getting words out without opening your mouth. Ventriloquism became popular because an open mouth was an inviting landing site for the pesky buggers.

They were a pestilence bordering on one of the 10 Old Testament plagues the Lord let loose on the Egyptians. There could be no moments of quiet contemplation in the woods or on the lakeshore because of the constant drone of the flies. Camping wasn't as much fun any more and even the Canadians were surprised by the problems they had caused by trying to help nature out.

An enterprising guide friend of mine, tired of the cloud of flies constantly buzzing around his head, took the time to capture several large dragonflies. He knew flies and mosquitoes were their favorite food. He tied two foot long threads to them and pinned the other end to his felt hat, figuring that since they liked flies that they would eat the cloud of them surrounding his head and soon he would be free of their drone. Success was fleeting however, as the dragonflies soon sated their appetites and a horde of additional flies soon replaced those that were eaten. It was found that insect repellents kept them from landing on you but the incessant droning never went away.

Soon however the scientists in their wisdom figured out a way to solve the problem they had created. They again flew over the park releasing yet more flies. But this time it was only female flies and they had been sterilized. As the male flies made whoopee, nothing happened, and as the fly lifespan is gratefully short, soon the fly population subsided and all the plagues disappeared. The guides and campers were able to retire their swatters and again pick up their fishing poles and enjoy the woods once again.

7

YUM, YUM, AND EAT-EM-UP

This story is not about food. As a person travels the myriads of lakes and streams in the boundary waters wilderness certain places acquire a reputation of their own. There are many places that the mere mention of their name brings back memories and can elicit stories enjoyable to hear. Some places have a special name that relates to the difficulty of getting there.

One such spot is called Eat-em-up portage*. It is a shortcut portage that cuts off several miles of river paddling and goes between Tanner Lake and the Darky River. In the year 2000, John Oosterhuis, a "Charlie guide*" friend and I decided to take a 12-day canoe trip with my son Matt and several of his friends. The purpose of the trip was to show him parts of the Quetico* Park that we remembered when we were guiding canoe trips years ago. Wanting the trip to be memorable for him the route we planned was to circle Hunters Island*, which is basically the entire perimeter of Quetico Provincial Park. The trip was a long one encompassing at least 175 miles and 56 portages. Eight of us hardy voyageurs* started the trip in high spirits. As each day would go by we would climb into our sleeping bags at night remembering the adventures of the day and all the beautiful lakes and country that we had seen.

Several days into our trip we paddled down the Maligne River into Tanner Lake. Looking over the maps at lunch break we noticed that we could save several miles of paddling if we would take the portage between Tanner Lake and the Darky River. On one of the maps the portage was labeled Eat-em-up. I don't know who the soul was who attached that name to the portage but he was right. The portage doesn't have any killer hills in it but it does eat up your strength. It is very long and very swampy. Several yards into the portage I moaned to myself "I remember this one now!" Sometimes a persons mind tries to forget the tough parts of a trip and remembers the good times. I had conveniently erased memories of this bad portage from my mind but as we began the trek they came flooding back.

The portage began in a cedar swamp with lots of tree roots to trip you up. It was actually drier than it had been the last time I had taken it over 30 years before. At that time we had to slosh through knee-deep loon* s##t(mud in the bogs) that clung to your clothes and was full of leeches. Half way into the nearly mile long trek there is a real swamp. It has logs laid across it to keep you from sinking in. Because they are very slippery I opted to skirt the edge of the trail and hopped from grass clump to clump and managed to make it through without many problems. Several of the others were not so lucky. Dave, carrying a heavy food pack stuck to the worn trail, slipped off the log and went in the muck nearly to his waist. He had to be helped out of his heavy pack and pulled from the mud. Jay, carrying a canoe, sank so deep he lost his boot for a time until groping in the mud two feet down located it. We all had a good laugh about the portage when we got to the other end with all our gear intact but it didn't seem like much fun at the time. But that is what stories are made of . . . overcoming hardships.

Another portage that is even tougher is yum yum. It is a 270 rod* (three-quarter mile) trek between Yum Yum and Kashapiwi Lakes. It is one of several routes into this popular trout* fishing lake but a route usually avoided by knowledgeable campers. There are a number of much easier routes to get into Kashapiwi Lake. The portage starts out gently rising up a rocky trail but the rise becomes steeper and then turns into a series of 18-24 inch high stair steps as the trail begins to ascend a series of rock ledges. A two-foot high step is doable without a load on your back but carrying a 90 pound food pack or a 75 pound canoe is pretty tough for anyone not in top notch shape. I lacked the strength in my legs to step that high anymore with a load on my back so I resorted to putting a knee up on each ledge and then standing back up only to face the next ledge. After negotiating this giant staircase, one faces a slippery rock slope that is nearly impossible to walk on if it is wet. At the top where you would hope to be able to rest your canoe, is a single boulder the size of a small house. It is too tall to rest the bow of your canoe on it so you have to just continue climbing on your aching legs. At this point you have climbed at least 150 feet above the level of Yum Yum Lake and the trail starts to go down hill . . . right into a swamp. The trail follows the base of a rock cliff abutting the swamp so there is no way around. The swamp path is marked with a bunch of slippery logs to walk on. Soon the trail leads out of the swamp.

After the last rise the path rapidly descends. One spot is so steep I sat down and let myself slide, pulling down on the bow of the canoe to put it in the dirt in a vain attempt to use it to stop me like a brake. The lake comes into view finally but it is still far down the hill. The landing is bad with many trees and big boulders blocking the path. If your canoe is wide you may have to tip it up on one shoulder to be able to thread between the trees on the narrow path. Only the great trout fishing on Kashapiwi makes this tough portage worth taking. If you have been over it you have something to brag about.

Another portage that is easy but incredibly long is Horse Portage at a mile and a quarter in length. It is quite flat and is an easy walk but I had a bad experience with a bear there once. (see the story Nutz") This portage has a lot of historical importance and follows the USA and Canadian border and bypasses several falls and rapids. It has been in use for hundreds of years by Voyageurs and Indians as well as loggers and modern day campers. You will work up a good sweat by the time you get to the end of this one.

Some campers dread portages but I look at them as a break from the tedium of paddling. It is a time to stretch your muscles and get the kinks out of your back. It is an opportunity to see some things not visible from the lake or river. If you are quiet it is a chance to see Moose, deer and other wildlife. Enjoy them when they come along and plan a little extra time for the hard ones.

8

A BOATLOAD OF FISH

The crew was struggling through the portage* from Bit Lake to Bell Lake. We had made decent time as this was only our second day of traveling out from the Scout base on Moose Lake*. The portage trail wasn't especially long but it was a rough walk. Doc, the adult advisor on this trip was the bowman in my canoe and he and I had already made it across the trail. We had already loaded our canoe and had pushed out a few feet into the small bay to make room for the boys and the other canoes that were following us. We were lounging in our canoe taking a short nap in the warm late afternoon sun. The sun angled into the bay illuminating the water and had made us a bit sleepy. We were intending to go on a bit further that day with Silver Falls as our ultimate destination. As we lay back against the gear piled into our canoe I glanced to my left at the shallow sunlit water and saw several long dark shapes that immediately caught my eye. "Wow, look at those northerns*!" I exclaimed as the advisor quickly sat up and looked where I was pointing. We both had the same thought simultaneously and we frantically tore into our personal packs looking for our tackle and fishing reels that we packed in a sock for protection. We untied our rods from under the thwarts*. He was quicker than I getting his gear assembled and put on a blaze orange flatfish*. "He ought to be able to see this" he said as he cast the outlandishly colored lure at the biggest fish.

Normally fishing in the border lakes involves casting or trolling from a canoe but it is rare treat to be able to see the fish before he strikes. The lure landed about two feet in front of the nose of a big three foot northern sunning itself just beneath the surface. "Come on, take it!" he urged the fish as he coaxed the lure into its characteristic wobble. The northern opened one sleepy eye and began to follow the lure but then within a few feet dove down and disappeared. "Shoot!" he exclaimed as he continued to reel in slowly. Suddenly water shot upwards as the lure was head butted five feet into the air as the big fish exploded from the surface and tail danced trying to snap at the flatfish. The cart-wheeling lure was badly tangled with the line as it fell back into the lake. The monster had missed its prey. "Oh no" Doc said as he frantically cranked the lure back in so it could be untangled. The northern didn't care that the lure wasn't working right and hit it again as it did the crappie flop on the surface, again clearing the water but this time his big mouth had engulfed Doc's lure and he was well hooked.

The crew, just now arriving at the end of the portage, was treated to the sight of our canoe motoring around the small bay just like in the movie "Grumpier Old Men". The northern was towing us around like a tugboat pulling an ocean liner and the advisor was yelling out orders "We're camping here tonight . . . grab your fishing gear!" The tired boys were spurred into action and glad to oblige Doc's orders, scrambled to assemble their poles and reels.

The crew was from Minnesota but most of the boys were inexperienced and didn't know how to fish for northerns, so after the advisor had landed his lunker, he and I paddled around dispensing advice on what lures to use and how to land the fish that they were already pulling in. We passed out band-aids to those who had painfully discovered that northerns have sharp teeth.

We must have been at the right place, at the right time, with the right lures. The fish bit at anything that moved and acted like they were starving. As we trolled around the small lake I spotted an empty campsite and threw out our packs in plain site to claim it. The other canoes full of scouts came by and also unloaded their gear, but all went back to fishing. I have never seen fish striking this consistently in any lake but on subsequent trips back to Bell Lake have never had the fantastic luck that we had that evening.

We reluctantly quit fishing at dark, which came at nearly ten o'clock in late June and headed into our campsite. We put up the tents by flashlight and quickly got a fire going and organized the kitchen area and put up the dining fly. I had the boys haul up a canoe and prop it on logs for a table to clean the fish on. "What's for supper?" the inevitable question was asked. I answered, "Fish of course." I directed the scouts to bring all their fish up to the overturned canoe and lay them out over the keel. There is something to be said about catch and release but the boys were so proud of the fish they had caught few had been thrown back. We had so many fish I threw back any that were alive knowing it would not be possible to eat them all before they spoiled. There were groans of dismay when a number of three footers were released. Even so, the entire length of the 17-foot canoe was covered in fish laid over the keel crosswise. There must have been over 200 pounds of fish! 10 or 12 of them went over 15 pounds. None of the boys knew how to fillet so I gave them a quick class in "cleaning fish: 101." Even with them all helping it took about an hour to clean them all. We made a fish dip out of flour and cornmeal with the appropriate spices and heated up the shortening in the fry pan. The boys ate the fillets as fast as we could fry them at first. Soon the shortening was all gone so we began using our butter. Then we even fried up bacon to get more grease and set up the reflector oven and began baking fish as well. As the eating slowed the fried fillets piled up, filling a couple two-gallon pails to the brim. The scouts were stuffed and could eat no more. At about one in the morning our fish-eating orgy was over and the scouts turned into bed. The whole cooking process had drained our supplies and it had been like 'the miracle of the loaves and fishes' as the fillets just seemed to keep multiplying.

In the morning when the boys asked the inevitable question "What's for breakfast?" I smiled and said, "Fish of course." I said it again at lunch and again at supper before all the fish were eaten up. I refused to waste food. The rest of the trip the scouts eagerly practiced the concept of catch and release.

9

THE DAY
THE DAM BURST

It was a high water summer in the border lakes region. The winter had been moderately snow free until mid-January and then it had cut loose. I was teaching school at Mountain Iron, Minnesota located in the heart of the iron range cities which made it about an hour and a half drive from the Boy Scout Base. The snow just kept on coming down every few days. By late February we had 60 inches on the ground. Every time the snow would settle a bit, another storm would move in and dump another few inches of the white stuff. The snow depth held for most of March and then the melt came quickly in the spring causing all the lakes and streams to be extra high.

Since I had been guiding for several years by then, Sandy Bridges, the base director, enlisted my help in assessing the danger areas caused by the high water. He made travel off limits on the falls chain and in several other possibly dangerous areas of the park until I could take a look at them on my first couple trips of the season and report back to him about the treacherous areas. Sandy had me route my first couple crew trips close to the falls and rapids so I could see if they could be safely negotiated. The high water was amazing. Some of the Indian petro glyphs* were under water. On the USA side of the border many portages were flooded out with the portage signs underwater. Some portages didn't need to be taken because the flood had connected the lakes. Other spots developed very dangerous rapids as flooded lakes tried to drain. At Kawanipi Forks the flooded lake made reading the map difficult as the whole shape of the lake changed. The 15 foot high cliffs at the gorge where the lake drained out were only sticking out of the water a few feet and the few riffles that were normally there had become a huge V several hundred feet long with 30 foot wide whirlpools six feet deep on each side that could easily swallow a canoe. Rebecca Falls was inaccessible from above or below because of the current and the huge standing waves.

Even at the scout base the high water was apparent. The multi level loading dock we had built the year before was all under water. Canoe launching became a bit difficult. The Moose Lake* chain, including Newfound and Sucker lakes are all interconnected and held at artificially high levels by the old logging dam at Prairie Portage* on the Canadian border. The 60 year old wooden coffer dam* had been erected during the logging era at the turn of the century. It was meant to facilitate the moving of rafts of logs between the lakes so they could be accumulated and loaded at the railhead that connected to Basswood Lake. After the logging was done around 1900, the abandoned dam was left and what used to be swamp at the south end of Moose Lake became a shallow bay. In time, numerous outfitting businesses and resorts had sprung up on the south end of the lake and they ran a thriving canoe outfitting and towing business. All of those businesses were very dependant on the dam keeping the lake high enough so the canoe parties and tow boats could start their trips.

The dam at Prairie Portage held back 12 to 15 feet of water depth. It was built of wood but all those years of being submerged had weakened its structure. Now the dam was asked to hold back its normal height of water plus the extra three or four feet of depth from the big spring melt. Normally just a trickle of water a few inches deep spilled over the top of the dam but now a torrent raged over the top several feet deep.

Late one night early in the summer the scout base received a radio-phone call from the rangers at Prairie Portage requesting help and equipment because they feared that the old dam was going to collapse. A number of the staff members and guides that were in camp grabbed cables, chains, come-a-longs and other equipment and hopped in several motor boats and canoes and set out on the six mile trip to Prairie Portage to help the beleaguered rangers. The work was dangerous, as cables and chains were strung and attached to large trees on shore to try to anchor the failing dam. All valiant efforts to save the aging structure were in vain and during the night the dam burst. I don't know how much water blew through to Basswood Lake but it scoured a new 200 foot wide channel down to bedrock for the normally small, ten foot wide creek and made a large floating island out in Bailey bay with all the trees and underbrush that was uprooted. Overnight Moose Lake dropped about 12 feet and Basswood Lake rose about two feet. Basswood is a huge lake and is said to have over 1000 miles of shoreline.

Moose, Newfound, and Sucker Lakes became separate lakes once again as they had been back in 1900. Now scouts had to take two portages before they could get to Prairie Portage. The flooded launching dock at the base now had a 30-foot beach below it before you got to the lake. All kinds of fishing lures, boat anchors and other lost objects showed up on the exposed bottom. It was a strange site especially at the shallow end of Moose Lake where all the outfitters were. Boat launch docks were hundreds of feet from the new lakeshore and much of the big shallow bay had become a mudflat. Resorts and outfitting posts were left high and dry. Business dropped drastically and outfitters had to quickly reschedule and reorganize trips to use other entry points into the BWCAW* for outgoing canoe campers. The forest service quickly built a temporary earthen dike at the north end of the lake to try to bring up the level of Moose Lake but it would take months for the creeks running into Moose to replace the lost water.

Quickly a new concrete dam was proposed for Prairie Portage and work began. Completed quickly, water began backing up behind it and by the following summer it was as if nothing had happened. I will never forget how fast the water went down and how much the look of the lake changed overnight. The Lord must have been watching out for the campers because there were no injuries or fatalities.

10

SPOTTED DOG, BULGUR, PACKSACK STEW AND OTHER GORMET DELIGHTS

I love cooking over an open campfire on canoe trips. Everything seems to taste so much better than at home. It is probably a combination of factors, the chief of which is that you are extraordinarily hungry because of all the hard work of paddling and portaging. It could also be that friends you bring with you don't expect to get the kind of meals that are possible to make in the woods if one takes a little care in the planning and uses a bit of ingenuity in the preparation.

The scouts that I would take out canoe camping would inevitably ask what was for breakfast or lunch or supper so often that I would take liberties with naming particular dishes. For example . . . Spotted Dog . . . It would get their curiosity up even if it sounded repulsive. Spotted dog is nothing more than rice with raisins and a little butter and brown sugar thrown in for flavor. It reminds one of 101 Dalmatians . . . thus the name. It's a great dessert.

Bulgur* is another food that most campers have not become acquainted with. It is a cracked wheat cereal that has the amazing capacity to grow. A little goes a long way and it really sticks to your ribs. It takes so long to cook that it is common practice to put a cup or so in a gallon of water the night before to let it soften up. In the morning it will have expanded to use up all the water. Mix in some powdered milk and sugar and you have a great filling breakfast. If you throw the uncooked granules in cake or muffin mix they end up slightly crunchy and you would have trouble distinguishing their flavor from ground walnuts. It must have a lot of fiber in it because shortly after eating a lot of it, one makes the bulgur-dash for the latrine. It is said that the ancient Egyptians used it to mine limestone and marble. They would drill a row of holes in the rock at the quarry and then pack them with bulgur and water. The holes were corked and then they just waited for it to expand and split the rock. It sounds reasonable to me.

Packsack stew* was always made for supper the last day of a canoe trip. It has no definite recipe but is just a big stew pot of all the food items that are left in the pack at the end of the trip. It tasted different every time. You could get rid of a lot of stuff in the pot. Rice, barley, left over loaves of bread, koolaid, if you wanted it a particular color or flavor, canned meat, fish, or whatever you had left in the pack. If the leftovers in the pack tended to be flour, pancake mix, cornmeal or oatmeal, one could throw in a few spoons of baking powder and bake it. Then it becomes something we called bannock*. With a little butter and brown sugar on top it was a very good coffee cake.

Ingenuity is important in campfire cooking. One does not have all the conveniences or tools that you would find in a typical kitchen. I have had to carve a spatula and serving spoon out of wood on a trip where we forgot the utensil bag. On a father and son campout in Inver Grove Heights with our church a few years ago, I had little time to pack for the occasion. I remembered the cake mix but forgot the eggs, oil and cake pan as well as water to mix in with the flour. We used a can of Mountain Dew for the liquid, skipped the eggs and oil and when it came time to put the batter in the pan I realized I had no baking pan. A quick survey of the campsite found no baking pan but led to the discovery that Craig had baby moon hubcaps on his pickup truck. We popped one off, rinsed it in the lake and poured in the batter. The cake turned out great in the reflector oven* in spite of the missing ingredients and we didn't even have to wash the pan thinking that it would self clean as he drove through puddles after the next rainstorm. Hub cake was such a hit the kids and dads still talk about it.

Syrup is heavy to carry so we make ours out of brown and white sugar, maple flavoring and if you like it to have more body, you can add a couple spoons of instant butterscotch pudding to thicken it. Instant mashed potatoes make a marvelous thickening agent for stews and sauces. They also work well for breading for frying fish. Homemade donuts can be made by mixing up a batch of pancake mix and then thickening is with ordinary flour or cake mix so it can be rolled out on the bottom of a canoe dusted with flour. Then you just cut them out with a cup and maybe the cap of the bug spray can for the holes and deep fry them. When they float up, roll them over in the hot grease. When they are nicely browned, toss them in a paper bag with sugar, cinnamon and nutmeg and you have something that will rival crispy crèmes. Spices can also make the mundane interesting. A capful of almond or vanilla extract does wonders to a pot of cocoa. I always carry cinnamon, cloves, nutmeg and mace for dessert dishes and spices like oregano, thyme and chili powder to dress up main dishes. Dried fruit can be cooked up into a fruit stew with brown sugar that is guaranteed to keep everyone regular on the trip. I add raisins to cereal, bread and cakes for added flavor.

Baking is very easy in the woods. Cakes, pies, cookies, brownies, pizza and anything you can make in an oven at home can be made in the woods. I prefer using a reflector oven but many campers like Dutch ovens*. There is even a small oven that is made to fit over a propane or gas stove, but I find them difficult to use and I like to bake larger quantities than they will hold.

Introducing scouts to natural foods is another interesting thing to do. Tea can be made out of a number of different plants such as wild roses, labrador leaves, various berries and leaves of a multitude of bushes. Cattail roots sliced up taste a lot like cucumbers. Cooked young milkweed pods taste like green beans and bell peppers mixed together. Leaves of the basswood tree make a credible lettuce and the berries can be made into a drink that tastes like chocolate. The fuzz from cattail tops can be mixed into pancake batter to extend it. Snapping turtle eggs can be used to make a good tasting French toast. I have even heard of using leeches in place of bacon in pizza.

Another fun activity is cooking without utensils, pots or pans. Eggs can be baked in the skin of a half onion or the rind of an orange. Water can be boiled in a paper cup as long as you keep it full to the top. Eggs, meat or veggies can be skewered and cooked like shish-kebabs. Potatoes can be baked in coals without burning if you coat them with mud about ½" thick. With a roll of aluminum foil the possibilities become limitless. Flat rocks wrapped in foil and properly arranged can make a reflector oven for baking. Many foods can be wrapped in foil and baked. You are only limited by your imagination.

A good friend of mine was expressing his concerns about what we were going to eat on a 12 day canoe trip we were planning. I tried to explain some of the things that were going to be on the menu, but he still had doubts because his wife, Pat, was a great Italian cook. Another friend Craig said to him, "Bob, Roy's cooking is just as good as Pat's but it's on a different level." He still talks about some of the things that we cooked up on that trip.

11

I'M NOT LOST . . . JUST CONFUSED

It was early June of 1969 and my guides-in-training crew was cooking supper. We weren't lost but we were a bit confused. With our usual guide bravado we had planned a trip that wasn't on a typical route of travel. We were at the present time camped on a rough-cut bulldozed roadway somewhere south of Insula Lake in the BWCAW*. The dirt road wasn't on our map and we weren't exactly sure where we were. The term GPS meant nothing in those days.

We had spent the better part of two days trying to go south on streams and small lakes that at least on the map connect Insula Lake to Isabella Lake. Using our maps and compasses and quite a bit of dead reckoning we had arrived at an area of the map where there should have been a long narrow lake called Arrow. It wasn't there. We had no idea where it had gone. The area had been partially logged over and maybe the lake had been drained we thought. At any rate we couldn't find it and had been portaging through the woods for quite some time trying to keep going in a generally southern direction. It was starting to get dark and we weren't anywhere near where we had hoped to be. It was beginning to look like we would have to camp in the middle of the woods and continue in the morning. Doing that would make meal preparation tough without water for cooking.

As we continued to brush-crash* through the woods heading south we came upon an old dirt bulldozed logging road that looked like it hadn't been used in a long time. Being the only flat spot we had seen in quite some time and the fact that there was a beaver pond close by for a water source, I announced that we would pitch camp here in the middle of the road. The very tired and bug bit swampers* (guides in training) breathed a big sigh of relief and all pitched in to help get the tents up, the fire built, and a wood supply secured and supper made. We conjured up some kind of one pot meal that was filling and baked up a nice couple of apple pies to top it off.

We were finished eating our stew and had just started to take the pies out of the reflector oven* when one of the guys asked "What's that sound?" He turned his head straining to hear as we all fell silent. In the hush we all began to hear the sounds of an engine laboring along. I thought this road had not been used in years but the sound of a truck coming continued to get louder. We watched dumbfounded as an old beat up dented pickup with a big camper on its box lumbered into view. A grizzled old man drove the truck with a younger man riding shotgun. Our campsite was completely blocking his path. He hit the brakes and gawked, squinting at the tents in the middle of the road. He was as surprised to see the road blocked by our camp in the middle of it, as we were to see his truck come down the unused road. He hopped out spryly to chat with us.

We explained to him why we were camped in the middle of the road. The man said he and his son were loggers who had taken the day off to do some fishing. They were from a logging camp on Isabella Lake a ways down the dirt road. I asked about the dented condition of his pickup truck and he explained that he had honked impatiently at a big bull moose* that wouldn't get out of his way on the road. The moose developed a bad case of road rage and had repeatedly rammed the pickup even though after the first attack the logger had slammed it in reverse trying to get out of his way. The moose finally gave up trying to chase away the intruder from his domain but not before inflicting a lot of damage to the truck, breaking a headlight, the mirrors, and badly denting the fenders and doors.

As the logger was recounting the moose story, Charlie, one of the younger guides, had caught the phrase . . . logging camp on Isabella Lake. When the story of the moose attack had been told, Charlie asked if this road led to their camp and were they heading back there now? The man said their camp was about 12 miles down the road and yes they were heading home.

We invited the man and his son to have some of our stew for which they were quite grateful. Charlie continued to look down the road and then back at the truck and then at our camp full of gear. Scratching his scraggly goatee he said "You know, I think we could get all our gear in your truck if you would be so kind as to give us a ride back to your logging camp." The man looked at all our gear and our three canoes and began to express his doubts. "It would all fit" we all insisted as we caught on to Charlie's good idea. Within 15 minutes the fire was out, the tents were rolled, and all the gear was packed into the camper. The three canoes rode crossways on top of the camper and all nine of us found places to ride, some even perching on the fenders and on the roof to help hold the canoes from sliding off. I rode in the cab with the logger and his son and expressed our gratitude to him for being willing to get us back on our trip schedule. He said we could stay the night in their cabin at the logging camp. I promised him a slice of the warm apple pies that were now riding on his dashboard, their sweet cinnamon smell out of place in the dusty old truck cab. Because of the bad road and the huge load of people and gear on his truck it must have taken three hours to get to his camp but it sure beat crashing through the woods. We got to stay in a warm cabin and we shared stories about the woods, fishing and logging until the wee hours of the morning.

Daylight came early as we put our canoes in the lake the next morning to set off once again. We waved good-by to our benefactors and paddled away into the mares tails of fog that swirled off the surface of the Isabella River, once again back on schedule for our guides training trip. I still wonder today whatever happened to Arrow Lake.

12

THE LOCH AGNES MONSTER

It is fun starting legends and telling tall tales. The scout crews coming up to the canoe base are out of their element, are very gullible and will believe most anything the guides tell them.

Dave Hyink, one of the 'Charlie Guides*' was an inspiration. He used to carry a little vial in his pocket. When showing the scouts how to fillet fish he would carefully cut out the anus of each fish and place it in the small vial giving no reason for doing it. Several days into the trip he would have quite a collection. Then he would prepare a big pot of stew and with all the scouts watching he would carefully empty the contents of the small vial into the stew. "For added flavoring" he said. The small donut shaped rings were actually spaghettios from a different jar. He would always get a big helping of stew that night as the scouts just picked at their food.

On a trip up the Maligne River, Dave was showing one of his crews an old wooden barge that was partially sunk lying near the shore. The barge was loaded with tons of logging chains from the early 1900's logging era and was in advanced stages of rot. It was old enough to have been built using hand forged square nails. The nails long ago had rusted away leaving rows of curious square holes in the planking.

When the scouts asked about the square holes Dave quickly came up with a tall tale for an answer. He shared sounding very knowledgable, "The holes are caused by the notorious Poohbah worms that abound in Poohbah Lake and the surrounding waters. That's why you have to be careful not to leave your canoes or paddles in the water at night lest they be set upon by the worms and eaten full of holes and ruined." As scouts take everything their guides say as gospel direct from the creator, a legend was born.

I decided to try my hand at story telling too so I came up with the idea of a huge fish that lived in Canadian Lake Agnes that we called the Loch Agnes Monster. I spent a bit of time on my day off shopping in Ely, buying a few necessary supplies to insure that my story would hold water. I had come up with what I thought would be a good way to perpetuate the story and make it more believable.

At Canadian Waters, a local outfitting store, I bought the biggest red and white daredevil* lure that they had. This big spoon must have weighed close to a pound and was fully 12 inches long. I don't think anyone ever thought it would catch fish but that it was good for only a conversation piece. At the local Ace hardware I bought about 250 feet of 1/8-inch diameter nylon rope and a three-foot length of 900 pound test aircraft cable. I also bought two cable clamps, a sturdy door spring and a big screw-eye.

Back at the base the next day I washed clothes and gathered my equipment and got organized for my crew that was coming in that afternoon. I took time to open the screw-eye and mount the door spring to it. I then mounted the screw-eye securely to the back stern plate of my canoe. Using the two cable clamps I made the aircraft cable into a very sturdy 900 pound test leader and fastened it to the big daredevil. I attached one end of the nylon rope to the leader and carefully coiled the rope and stashed it away into my personal pack to be revealed at just the right moment.

That afternoon my crew arrived and we went through the mini training sessions that I give all my crews so they are prepared for their trip. We packed up our food from the bulk bins and then spent some time together planning where to go on our trip. The crew of course wanted to catch lots of fish. In front of the big map board I pointed to Lake Agnes and let the story of the Loch Agnes Monster out of the bag. Of course the scouts wanted to include paddling up Lake Agnes on their trip. It doesn't take a rocket scientist to know that the scouts are really open to suggestions from an older experienced guide. You can usually talk them into going anywhere you would like to go. I convinced them further of the wisdom of 'their planned trip' by explaining that I had hooked the monster numerous times but he had always snapped the line. But now I had a sure-fire secret weapon with my heavy duty fishing rig that I had put together. We just had to go there to try it out on the monster.

We set out on our trip the next morning in our three Grumman* canoes and my Seliga*. The lake was pretty calm and the trip up the chain of lakes to Prairie Portage* took only a couple of hours and then we were in Canada. That afternoon we crossed Ranger Portage out of Bayley Bay on Basswood Lake and entered Burke and Sunday Lakes. We camped early and the boys set up the tents and we soon had supper on the fire. There was time to do some fishing and the boys landed some nice bass. The next morning we headed for the two long portages into and out of the small Meadows Lake. Later, at the end of the last portage, we stood looking at the 20 mile expanse of Lake Agnes.

It was a beautiful day with scarcely any wind and we began our trek up the 20-mile long very deep lake. An hour or so later it was time for lunch so we pulled the canoes together and made lunch on the water. We dipped water out of the lake in the canvas bucket and stirred in the punch mix with one of the boy's paddles. The cook dug out the flat folded up reflector oven* to use as a countertop and made each of us two thin peanut butter and jelly sandwiches out of the squashed bread. To save space in the food pack, we routinely punctured the loaves of bread and squeezed them down to about two inches like an accordion. The nutrition was there but not the fluffy. We topped off our lunch with a big handful of raisins.

We put away the lunch fixings and I announced that we were in a deep part of the lake and it was time to try to catch the Loch Agnes Monster. I unveiled my secret heavy-duty rig. I tied the coil of nylon rope to the door spring mounted to my canoe stern plate. One of the boys asked, "What's the spring for? "To take up the shock of the big strike when he hits this," I said, as I pulled the 12-inch daredevil with its attached leader out of my personal pack. The boys eyes all opened wide when they saw the size of the red and white daredevil. I tied the free end of the leader to the loose end of the rope and I was ready. I knew the heavy lure would sink like a stone so we had to get up a pretty good head of steam before I dared to pitch the lure out. When I thought our canoes were going fast enough I quickly laid my paddle down, grabbed the lure and twirled it over my head launching it about 100 feet behind my canoe. I grabbed the paddle and stroked to keep the trolling speed up and gradually eased out the rest of the 250 feet of nylon rope until it was all trailing behind my canoe securely tied to the big door spring.

Things were looking good and we trolled that big lure off the back of my canoe for about a half a mile. I began to think that maybe a big northern might actually strike the lure as we paddled up the center of the lake at a pretty good clip. I guess I was getting suckered into my own tall tale. Agnes is a very deep lake, scoured out by glaciers, but I knew if we got to an area that wasn't at least 100 feet deep I might be in trouble trying to troll something that heavy.

Suddenly disaster struck! The lure found a rock on the bottom to anchor itself to and my canoe came to a screeching halt as the rope and the leader went taut. The stop was so sudden the bowman flew out of his seat and almost went in the lake over the bow. "I've got him!" I yelled to the crew close by, trying to cover the fact that I had snagged. As the canoe ended its forward momentum the door-spring took up the shock as I had planned, and it stretched out and out an unbelievably long distance. We were almost stopped and I expected to be pulled backwards by the spring. I guess I miscalculated. A canoe full of people and gear is far heavier than a screen door. I had no idea a spring could stretch that far. The leader and rope held but the overstretched screen door spring snapped, whip-lashing both my butt cheeks bad enough to leave me a bruise that didn't go away for over a week. "Aw, dang it! He broke this line too!" I groaned to the crew with tears in my eyes as I furtively rubbed my smarting rear end. And a new legend was born.

13

THE BARE

A group of my friends and I were on a short four day canoeing and fishing trip to Wind Lake. It was warm for early September. The weather had been great although it was a bit windy making the lake rough. We had good luck catching mostly northern pike* and smallies*. Our campsite was situated on the big sand beach in the back of the mile wide circular bay.

We were sharing the lake with some black powder bear hunters who were camped on the point campsite right at the entrance to the big bay. We stopped to chat with them each time we would paddle by to see how they were faring with their hunting expedition and show them the stringers of fish we were catching. They had a spot where they had been putting out bait for the bears. They would use old donuts, bread, cooking grease and whatever foodstuffs they could find to get the bears used to finding the food and feeding at that spot. Hunting consisted of waiting for them to come in to feed. They said they had seen bear sign and had evidence the bears were feeding on what they were putting out for them but hadn't seen any yet.

On the south shore of the bay within shouting distance of the bear hunters campsite was another small campsite that was evidently occupied because we saw a couple of tents set up there. We hadn't stopped to chat with those folks because we had yet to see any people there.

The next morning was still breezy so we opted to lash two canoes together to make a catamaran* to make a more stable platform for fishing. We rounded up some birch poles and lashed them across the gunwales* at the thwarts* and set out with six of us aboard to see what we could catch. The homemade catamaran was stable enough that you could stand up to cast your lures. Some of the crew stayed behind to fish near the campsite out of the single canoe that was left over. We used our raincoats held up on our paddles for makeshift sails whenever the wind was at our backs. We sailed through the narrow neck of the big bay seeing no one at either of the occupied campsites. The day was spent paddling, sailing and fishing in the calm water spots we could find along the shoreline.

My son Matt had been bragging, saying, "I am the man!" as far as fishing went, and was proving it with several nice catches. He had caught 22 fish so far on that trip. Even though his fishing prowess had been learned from me, I was still skunked! Not one fish! I couldn't believe it. As we trolled past a small bay in one of the arms of the lake near the portage to wind bay I finally got a strike. It wasn't much of a hit and it had little fight but it was definitely a fish. As I reeled him in he felt like a waterlogged branch, we were all surprised that it was a walleye* and a huge one at that. When I got him landed and put him on the de-liar* scale he weighed just over eight pounds! We found two things very interesting. I had fished Wind Lake many times over the years and had never caught a walleye. We had all thought northerns and bass were the only fish in the lake. The size and the species were a surprise as was the scars the fish displayed. Across both sides of the belly were teeth marks in a wide arc of perhaps six inches. They were barely healed. A much larger fish, probably a pike* had tried to eat my fish crosswise but he had gotten away. It proved to be the only fish I caught the whole trip but it was the one everyone talked about. Much to my disappointment I later lost the gold colored lure I caught him with and have been unable to find a replacement anywhere.

The sun was starting to approach the horizon so we decided to head back to camp and make some supper. With all six of us paddling the catamaran made good time and we were soon passing through the narrows into the big bay. The bear hunters were evidently still out hunting so we couldn't chat with them to show off my big walleye. We swung a bit south and paddled by the other occupied campsite. We saw a college-age dark haired girl swimming 20 or 30 feet out from the shore of their camp. We started to swing closer to say hello.

When we were about 75 yards away she swam to shore and stood up in the shallow water. She had been swimming with a life jacket on. With only a life jacket on! We hadn't seen any women on our trip and as if petrified we ceased paddling and gawked at the sight. We still didn't quite realize that she had nothing on. As she removed the life jacket I commented "That is the smallest black string bikini I have ever seen," as I strained to see the strings that weren't there. Todd stated "I think those legs go all the way up!" As she pranced up to the shore dangling the life jacket from one hand and confirming what we had all suspected with the view of her behind side all Jay could say was "God bless America!" We were obviously ogling and I am sure all our mouths were hanging open. She made little effort to hide the fact that she had nothing on and grabbed a towel and came back down to the waters edge to paint her toenails. The towel dropped off and she didn't bother to pick it up to cover herself. We heard her girlfriend say, "They are staring at you. "Why don't you put on a show"! We thought she had put on a pretty good show already and knew we shouldn't stay to see any more. I croaked out a "Hi . . . how was the water" but she didn't answer. Reluctantly we paddled on as the two girl's boyfriends came down to the lake from the tents. We wondered what kind of folks they were to possess so little modesty.

When we got back to camp we mentioned to those who had stayed behind that we had seen a bare. "Did the hunters get one?" they asked. "No, we just saw one" we said. We further explained what we had seen and they were all wishing that they had come along and made our fishing platform a trimaran by tying on the last canoe.

The next morning we broke camp and headed back toward Moose Lake* and home. We hugged the south shore hoping for another sighting of the bare but our hopes were in vain because there was no visible activity at the bare campsite. We stopped to chat with the luckless bear hunters as we went through the narrows. They were busy eating breakfast. We told them we had sited a bare. "Where'd you see a bear? They asked excitedly. "We saw a bare in the next campsite." We explained grinning ear to ear. "Oh, we have been keeping an eye on that bare too with our spotting scope" they both said as they broke into big smiles.

14

MINOR MIRACLES

Sometimes things happen while you are out camping in the woods that just make you pause and look up expecting to see the smiling face of God and hearing him say "What did you think of that, huh?"

In the summer of 2000 we took a trip around Hunters Island* in the Quetico*. There were eight of us and we were having a great time. My son Matt was along. I was enjoying showing him the places I loved from my guiding days 35 years before. We were about three quarters of the way through our 12-day trip and were on the home stretch. A hot shower was sounding pretty enticing. We had had good luck finding campsites up to this point and were now around Lower Basswood Falls looking for a spot to park for the night. Every campsite we found though was occupied, and we pressed on with a sense of urgency as the weather had begun to look threatening.

Each night when we camped we would erect tents and do all the camp chores and then get comfortable by slipping out of our wet socks and boots and donning a dry pair of socks and our moccasins or tennis shoes. It was almost as good as sex. All of us enjoyed the pleasure of dry footgear except Jim Krech, who had forgotten to bring a spare pair of shoes. He had to keep his wet boots on in the hope that they would dry out if he hung around the fire long enough. Usually, his waterlogged feet looked like pale prunes when he took his boots off at bedtime. He was missing out on one of the great pleasures of canoe camping . . . dry shoes and socks.

Finally we spotted a rock formation that looked like it might be a campsite. As we approached, it was confirmed that it was a campsite and it was empty. The thunder and lightning to the north made it imperative to check it out quickly to see if it would be usable for our group. From the river it didn't look like much and the canoe landing spot was less than ideal. Jim hopped out, waded a few steps to shore and ran up to the fire grate and looked around to see if it had enough room for our crew and if it had decent tent sites. He hollered back, "this will make a fine home for tonight" and we began to unload our gear. As he glanced around the area Jim spotted a brand new pair of tennis shoes and a pair of clean white socks sitting on a log next to the fire grate. They looked like they had never been worn. He picked up the shoes and noted they were size nine and a half, just what he wore. Coincidence? I don't know but Jim didn't think so as he looked up and mouthed "Thank you Lord."

On another trip, years before, with a group of scouts from Kearney, Nebraska we were out for my first 15 day long trip. On a trip that long, without a chance of re-supply, the food packs were pretty heavy and there were five of them. We had to double pack the portages* to make it across in one trip until enough of the food was eaten to cut down on the number of packs. There would have been even more packs but we were baking bannock* each night for the lunch the next day so we didn't have to carry bulky bread. We were also counting on catching a lot of fish to keep the food volume down. Our trip was around Hunters Island with a jaunt to the north to the town of Atikokan, Ontario where we took a layover day*. We were to meet the sister crew*, who took the reverse of the same route as we were taking,—and Atikokan was the half way meeting point.

The fishing had been great so far on the first half of the trip. In Cirrus Lake I latched onto a 48 inch northern* and got him up to the side of the canoe. I got my hands on him twice but he was barely hooked and managed to spit the lure and get away. My other disappointment was losing my favorite top-water black hula popper*. We had been fishing at Chatterton Falls in Russell Lake a few days before. The lure was deadly on bass*and pike*, but I had to leave it hooked to a stump I had snagged below the falls because the water was too dangerously fast to try to retrieve it with a canoe.

On the return leg of our trip we camped on the island at Rebecca Falls in McAree Lake. Jim McKay, the crew advisor and an avid fisherman, suggested that he and I should go catch some frogs for bait for the big northerns that like to sit just below the falls. We grabbed a canoe and paddled to the shore opposite the falls and beached our canoe. We hiked the sandy shore catching a number of frogs that we placed in the number two cooking pot we had brought along. I commented "Sure wish I hadn't lost that black hula popper . . . . would have been great for this spot." "You mean like this one" he said, as he stooped down and picked up out of the sand, a lure alike in every way to the one I had lost seven days before. It had the white skirt and a red eye but lacked the teeth marks from fish that my old lure had. "Yeah, just like that one" I said as he handed me the lure. We both looked up and said a short thank you to the Lord who I know was getting a kick out of our wonderment.

Once on a trip to Northern Lights Lake with a group of scouts, we had made camp early and we were all out fishing. The boys were wishing they had brought more tackle because the fishing was great. The boys hadn't brought many lures so when one was lost it was a major catastrophe. One of the scouts latched on to a pretty good-sized pike of perhaps 10 pounds, so I started to paddle my canoe over to give him some advice and help with landing him. The scout was really excited and didn't wait for my help. He didn't try to tire the fish out but cranked him right in and tried to lift him into the canoe with his rod. That technique just doesn't work with ten pound thrashing fish. The fish flipped and broke the line right at the leader and got away before I could help. "Rats" he lamented, "That was my only rapala*." Dejected at the loss of the lure, he tied on a new leader and a doctor spoon and kept fishing but without success.

In the morning the scouts were up early enough to get in some more fishing for a while before breakfast was ready. The scout that lost the rapala went out to try his luck again. He soon had a good sized northern on and followed my advice and was able to land him. Next to the doctor spoon hanging out of the ten pounders mouth was the well hooked rapala that this same scout had lost the night before. Just luck? . . . I don't think so . . . do you?

On a weekend excursion to Wind Lake late one summer we had left very early in the morning from the Twin Cities so that we would have enough time to get to the lake, set up camp and maybe get some fishing in as well before dark. We paddled in and found the point campsite vacant and unloaded our gear and set up our site. We ate a leisurely lunch and everyone took a hour-long nap to make up for lost sleep. In the afternoon we did some fishing and using boulders from along the shore, my friend Wally Krech directed the building of a nice pier of rocks for landing the canoes. It was to be a relaxing weekend and we were all feeling renewed by being in the woods. In the late afternoon a thunderstorm passed over causing a beautiful double rainbow to form in the east. We scrambled around taking pictures of the sight. To this day it is my favorite picture of the boundary waters with the rainbow coming down through the trees just above the dimly lit canoe. It is the photo on the cover of this book. It had been a great day.

That night we sat around the campfire telling stories and watching meteors. The storm had ushered in a cold front and the temperature began to fall rapidly in the clear cold night air. The huge pile of firewood we had originally gathered began to run low. Someone commented, "We should get more wood." Sitting by the warm fire listening to stories and sipping hot cocoa held more allure than crashing around in the woods with a flashlight in the dark looking for wood so there were no takers to the suggestion. No one was tired yet and the stories were still being told when the last piece of wood was put on the fire. As the fire died down to coals a bit later I again offered the suggestion that if we were going to stay up we needed more firewood. Still no takers. The night was dead calm and it was really getting cold. You could see your breath and frost in the morning was a real possibility

Suddenly there was a loud crack and then a big crash as an old dead spruce perhaps eight inches in diameter and 30 feet tall fell to the ground not 10 feet behind our crew huddling around our dying fire. Surprised and scared by the near miss we wondered what had tipped it over. We opined that the Lord must have reached down and given it a gentle shove in our direction to provide the firewood so we could continue our fellowship around the campfire. Why else would it have fallen just then with no wind pushing it our way?

On another 10-day trip we were lounging in the warm sun on Table Rock in Crooked Lake after a generous lunch. A nap was just what we needed. My friend Craig commented, "It don't get no better than this!" as he had dozens of times during the trip, whenever big fish were caught, or an exceptional meal was served, or a beautiful sunset or waterfall had come into view.

Table Rock is a curious geological formation in Crooked Lake just before it connects to the Basswood River. The rock, must weigh 30 or 40 tons, is very flat, and only about a foot thick and about 20 feet across. It sits out on a flat bedrock point of land perched on three or four two foot boulders that act like table legs.

Lazing in the sun and just starting to doze off Craig just had to say it again "Nope, it sure don't get any better than this." Not five seconds later three canoe loads of bikini clad college coeds paddled around the point to stop for lunch at the popular table rock that we were all napping on. Yes, it can get better than this we all realized.

15

THE PERFECT CREW

Every guide, (or as they call them now . . . interpreters*) at Northern Tier High Adventure Base likes to brag a bit. It was the same for the guides back in the 1960s when the base was called Charles L. Sommers Wilderness Canoe Base*. Each of us back then touted our cooking ability or our fishing prowess or the feats we accomplished in the woods with an extraordinary crew. We all wanted to go the farthest or paddle the fastest or do unusual things with our scout crews. Most crews were an average bunch of scouts but occasionally you would encounter an exceptional bunch of boys.

Every guide dreamed about getting assigned the perfect crew.

To take a record-breaking trip, the crew, including the guide, had to total nine people. That put three people in each of three canoes and meant that all the gear could be carried across portages in one trip. That number was the most efficient for traveling, for campsite setup and for portaging. They would all have prior training in canoe paddling, map and compass orientation, and be experienced campers. The scouts needed to be built like linebackers so they could shoulder the loads on portages. They would all arrive with small lightweight goose down sleeping bags and compression stuff sacks so personal packs could be easily packed with three boys to a pack. If all these factors came together and the crew was willing, they could plan the ultimate super long trip. It almost never worked out that way.

I thought I had that crew once. They were from Texas and they were big. All of the scouts were bigger than me and I wondered what football team they played on. We planned a long trip as they assured me that they could handle anything I would plan out for them. In the morning when we began loading up the canoes I was prepared for a great time. When I said, "Lets load up and get underway" they stated that they didn't have all their gear brought down to the waterfront yet and they all ran back up to their tents to get the rest of it. "Oh oh" I thought as I counted the personal packs. They came back down with their sleeping bags that were rolled up tight but were the size of 30-gallon oil drums each packed in a waterproof duffel bag. The guys were so big that not even one of their oversized sleeping bags would fit in the Duluth packs where I had instructed them to pack three to a pack. We spent an hour or so trying to repack and reduce the volume of the gear but the bulky bags defied getting jammed into the packs. The duffels just had to be stacked on top of the other gear in the already precariously loaded canoes. The gear was piled so high in my canoe I couldn't see ahead to steer so I had to raise up in a crouch once in a while to check to see where I was headed. This didn't bode well for the long trip we had planned. I am sure the boys had a great time but portaging was tedious because we had to walk all the trails twice to carry the extra gear across. The scouts were lazy in camp and loved to sleep in. After a couple of days we resorted to shortening our trip route by half to stay on schedule.

Later that summer I had a crew from Brainerd, Minnesota. The scouts were all small in stature, but looked tough and wiry. There were seven boys and two adult leaders so the crew was ten counting me. "Not the ideal number for a crew because we needed to take four canoes" I calculated in my mind. Only a couple scouts brought fishing poles and the crew announced to me that they wanted to set a record for the longest trip any of the crews had ever taken. I was impressed with their desire but tried to discourage their plan because of the small size of the boys and the less than ideal number in the crew. They explained that they had been training hard for this trip and knew they could do it. After much discussion about the hardships of the trip I finally relented and we sat together in front of the map board and laid out our proposed route. Our trip was ambitious, circling the western half of Hunters Island* but digressing northward into Upper Sturgeon, Cirrus, and Quetico Lakes and returning through Beaverhouse, the Namakan River and Lac La Croix . . . a distance of about 250 miles and over 50 portages. We quickly packed up the food and pulled out our canoes and got paddles and life jackets all down to the waterfront for a really early start in the morning. After the evening campfire the scouts hit the hay early for our morning start. As soon as breakfast was over the boys ran for the dock with their personal packs, and we were quickly loaded and on our way a couple of hours before any of the other crews on our shift* were ready to go. In five minutes I knew this crew was something special and we would probably be able to pull off the trip we had planned. The boys steered the canoes like pros, knew how to navigate and orient* their maps and were so fast I struggled to keep up with them.

The very first night we made it to the north end of Canadian Agnes just at dark. Most crews take two or three days to get that far. It was a clear night so we slept under the stars not bothering to take the time to set up tents. It was mid-summer and the worst of the gnat and mosquito season was over. The scouts sacked out immediately after a quick supper. Our meals had been planned out to take the least time to prepare and we didn't expect to do a lot of fancy cooking or baking because we needed to spend time on the water . . . up to 12 or 14 hours a day paddling to go the distances we had planned. The weather cooperated with only one short shower one evening. We never set up tents on any night and we crawled under the dining fly to escape the rain on the one night that was wet. We were up before dawn and the sun was just peeking over the trees as we pulled away from the campsite the next morning with our bellies full of warm oatmeal.

Night two was in Upper Sturgeon. Night three was in Cirrus Lake. I was really proud of the scouts and the crew could scarcely believe we had already covered 100 miles . . . . over 30 miles a day! We arrived in Cirrus early enough to investigate the sound of a waterfall on the north side of the lake. The map showed there was a rapids, but upon investigation we found a beautiful series of falls and cascades that dropped about 125 feet into Cirrus Lake. Night four was spent in Beaverhouse Lake. Day five was an easy paddle on the Namakan River to the sand beach by the First Nation Indian Village on Lac La Croix. We had covered so much distance so fast that we had seriously considered making a run over to Namakan Lake but decided we wouldn't chance it in case the weather or wind went against us. Night six was at Wheelbarrow Falls on the Basswood River . . . a 40-mile day! At lunchtime a totally fearless deer strolled up to our crew as we ate sandwiches and acted like he wanted a handout. I stood up and slowly approached her with my P B and J sandwich extended at arms' length but she wouldn't let me get closer than three feet. I am sure the doe had never seen humans before.

We were ahead of where we had planned to be so we took a layover day and caught up on some sleep and cooked a fancy supper. The boys did some exploring of the falls that day and got pictures of a shy yearling bear that paid us a visit at lunchtime. On day eight the entire crew dog-trotted the one and a quarter mile long Horse Portage*, and we crossed it in a record setting pace of 18 minutes. We camped our last night on the sand beach campsite on US Point and made it back to the base by the middle of the afternoon on the ninth day.

Dave Hyink, my good friend and fellow guide, was able to take a crew on this same route later in the summer but they ran into headwinds on Lac La Croix so he routed his crew through some small lakes to the south before getting back into Crooked Lake. This made his trip a few miles longer than the one I took with my Brainerd crew. He however, paddled every day and did not take a layover day. Technically my crew did the trip in seven and a half days, so I feel like we still set a record.

After the long trip, I was really worn out and my next trip that I took out a couple of days later was the shortest I ever took. We covered only 50 miles on that one but cut many portages to small, unknown and unvisited lakes to make it interesting. We must have walked at least 15 of the 50 miles that we covered. You always have to give the scouts something to brag about and it makes good story telling fodder for years to come.

16

THE TOUGH TRIP

The crew came from Brookings, South Dakota. I had worked with the scouts and their troop while I was going to college there and I knew most of the boys. I was instrumental in getting them interested in taking a canoe trip through the Sommers Base. Steve Bibby was the crew chief and his dad was the adult advisor. It was a good crew with a fair amount of experience so we planned a trip to the northeast corner of the Quetico* and on out of the north end of Northern Lights Lake. We then intended to go through Mowe, Plummes and Cannibal Lakes then on to the rarely visited Sleigh, Deatys, and McGinnis Lakes. From there the plan was to bushwhack* a portage* to a fairly large lake with no name, go out the other side and cut a portage to the Wawiag River and come home on well traveled routes through Kawa Bay and Agnes. It was a moderately long trip with a lot of unknown factors thrown in. Unknowns can be troublesome.

The boys did great the first three days and we reached Saganaga on our third night. Day four was harder with a lot of portaging but we reached Sleigh and were still on schedule. On day five we paddled to the north end of Sleigh where a 212-rod* portage (1 rod equals 16 ½ feet) was shown on the map. It would take us a half hour or so to cross it I estimated. Wrong!! We looked for over an hour and found no sign of a trail. Even worse, a tornado had gone through the north end of the lake and the trees were down everywhere making a passage close to impossible. We should have changed our route, but not being one to back away from a challenge, I armed myself with my compass and axe and proceeded to chop my way north out of the Sleigh Lake heading toward Deatys Lake. It took nearly eight hours to cover the three quarter mile trek. We sometimes didn't touch ground for 50 yard stretches as we dragged the canoes over the jumble of downed trees. We needed to be in McGinnis Lake that night but there was no possibility of getting that far with all the daylight we had burned up just crossing that one portage. We took one more portage before dark and camped on an island in a swampy no-name lake. We had to make our own campsite and there were no rocks with which to build the fireplace. After traveling 30 miles a day at the beginning of the trip the two miles we had covered that day looked pretty meager. We cooked a supper in the dark and suffered through lots of mosquitoes. After breakfast the next morning, we discovered that the fire had burned deep down into the duff* and it took over 50 three gallon buckets of water before we were assured it was out. That night we finally made it to McGinnis Lake and were now one full day behind schedule.

We got an early start the next morning trying to make up lost time. We were hoping the tornado damage had been isolated because this was the day where we planned to bushwhack two new portages. By late morning we had finished cutting a trail to the lake that lay between us and the Wawiag River. We gobbled a quick lunch and began heading north into the woods toward the river. One good thing was that it was mostly downhill. The distance was perhaps a mile. We could almost see the river down in the valley as we crested the first ridge. We had no topographical maps to help guide us around difficult areas. When we came to a series of three or four rock cliffs we were further delayed as we resorted to lowering canoes down them with ropes. Mountaineering is a skill not expected to be needed at the canoe base. By late afternoon we finally arrived at the bank of the river. We now faced 25 miles of river paddling to stay only one day behind schedule and twilight approached. We snacked on some sandwiches and raisins for supper and then quickly loaded the canoes and set off down stream in the waning daylight.

With no choice but to go on, we dug in and paddled the meandering river well past dark. It was a cloudy night so visibility was meager. You can't get very lost on a 50-foot wide river but you can run smack into islands in the dark. Without any starlight, you couldn't even see your hand in front of your face. Once, we almost dumped the bowman out when we ran into a three-foot diameter pine tree that had fallen across the river. We struggled through the flotsam of debris and the branches by the light of flashlights and pressed onward.

At about 1:00 A.M. we heard the roar of fast water in the calm night air and we knew we were approaching the seven-foot waterfall shown on the map. Never having been there, I didn't know which side the portage was on. We guessed the left and eased closer hugging the shore. Luckily we were right and the portage was there but it started right at the top of the falls. We all wearily unloaded the canoes and I saw that the portage was pretty flat and sandy. The fight had gone out of the boys and they were exhausted. I called a halt and told everyone to roll out their sleeping bags on the trail and get some shut-eye. I was praying that the clouds wouldn't leak any rain because we were too beat to set up the tents. Within ten minutes the sound of snoring could be heard.

It seemed like only moments later when I was poked in the ribs by the scout next to me as he tried to wake me up. He said, "A moose*, a moose!" I cracked one eye open and caught a glimpse of something going off down the trail into the woods. The scout said that the moose was right there and pointed next to my sleeping bag where I saw fresh tracks. I don't know how he managed to thread his way down the trail through all the sleeping bags filled with snoring scouts without stepping on any of us. I've never gotten that close to a moose before. I looked at my watch and saw that it was 7:30. Time to get going!

After a quick breakfast of hot cereal we were off and made it to the end of the river and Kawa Bay by about 10:30. We couldn't waste time as we had only one more night of camping left and then we had to be back at the base the next afternoon. We faced 70 more miles of paddling and to make it worse the wind was whistling from the southwest blowing up some pretty big whitecaps. We took off into the waves struggling to make progress, expending what little was left of our already sapped strength. We were trolling fishing lures to try to nail a few walleyes for supper as our food supply was becoming diminished. By 10 that night we gave in to weariness and found a campsite about half-way down Agnes. We cooked up the fish we had gotten and hit the hay at about One A.M. again.

We still had 25 or 30 miles to go to get back to the base so again it was an early start. We cooked packsack stew* for lunch at the end of the first Meadows portage and put back in the water for the home stretch. As we finally neared the base we heard the supper bell ringing. We made it just in time to eat but they gave us our own table in the corner because we were badly in need of showers and our late arrival meant we had to take them after supper. I am sure we smelled bad enough to cause people to lose their appetites.

After a shower and a sauna we all felt better. At the campfire that night each of the eight crews that had come off the trail that day got to share a little bit about their trips. When the others had told their tales and shared where they had gone, my crew realized what a feat they had accomplished. They proudly told the story of our trip and even the other guides couldn't believe how far we had gone and how hard we had paddled the last few days to get back to camp on schedule. I think a number of boys became men that week and they will never forget their trip.

17

BAD AIR

A guide is all about being a macho man. The scouts all hold you in awe as they see you handle a paddle and go all day long without switching sides. They can't believe you can carry a pack and a canoe across a long portage without a rest stop. Spellbound, they listen to your tales of adventure in the woods. All guides love to impress people with their prowess and skills.

I once took a crew on a trip ending up on the beach at Shagawa Lake in Ely. I always made it a point to try to visit at least one new lake I had never seen on every trip I took out into the woods. After several summers of guiding and after about 25 trips, it was becoming increasingly difficult to do so, thus the unlikely trip through Shagawa Lake.

We then portaged* from the beach up the hill to Elys' main-street, relishing the stares of all the astonished tourists. As we plodded up the hill, carrying our canoes and dripping water and looking very bedraggled, we were flagged down by Eric Rosher, who owned Fisherman's Headquarters at the time. He and Judge Sammy sponsored and taped a popular weekly radio program on KELY out of his store and they were always looking for interesting people to put on the air. The program was a come-on for tourists and was good for business. He saw us walk by the front of his store and ran out to interview us.

He said to wait and he ran back inside returning with a small cassette recorder. He asked where we were from, and where we had gone on our trip, and how was the fishing? I knew Eric because I bought most of my fishing gear in his store and he was always very helpful. He also had a couple of very beautiful teen-age daughters who worked in the store and I had dated one of them a few times. It aired on the radio that week and was great fun for the crew. It was all about being macho.

We then proceeded to finish our three-mile portage down main street, to highway one heading south and on to White Iron Lake. It took us about two hours to make it but it saved a lot of miles of paddling. We paddled down to the Outward Bound School* on the Kawishawi River. We had heard the girl campers were on base but it turned out that they were out on their training trip. The scouts got to try the ropes course* and we got to take a nice hot sauna* and then dove into the Kawishiwi River to cool down. We returned to the base through the back door, portaging in from Flash Lake and ending up right in tent city. What a cool trip!

Our haircuts, beards, and clothes also helped to give us the mountain man image. I wore a deerskin fringed war shirt bedecked with rattlesnake rattles and cowhide leggings with a white headband when I was out to make an impression. My boots had old cut up snow tire rubber tread nailed to the bottoms because I had worn holes through the soles and my footprints gave away my whereabouts more than once. I carried a huge homemade six-foot paddle all painted up with an Indian chief design. Each guide had his own persona to convey but we all tried to be macho to the max.

On the trail it was even more fun impressing the "tourists." We called any inexperienced canoeists that, not to be degrading, but just to show our scouts how canoe tripping should really be done. Even our scouts began to show off for the tourists. We would often see the tourists trying to two-man-carry their canoes or even drag them over portages fully loaded making a terrible racket. Most of them brought way too much gear . . . giant tents, cots, lawn chairs, big lanterns and all the comforts of home. That is not canoe camping, its an ordeal getting all that stuff across the portages. It was no wonder that most of them never got to see that much of the wilderness because after one or two portages they could go no further.

We would often arrive at a portage with tourists blocking our way. Our groups were so organized that within a couple of minutes all our gear would be off-loaded and on its way across the trails along with the canoes. They would stare dumbfounded at the speed we could get our gear across as they were struggling with too much gear and a real lack of knowledge of how to flip up a canoe on their shoulders. Often the scouts would run back and help the poor souls get their gear over the trail when we were done hauling ours across.

Once, I came across several great big guys struggling with their gear. They had ultralight Grumman* canoes and were struggling to get them up on their shoulders even with two working together. I couldn't resist. I flipped my canoe off and stopped to chat with them. "I see you have the ultralights . . . could I try one on for size?" I asked. "Be our guest" they answered. I walked over, reached down with one hand, and flipped the canoe to my shoulders with ease. "Wow, these are really light . . . must be only half the weight of my Seliga*" I exclaimed flipping it back to the ground as their mouths fell open in amazement. I had a big grin on my face as I flipped my Seliga back on my shoulders and dog trotted down the trail leaving them gawking.

Sometimes being such a show off caused a bit of embarrassment. On the big sandy beach at Ranger Portage a large group of girl scouts were getting ready to portage as our crew arrived. "What a perfect time to show them how a real macho man does it", I thought. I shouldered my pack with a long-practiced shrug and reached down and flipped my hundred pound Seliga to my shoulders making it look easy. I took off for the start of the portage at a dead run. I forgot about the sand. My loaded body took off but my feet bogged down in the soft sand and couldn't keep up and I fell flat with the canoe landing on top of me. Red faced, I crawled out from under the canoe, gamely reloaded and set off at a more leisurely pace skipping the running idea.

One warm evening at the base a bunch of the guides, me included, decided to go skinny-dipping in Moose Lake off the loading dock. We challenged each other to swim across to the big island several hundred yards away. Half way across several canoe loads of older girl scouts led by Ma Harry came along. We kinda forgot we were buck-naked and swam up to the canoes to chat with the girls. As the first guide reached the canoes, Ma looked down over the side and calmly stated, "I can count your toes." Oops!

Canoeing means wet clothes and boots all day. We taught our scouts to hop out and unload the gear and reload the canoe while still in knee-deep water. This saved the canoes from a lot of damage and indeed lengthened their life to many years. We call it "Wet footing it". The base is still using some of Grummans that I used 45 years ago.

The problem with wet footing it all the time is that I swear the human body can absorb water through the feet because at the beginning and end of nearly every portage I had to urinate at the nearest tree. It wasn't my prostate and it wasn't only me. More than once, I or one of the scouts was interrupted mid stream by tourists. One could only turn away and finish as fast as he could and hope they would understand.

Another common problem was caused by the high carbohydrate and cheese diet with its complement of dried fruits and raisins. The fruit was necessary to counterbalance the constipating effect of all those carbs, but the side effect on most of the scouts systems was the production of prodigious amounts of gas. Flatulence to the Nth degree.

On one trip, the guys started announcing, "Bad air!" whenever they were about to break wind. This got everyone's attention and we would quickly check wind direction and move upwind of the offender. Compliments were often made if the offense was exceptional. "Bad air" caught on and soon everyone was saying it when the need arose to reduce internal pressure. Even I started saying it . . . after all I read somewhere, the average person passes gas 13 times a day so why not celebrate the event. The atmosphere in a tent at night with six scouts sometimes gave you a headache.

On the last portage into Moose Lake from Wind, I was well ahead of the boys I thought. As I headed down the last hill to the lake I heard footsteps behind me . . . one of the boys was catching up to me I assumed. The fruit stew hit me right then. If I pollute the air behind me I'll get first chance to set down my canoe I reasoned. If farting could be an Olympic event, I would have brought home a gold medal!

It was an eye watering, plant wilting, butt cheek blistering blast of the first order! As a seismic event it would have rated about an 8.5 on the Richter scale! I tooted like a tuba! I loudly announced, "Bad air!" A fart of that magnitude deserved a reaction from those near enough to experience it. I expected an "Oh, wow" or at least some muffled gagging. From right behind me now I heard a sexy feminine voice say, "Sure is!" It is hard to describe the embarrassment I felt when I realized he was a she and not from my crew.

18

NUTZ

I once had a dog, named Nutz. I'm a bit fuzzy why I stuck that handle on her. She was a pretty well mannered yellow lab and though untrained, was a pretty good retriever of pheasants and ducks. Most summers I found people to take care of her while I worked at the scout base. She wasn't too hard to care for, but she wasn't spayed, and she enjoyed the company of any dog, if it was of the opposite persuasion when the fancy struck her. The last folks that took care of her presented me with eleven puppies when I came back for her in August. "Nuts!" Maybe the name was a premonition.

It was June again and school was out. I just couldn't find anyone to take care of her as she had worn out her welcome at the place she had spent the last summer and I didn't want a repeat performance. Pups are cute . . . but eleven and of questionable vintage? "Not again" I said as I determined that taking her with me into the woods up at the scout base would keep her away from any undesirable suitors.

On the way up to Ely, she was almost killed when a big Buick ran into her on the highway at a gas stop. She got a skull fracture and lost an eye but she would survive the vet said. He stitched up her lacerations and dosed her with antibiotics and said to keep her quiet for a couple of days till she stabilized.

Upon arrival at the base she promptly took off after a wayward woodchuck. The barking alerted the base director, Sandy Bridges, to her presence. I explained my situation and although he didn't like the idea, Sandy said the dog was my responsibility and he would tolerate the situation as long as she didn't cause any trouble.

At camp she was everyone's friend, especially the dining hall steward who kept her supplied with bones to chew on. At the big steak fry for the staff at the end of training week she was in seventh heaven, feasting on over 100 leftover T-bone steak bones. She got as fat as a pig.

When I was assigned my first crew the dog had to go along

She had never ridden in a canoe before but soon got used to curling up on the bottom in the sun and snoozing away as we paddled along. Every portage* was a new adventure for her and she eagerly scoped out each portage trail ahead of us. She slowed us down a bit with her digressions into the woods at the end of some of the portages when she discovered a partridge or a pesky squirrel. We carried no dog food for her as she subsisted very well on tidbits from the scouts and did a pretty good job pre-rinsing our cooking pots when we had leftovers. She would eat almost anything. Once though, she showed her displeasure at some leftover "spotted dog" (rice and raisins), by squatting and peeing in the kettle we set out. I don't know if she didn't like raisins or if the name of the dish offended her.

She would get pretty excited when we were fishing and it was all we could do to keep her in the canoe. It was the retriever instinct I think, that made her want to go after the lures. Especially top water lures! The first time a big northern* was landed she went ballistic as it flopped around in the bottom of the canoe. The scout riding garbage* (mid-ship), fearing the dog would tip the canoe, grabbed his big Bowie knife and stabbed the fish three times. The fish died, Nutz calmed down, but now water geysered up through the three slits he had poked through the canoe bottom with his fancy knife. I handed him a cup to bail with and told him never to do that again. We patched the holes with pieces of the tail of my shirt and some Ambroid model airplane cement at the next portage. This was in the days before duct tape.

Paddling through Sarah Lake, with Nutz riding garbage, later that summer, I spotted something up ahead swimming out to an island. I swung the canoe toward it to investigate. Nutz sensed the change of direction and sat up on alert. Just as I realized the swimmer was a black bear Nutz saw it too and launched herself with a 10 foot leap off the starboard gunwale*, intent on retrieval of whatever it was. She moved too quickly to stop and nearly rolled the canoe with her excited jump and was rapidly closing on the bear. My yelling at her fell on deaf ears, so we quickly paddled up along side of her. Within a few feet of the frantically swimming bear, we got hold of her collar and hauled her back into the canoe. Needless to say she got a severe scolding.

Most of the time she was fun to have around but I am sure she kept us from seeing as much wildlife as we could have. She made a good pillow and on cool nights a good foot warmer in the tent. She was treated as a regular member of the crew whose job it was to scout out the trails ahead of us and protect us from whatever dangerous creatures might be lurking in the woods. Whenever she encountered a rabbit it could easily get away if it took and abrupt left turn because that was the side with her blind eye. Her handicap never kept her from trying to catch the speedy critters.

On another trip with Nutz, we were returning to the base from Darkey Lake. We were entering the Basswood River from Crooked Lake. In the river are a series of falls and rapids. National geographic sponsored an expedition with skin divers that summer to look for trade goods below these turbulent waters. This route was a common route taken by the Voyageurs* in the days of the fur trade 300 to 400 years ago. They found little below the big waterfalls but uncovered trade beads, clay pipes, flintlocks and other relics below the smaller rapids. The voyageurs had to portage the big falls but often tied ropes onto their birch bark canoes and lined them down the rapids to avoid extra portaging. Those spots were where accidents sometimes happened and canoes were dumped losing the goods.

Horse portage bypasses a number of these rapids and falls. It is about a mile and a quarter long. We paddled up to the start of the portage and my crew and I loaded up our packs and canoes and began the trek across. Nutz led the way followed closely by me and the crew struggled along some distance back. As I neared the far end a half hour or so later, Nutz bolted and began barking at something up a nearby tree. "A squirrel", I thought as I couldn't see what it was with the canoe on my shoulders. I stepped into the water and flipped off the canoe and turned to see what had her so riled up. Her frantic barking turned to a nervous whine as I looked up the tree. A big sow black bear was backing down the tree to protect her cub, on a branch above her, from this noisy intruder. Nutz's tail went between her legs as she backed up. If she could talk it would have been "Oh s_ _ _, what have I done?" The bear hit the ground running after her and she turned tail and ran into the woods with the bear hot on her rear end. At least she was smart enough to run. Nutz raised a cloud of dust in her haste to shake the angry mama bear. There was some crashing around in the underbrush and I feared for the life of my dog. You don't want to cross any wild creature with a young one close by.

A few seconds later, Nutz bolted out of the woods and did a perfect heel at my side. I grabbed her and pitched her into the canoe. Unfortunately the bear hadn't given up the chase and came running up right behind her. The bear stopped about 10 feet away from us, drooling, snorting, and rocking her head back and forth in anger and spewing saliva in a show of force. I had only a paddle in my hand and stood my ground with one foot in the canoe and one on shore ready to shove off. My not so smart dog, shivering in fear, was by my foot in the canoe barely peeking over the canoe gunwale*. The rest of the crew-members were just starting to show up at the clearing at the end of the portage and I yelled at them to stay back. The bear and I had a stare down with me screaming at her at the top of my voice. I have no clue what I yelled at the bear but it finally turned back to its tree and climbed back up. I like to think I scared it away, but I'm guessing it felt outnumbered by the arrival of the scouts. My sheepish, foolish dog had her tail between her legs and her ears laid back as she hid in the canoe bottom. She was pretty subdued the rest of the day and the rest of the summer she left the bears alone.

19

THE ISLAND OF RODENTIA

In the animal kingdom under the groupings of the vertebrates and mammals is a class or order of creatures labeled the Rodentia or in layman's language the rodents . . . It includes rats, mice, squirrels and the like. Mice! We have discovered a place where they thrive. Not only thrive, but exist in prodigious numbers with uncontrolled reproduction. Their numbers are impressive.

My friends Dave, Mark, Parker and I took a 10-day trip into the Quetico* a few years ago. We were able to travel fast with only two in each canoe. We were intent on doing some serious fishing and headed toward the western end of the park. We spent most of our days hanging around Curtain and Rebecca Falls and also diverted over to Darkey and Argo Lakes. During waking hours more often than not we had fishing poles in the water.

Our trip started with a fire ban in place, so all our cooking was done on a small Primus gas stove*. We didn't need to hunt for firewood and the pots stayed cleaner. Some people like cooking that way, but the single burner canceled out most of our plans for fancy seven course meals and baking was really tough so the cakes and pies we like to make in the woods were off the menu. It was a drag not only because of the simplified cooking, but without a campfire drying out wet clothes was impossible and who ever heard of sitting around the Primus telling stories.

A few days into the trip we got hit with a pretty good thunderstorm and our tent was found to be a leaker. In the middle of the night we woke up during the storm, lying in our saturated sleeping bags, shivering. Parker looked over at Dave who was still asleep. Dave was lying on the downhill side of the tent. It is amazing that a tent can leak so much water in and not let it leak out. It was a good thing Dave was laying on his back or he would have drowned! Only his nose and eyes projected above the small lake he was laying in. Any deeper and he would have had to tread water. "Dave . . . DAVE . . . Wake up!" cried Parker. Dave came to, alarmed at the water depth. He scrunched up against us on the high side of the tent asking "Why did you wake me up? Now I'm cold." We spent the rest of the night huddled together sharing what little warmth that generated. Now we really wished for a campfire but we had no way of knowing if the fire ban was lifted. Thankfully, the next morning was bright and sunny and we were able to hang everything up to dry.

At Curtain Falls we had to camp on an Island that we assumed was on the Canadian side as there was no fire grate or Latrine. Any group taking the portage around the falls passed right by our little island. What I am saying is that it was a pretty public spot. The half—acre island was all forested with small red pines with little undergrowth. Privacy was out of the question and the only place we had to make a latrine was where two big flat rocks made a vee shaped crack between them. You could put one cheek on each rock and leave your loaf in the crack. There was a small cedar on each side but it still commanded a pretty good view from the lake. One morning, as Parker was taking an extended bathroom break, (the fruit stew hadn't kicked in yet) a group of tourists paddled by. All he could do was sit there and wave and pretend he was just enjoying the view.

Later that day, Parker took advantage of a large rock projecting out into the fast water below the falls to do some fishing. Parker likes to use spoons where I would prefer to use plugs for artificial bait. Casting a Mepps spinner into the fast water, in the course of a few minutes, he pulled in a bass, a northern, and a walleye from that spot using the same spoon for them all. He almost made me into a spoon man. Boy those fish tasted good. It was even better because we had heard from some passers by that the fire ban was lifted so we were back to cooking over an open fire. We were also able to burn our big bag of burnable garbage and further dry our bags and clothes.

A day later we took a side trip over to Darkey Lake to do some serious bass fishing. Darkey is a big deep lake and contains all the species of fish that are found in the boundary waters including Lake and Brown Trout*. It is a great bass* lake because of the several streams that flow in and the accompanying lily pad beds. We had a blast fishing top water hula poppers* and jitterbugs and caught a fair number of smallmouth bass. We fished our way to the north end of the lake and claimed the empty campsite on the giant hog back of rock near one of the bass streams. The fire place was built against a big round rock at the top of the site providing a good reflector for baking.

While cooking that late afternoon, we occasionally caught a glimpse of a mouse investigating our presence. We had to shoo them away from the food that we had spread out on the tarp. It looked like they were going to be pesky. A big golden eagle and a bald eagle began a ruckus as to who got to sit in a perch on a nearby tree. I think what they were really arguing about was who got the good observation spot because of all the mice that were available for them to catch and eat.

We didn't dare to turn our backs on any of the food or the mice would show up in numbers and begin nibbling on the food bags. Soon, many of the plastic bags were leaking their contents from the holes the pesky critters had gnawed in them. We had made more stew than we could eat for supper so the leftovers were set aside with the rest of the dirty dishes while we waited for the dishwater to heat up. A few minutes later as we sat around the fire warming ourselves against the descending night-time chill, we began to hear the dishes and silverware rattling around piled inside the big stew pot. Normally the first thought is . . . it's a bear!

Mark put his spotlight on the pile of dishes and about 50 mice bailed out of the stew pot and ran for cover. He pitched a small log at the pile of dishes and even more scattered. We discovered mice are highly nocturnal creatures . . . the numbers we saw earlier did not compare to what we were seeing now. They had licked all the pots clean and the leftover stew was gone. They came out of the woodwork. It was like in the movie "Never Cry Wolf" where the naturalist's camp was over run by the vermin. Alarmed, we turned the light on our food still laid out on the tarp. They were all over the food bags. We scrambled to save what we could and put a lot of it in the cook pots and put the lids on weighting them with stones. The rest went back into the pack but many bags were leaking ingredients all over.

Dave's one-pound sack of sunflower seeds, were all shelled into a neat pile, all eaten. It must have been their favorite food. We gathered the pre-rinsed dishes and washed them in the heated dishwater. I think the local mouse herd was supported by all the food that was provided for them by the campers that used the popular campsite. During the night the mice kept us awake with their antics. I swear they were running up one side of the tent and sliding down the other side like a ski slope. I swore I could hear a high pitched "whee" once in a while. I think they were enjoying themselves. Dave even had one run over his face during the night. It was like the 10 plagues visited by the Lord upon the Egyptians in the Old Testament.

I had mentioned to my friends earlier in the trip, that I had never lost any food to bears, but that I had lost a lot to chipmunks, mice and squirrels. They found out the truth to that statement the next morning as we surveyed the wreckage to our food supply caused by the little buggers. We would remember the Darkey campsite for a long time because of the plague of the mice.

20

BUGS

Officially we all know that the Minnesota state bird is the Loon. Unofficially it's the mosquito. There are several species in the state but I only am concerned with their abilities. Some have the ability to pass through screen doors where others I swear can open them. I hate 'em all. I know they feed the fish and are part of the food chain but "Dad gum it! They can sure make life miserable for all warm blooded creatures such as humans" I swear. They are worst early in the summer but if it is a wet summer they will persist clear till frost. The last few years since the big blowdown on July fourth, 1999 have been bad. My theory is that the 25 million trees that went down in that storm left a lot of potholes as their root balls were wrenched from the ground, and all those holes in the woods served as collecting points for stagnant water that has given the pesky buggers untold numbers of perfect breeding ponds.

Usually, August is relatively mosquito free and I have been on 10-day trips where I never had to smack a single one. The worst encounter I ever had with them was on a trip I guided down the Wawaig River. The paddle is a long 30 miles or more and to canoe the whole river in a day is normally the plan as there are no campsites along its banks. Usually, with an early start you can just get to the end of the river before dark. On this trip it was already almost 10 PM as we approached the mouth of the river and we could hear the drone of the hordes of mosquitos before we got to the campsite located where the river flows into Kawanipi Lake. They hadn't bothered us too much as long as we had been moving but when we stopped at the site to unload our gear and set up camp they became blood thirsty. The crew set up the tents in record time and dove into them for cover. I braved the clouds of bugs and got a one pot supper cooked as quickly as I could. I was getting bitten through my jeans and shirt and I began to feel like a pincushion. Where I had holes in my clothes they attacked with a vengeance. I carried the pot of food around to each of the tents and the boys ate their food under cover. I doused the fire after serving the food and grabbed the can of bug killer. I went around to each tent and sprayed to kill the ones that had made it inside. The boys all hunkered down and crawled way inside their bags to escape the humming horde and the cloud of pesticide. The dead mosquitos in each tent could be literally swept into a pile. About three in the morning I woke up and needed to go to the bathroom. I crawled out of the sack and made my way to the door of the tent careful not to step on any of the five boys sleeping in the tent with me. I shined my flashlight on the mosquito netting looking for the zipper but quickly changed my mind about going out there. The warm breath of the boys and the promise of a blood meal had the mosquitos swarming nearly two inches thick on the outside of the mosquito netting. They had been attracted to us like iron filings to a magnet. I thought, "If I go out there I'll bleed to death before I can finish." Thank God I didn't need to have a bowel movement. I opted to pee right through the mosquito netting and climbed back into my sleeping bag. Thankfully in the morning the wind had come up and the cloud of mini vampires were blown back into the woods.

Just before the mosquitos make their appearance each summer, the gnats or black flies appear. They are also after blood and once they get you bleeding a bit then they call in all their relatives and family for the feeding frenzy. Some people are allergic to the enzymes that they inject into you to keep your blood from clotting as they bite. I once had an advisor whose face swelled up so badly from them that I seriously considered taking him back to the base and shortening our trip but he gamely said he didn't want to ruin the trip for the boys. He doused himself with bug dope to ward them off and soon the swelling went down. The gnats go for blood around the hairline and behind the ears. Once you start bleeding more come to feed and pretty soon you are leaking blood and itching like crazy. They don't die as easily as mosquitos when you smack them and are really pesky. Further north in tundra country they are far worse and have actually driven people mad.

Another noxious critter is the no-see-um. These are smaller than gnats but can be equally troublesome. They are so small you may wonder what is biting you, thus the name. Repellents containing DEET* work really well on them. We really stirred them up at one campsite as we tried to sweep off the tentsites of debris while setting up camp. Soon, everyone was scratching and itching. The sun beams shining through the trees lit up the clouds of them that we had disturbed in our clean up. After sharing our bug dope with everyone they left us alone.

Ever hear of chiggers? These are really tiny red spiders whose bites leave nasty welts around the ankles and lower legs as they crawl up inside your pants. Again, repellents work quite well to control them.

Early in the summer wood and deer ticks abound. I have picked dozens of ticks off myself at one sitting after a hike in the woods or crossing a portage. Some years they are worse than others. Deer ticks can transmit Lyme Disease and they are much smaller than the ordinary wood ticks. Ticks can also transmit Rocky Mountain Spotted Fever although I have not heard of a case in the boundary waters area. It is wise to check each other over at bedtime to see if any are on you. One poor guide had found one firmly imbedded on his male member while he was in the shower back at the base. He could find no volunteers to help him remove it. He finally got it to back out by touching its behind with a hot match. Burying the tick in Vaseline will also make them back out with their air supply cut off. When I get bit the ticks leave huge welts that take quite a while to heal up. The danger of pulling them out is that their head may be left buried in your hide and that makes the healing process even longer. Ticks are hard to kill and generally I like to throw them in the fire or smash them with a stone.

"What is it with deer flies?" They love to land in your hair. They sit there for quite a while and then bite and start to draw blood.

They usually fly away when you smack them and are really hard to kill. Repellents work marginally on them. They are virtually indestructible. They are worst in hot, dry weather later in the summer.

In dry summers ground bees or yellow jackets can become a problem. They are attracted to sweet foods and drinks and a person needs to be observant so you don't bite into one or swallow one. Their nests are next to invisible until you step on them and then they can be quite aggressive.

Hornet nests are usually large and easily seen hanging from tree branches or in bushes. They are quite aggressive but by being always observant you can usually avoid them. Once with the canoe on my shoulders, I accidentally bumped a low hanging nest of them with the stern of my canoe. I was at a curve on a portage trail, and I never saw the nest but I sure saw them. I finished the portage in record time on the run. I had quite a few buzzing around me as I carried the canoe but never got stung. The rest of the crew had avoided them and showed me the nest later. We threw a rock at the nest and really got them riled up. Believe me, avoiding them is the best policy. If you are allergic to bee stings it is a wise plan to carry a bee sting kit.

In spite of what I have described, most of the time spent on canoe trips is relatively bug free and quite pleasant. Do not let the threat of bugs deter you from canoe tripping. If you are bringing children on a trip I would avoid going in the spring and early summer but would take them later on when it is more bug free. Modern repellents work very well and it is best to come prepared. Long sleeved shirts and pants are always along on my trips for protection from not only the bugs and sunburn but also the chilly nights. Enjoy your trip!.

21

FISHING IS A BLAST

Boy, do I love to fish! Especially with top water lures! I have absolutely no desire to own a big fancy boat and motor. Trolling a lure, out the back of a canoe, suits me just fine. We don't often use live bait due to the extended length of our trips and the fact that the use of minnows is prohibited in the Quetico* park. I like to keep it simple. There should be a law that if you go into the boundary waters you have to take a rod and reel. I almost insist that anyone that goes with me into the woods has one along. It's the first piece of equipment I assemble whenever I start to pack for an upcoming trip. If I were allowed to take only three lures into the woods they would be a jointed rapala*in black and white, a red and white daredevil*, and a black hula popper*. I would catch a lot of fish with the first two lures but I would have the most fun with the hula popper.

You know, even if you don't have any luck using one on a particular afternoon, you still can have a great time just casting a hula popper or some similar top water lure trying to tease the fish to the surface. I get enjoyment just trying to see how close I can land a lure to the edge of a bunch of lily pads or near a likely branch hanging down in the water.

Usually in calm water, I will drift the canoe about 75 to 100 feet out from a likely shoreline and work the shoreline with the popper. If the shore has lily pads, a bed of reeds, or trees lying in the water, it will be all the better for fishing. This is when the fun begins. The hula popper imitates a frog. Frogs hop from shore or from lily pads into the water. To interest the fish, you have to cast your lure as close as you can to frog habitat and then let it sit. Any fish, particularly bass*, but often northerns*, that are close by have already taken note that something hit the water. Wait carefully until the ripples from the splash from your lure have spread out to about 10 feet in diameter. Now, while you still have the fish's attention, let them know that this object is indeed alive and twitch the tip of your rod, making it pop. Wait a few seconds and do it again. After five or six pops chances are no fish were in the vicinity. By teasing them this way you can usually pull a strike right away. Set the hook solidly and you have a great fight on your hands.

In time, all that casting will improve your skill and accuracy. At first you will tend to cast short. As your skill increases and you become more daring you will reach out farther and farther until you start making great casts right next to likely bass hideouts. You will make your share of overshoots and land on shore or in trees or bushes, but it is a top water lure and you are in a canoe, so recovery is usually not too tough.

Several fishermen I know have found that sometimes a fish will follow a lure all the way back to the canoe and strike at the last second. They often will leave the lure in the water for a few seconds and drag it in a figure of eight pattern to draw that last second strike. Don't ever think you can crank in a lure faster than the fish can swim. And do be ready for the occasional strike the instant the lure lands in the water or sometimes just before the lure hits the water. I heard a story about a big northern jumping up to consume a squirrel that was on a branch that hung down close to the water. They can get that big and they are out there! Sometimes a fish will clear the water going after a lure before it even hits the surface.

I once cast near shore, trying to plant my hula popper just beneath an overhanging branch. I cast too high an arc to get under the limb and tried to pull up short to avoid getting snagged. The lure sailed just over the branch as I tried to stop it and centrifugal force wound the line around the branch several times, leaving the popper swinging about 18 inches above the water. Your lure doesn't have to hit the water to interest the fish. An 18 inch small-mouth leapt up and impaled himself on the lure with his tail just touching the water as he thrashed about trying to get free. Wow!

There is nothing like a top water strike to get the heart pumping. Forget cardio exercise . . . just fish more. Even if the fish misses the lure the excitement is there and you just want to try again. I treasure the looks on camper's faces when they first try a top water lure. I have loaned out top water plugs to campers many times, knowing they will soon be hooked on fishing that way.

There are lots of other top water lures that work great too. A jitterbug is another favorite of mine. Another is a wire and double blade contraption that makes an obnoxious clanking and splashing sound and leaves a wake and commotion that looks like a small bird trying to get airborne. You have to retrieve rapidly to keep it on the surface of the water, as it will sink fast if you hesitate. It often will pull the big ones up from the bottom like nothing else. Even a floating rapala is a good lure for top water, if you twitch it imitating an injured minnow. If you have ever teased a kitten by pulling a string along the floor you will have a good idea of how to use top water lures.

If you are in a lake with big northerns that are hungry you can generate awesome strikes. Be sure to put a short steel leader on your lure so you don't get your line sliced by their teeth. I use six inch ones so I won't interfere with a lures action or ability to float. I have seen large northerns over three feet long clear the water trying to get a top water lure. Don't fish for them if you have a weak heart! On the other hand, what a way to go!

Several years into my first marriage I talked my wife Kathy, into going with me on a short weekend trip to fish Wind Lake. After we had set up camp we trolled the shoreline for northerns and stopped in calm bays to cast top water lures. I was a bit short on gear so she was using an ultra light open faced reel that I had fastened to an old fly rod with electricians tape. It wasn't the greatest set up, and the rod tip was missing, but she had caught a few fish on it and it had good action. It was nearly time to make supper so we had decided to head back to camp. Our five year old son Matt who was riding in the middle of the canoe was getting hungry.

I turned our canoe around and started crossing the channel to the other side. Out in the middle, far from shore, I heard a splash behind us. It sounded like a beavers tail smacking the water in alarm. I looked back and noticed Kathy's rapala was tangled up and doing the crappie flop* on the surface. I told her she needed to reel in and untangle the lure. She gave the reel a couple of cranks and then there was an even bigger splash as a big northern nailed the lure. I suspect the lure had gotten tangled at the pikes* first attempt at hitting it. The fight was on! Twenty minutes later we had the 15-pounder on board. It was a stoutly built big feeder pig of a fish . . . not at all a hammer handle*. Our stringer was one of those metal chain gismos with all the spring-loaded clips. I didn't trust one clip to hold this fish so I put two of the clips through his lower jaw and locked them shut. I returned the stringer with the big northern and the three other fish we had caught to the lake, and locked the stringer to the thwart*. We pulled in our lines and started to stroke toward camp. The big northern took this opportunity to start a ruckus alongside the canoe and drenched me with his thrashing about. I thought I had better check on him and lifted up the stringer. He was gone! Both steel clips were bent out straight! I never heard the end of it and that stringer went in the garbage when we got home.

Back at camp that evening, I spotted a big snapping turtle at the bottom of the lake just off the campsite, easily visible in about 10 feet of water. He was munching on fish parts that were lying on the bottom. I grabbed a rod and pitched a daredevil just beyond him and dragged it back over him. I Missed. On the second try I hooked the edge of his shell. I hauled his 30-pound hulk to the surface but when he saw me he turned tail and headed back to the bottom, straightening out the hook on the lure and got away. He went right back to eating the fish guts. I grabbed my pliers and bent the hook on the lure back and tried again. This time I snagged him in the web of his front foot. My rod tip yo-yoed back and forth with every stroke he took swimming mightily trying to escape. I finally landed him and grabbed him by the tail, holding him as far away from me as I could. Their powerful jaws could take off a finger or get a big chunk of flesh if he got hold of me. He hissed and snapped at me generating a lot of respect,

Matt, who had been watching, ran up to get the axe. We chopped off the turtle's head. Since turtles don't die easily the head lay there snapping and soon the detached head had latched on to the tail of the headless carcass. The gruesome sight became even weirder as the body was still trying to walk away dragging the cut off head hanging on its tail. This was my first experience cleaning a turtle and I have to admit it was a bit of a job. We paddled out the next day with about 10 pounds of turtle meat in the packsack. We ground it up when we got home and turned it into turtle burger. The meat had the flavor of several kinds of meat with a faint fishy aftertaste . . . not too bad we thought. The big fish and the turtle had made for an exciting weekend but the excitement of top water fishing is what made that weekend trip truly memorable.

22

BULLWINKLE

Moose* and the boundary waters go hand in hand. It's their habitat. Seeing one on a canoe trip is a highlight to cherish. Since my first canoe trip in 1959, I have lost count of how many moose I have seen in the woods. On canoe trips I have seen many more moose than deer but then it is hard to miss a moose.

Traveling the length of the Cache River with a crew of scouts we saw 12 of the big critters in one day of paddling. Occasionally we caught the pungent scent of their droppings . . . smelled a lot like a cattle feedlot back home in farm country.

On another trip with a crew of scouts we were traveling down a creek out of Phoebe Lake on the U.S. side of the border. In a shallow stretch of water we were walking our canoes downstream to avoid a portage*. I was about 50 feet ahead of the crew with my bowman. The scouts were making quite a bit of racket and were horsing around, splashing water, and having a good time getting each other wet. I thought, "We're never going to see any wildlife with all this commotion." Suddenly, a big bull moose blundered into the creek about 75 feet in front of me. He spooked when he heard us and quickly vanished into the woods on the right. I had tried to get the scouts' attention at his appearance, but couldn't in time for them to see him. I waited for them to catch up and told them about the moose. I saw disbelief on their faces. I whispered to them, "he's standing just a little ways into the brush on the right side of the creek."

Quietly now, I led the disbelieving boys downstream to the shore where I had seen the bull head into the woods, and we all carefully climbed upon a large fallen white pine that was leaning on another tree. When we had scaled the ramp and had a good view of the woods from our 15 ft high vantage point I looked around and spotted the bull. I could see only his back end in the brush and whispered, "There he is!" to the boys. Most still didn't believe the big dark brown lump was the moose even when I carefully pointed him out because it hadn't moved, so I grabbed a chunk of bark off the big pine and pitched it at his rear end about 30 feet away. It was a direct hit. The woods erupted as the startled moose ran for cover. The boy's eyes were big now! I admonished them to be quiet when we were wading the creek and sure enough, 10 minutes later another big bull crossed in front of us and all saw him. Five minutes later we saw two cows each with a calf. Six moose in less than 20 minutes . . . Wow!

On another trip a couple of canoe loads of scouts had challenged each other to a race to be first at the start of a portage. I don't know why they were racing because the portage* was nasty, starting on a floating bog or muskeg*. At racing speed and only about 40 feet from shore, the scouts were startled by the head of a big bull rearing up out of the water. He had lily pads and algae dangling from his ponderous rack and he was frantic to get out of their way. As the scouts back-stroked mightily trying to avoid a collision, he managed to get his front legs up on the muskeg and struggled to haul his bulk out of the water. Within a few seconds he was gone down the trail like a ghost, the rocking, bobbing muskeg the only evidence that he had been there.

Traveling the Little Indian Sioux River with a crew of guides on a training trip the next summer we struggled in the shallow river with all its twists and turns. We weren't making very good time. Around one meander after another, I was hard put trying to steer and not hit the shore. Suddenly, pivoting around a blind corner, we encountered the rear end of a big bull four feet over our eye level and only ten feet away. I quickly stuck my foot out and dragged the canoe to a stop in the sandy bottom. He was oblivious to our presence and continued to feed.

Evidently he had not heard or smelled us and was facing the wrong way to see us. I think we were the first humans he had ever seen, because when he finally turned and saw us he just stood there dumbfounded, and curious. We waited patiently but finally I yelled at him to move it and he clambered up to shore and stood and watched as we paddled onward.

On another camping trip on an island in North Bay of Basswood Lake I arose early one morning and walked from the tents down to the lakeshore. I spotted three moose wading and feeding in the shallow beds of reeds jutting out from the mainland a mere 100 yards away. I have encountered dozens of moose swimming across lakes and have paddled up close to them but have never had the courage or perhaps foolhardiness to climb out and jump on their backs and ride them in the water as I know several of the guides have.

One warm sunny afternoon, my son Matt, my grandson Zack and I were fishing in Wind Lake near the portage into Moose Lake*. We were paddling the shoreline, trolling for northerns* and had a couple nice ones on the stringer. As we made our second round of the bay we noticed a large dark shape on a small beach ahead that hadn't been there the first time we had been by. We argued briefly over what it was . . . . a stump, a bear or something else. We hadn't seen it move. Paddling closer to investigate we realized that it was a big bull sleeping on the warm sand. When we got about 50 yards away he saw us and stood up. Zack's eyes got big when the long legged, ungainly critter finally got his legs under him and stood up at his full height. "He's as big as a horse!" Zack exclaimed and he was right.

On the same lake the next spring on a trip with a bunch of friends, the kids challenged the old-timers to a fishing contest. We all set out to win the prize of a few dollars that had been thrown in the kitty. Later when it started to drizzle, the kids having more sense than the adults, headed back to camp and their warm sleeping bags. The die-hard old timers kept on fishing. We had not had much luck and pulled up on a small island for a potty break and to pick some blueberries. My friend Jim Krech wandered up the small hill to the top of the island looking for berries but soon scurried back down to us wide eyed. He had his thumbs in his ears with his fingers outstretched imitating something.

He whispered loudly "Moose . . . up there" and pointed up the path. I said, "Lets' go see." "What if he charges us?" Jim questioned. "Get behind a big tree", I suggested. Dan, Jim and I crept up the hill and there he was in the middle of a small empty campsite. It was a small bull. As I slowly approached him he backed away, never letting me ease closer than about 30 feet. We followed him down to the water and he waded out and began to feed in the lily pad patch near the island. We watched fascinated, and he was still there later when we paddled out to fish again.

Once, on a small creek our crew ran into a family of moose. One of the canoes got between a cow on one bank and her calf on another. I shouted "back up and wait for the calf to cross over". It is prudent never to get between a wild critter and it's young as it can infuriate the mother and put you in danger. Most animals have a very strong instinct to protect their young. It is also wise not to provoke a creature much larger than you are. I once saw a pickup with thousands of dollars damage from an angry bull moose that had repeatedly rammed it.

I have had a moose literally step over me and a bunch of my scouts as it picked its way over a portage trail where we had made an impromptu camp after paddling late into the night. We were all sound asleep but woke to catch a fleeting glimpse of his rear end going down the trail and found evidence that he had carefully and silently avoided stepping on us by following his trail of fresh foot prints in the sand.

The closest I ever came to a live moose happened late one night on highway 1 south of Ely. My brother Paul and I were traveling north from Duluth up to the scout canoe base northeast of Ely for a weekend visit. Sandy Bridges had just retired as director of the base and they had a nice party for him in Duluth. After the event Paul and I left for the base. About 11:00 PM I mentioned to Paul to be on the lookout for deer on the road. They can usually be easily spotted by the glow of their eyes in the headlights. The words had scarcely left my mouth when suddenly I saw not glowing eyes, but instead what looked like four black trees growing out of the blacktop ahead. I cranked the wheel to the left and stood on the brakes. I wasn't going more than about 45 but the antilock brakes kept me going straight ahead and I didn't quite have enough room to stop. A rack of a big bull caught my eye at the last second as he slowly sauntered across the road. I clipped his rear legs with the bumper of my mini van and dumped his bulk onto the hood. His rump smashed into the windshield spider-webbing it and spraying us with glass. The collision broke off the mirror and the antennae and dented the post on the windshield on the right side. The hood was a crumpled mess. The windshield had held but the moose's bowels hadn't. He had unloaded on the hood, windshield, roof, and even the back window somehow. "We scared the s_ _ _ out of him!" Paul exclaimed as we surveyed the damage. The collision hadn't broken any lights, killed the engine, or even set off the air bags but had done $2500 damage we found out later. We checked each other over but found no blood. The moose had gotten up and walked away. We limped our way up to the base driving slowly so we wouldn't dislodge the broken but still intact windshield. There we braced the dished windshield with a piece of Plexiglas until we could get it repaired. We said a prayer of thanks because we could both have been killed or seriously injured. It's pretty tough to win an argument with a moose.

23

THE COUGAR

It was late September and the leaves were in full color. It was a beautiful, warm fall day when 16 (this was before a size limit was required) of us set out for a trip to the BWCA*. The group was made up of my wife and I and our church youth group with their youth advisor and his wife. Our pastor also came along on the trip. Included in the group of teenagers, was my son Matt. We paddled across Moose Lake* and took the half mile portage leading to Wind Lake where I had promised the group some good fishing. Our outing was only for a long weekend, but it was the first experience canoeing for many of the farm kids we had along.

We set up a nice camp on the beach in the big bay and did all the camp chores, gathering fire wood, stringing clothes lines and cooking supper. Sunset turned a bit gray as a cloud bank approached from the west. A few in the group went out and caught several nice pike that we saved for breakfast. The kids turned in and the adults stayed up sitting around the campfire drinking coffee and telling stories. As it got later we sensed that it would probably rain so clothes that were left out were picked up and the food was packed away under the dining fly. The canoes were stashed safely and we all climbed in our sleeping bags and were out like a light in minutes. A couple hours later the wind came up and the rain came down in buckets. It didn't take long to discover a few leaks in the tents as the bags soaked up some water.

In the morning it was quite a bit colder and you could see your breath. It was still cloudy but the day didn't seem like it would be a total loss. It was a bit of a challenge to get the fire going with the soggy wood but soon there was a nice bed of coals. We cooked up bacon and eggs and fried up the fillets of the northerns from the night before. We topped off the good hot breakfast with several cups of hot chocolate and then the kids all wanted to go fishing. We all set out and had pretty good luck landing plenty of pike and bass to eat for the next meal. The sun popped out briefly and it looked like it might be a nice day. After a few hours most of the youth group had returned to the campsite. A bit later Ben, the youth leader and I were still out fishing on the far side of the bay along with one other canoe when I noticed some pretty dark clouds coming in from the northwest. We quickly cranked in our lures and began paddling hard for our campsite a mile away. The wall of heavy rain from the storm soon caught up to us and we began three manning it*, trying to get ahead of the storm. Slowly we pulled out of it as we raced to camp. For a while the bowman was staying dry while the stern man was getting drenched because the line of rain was so definite. We beat the storm to camp by only a minute. We dove in our tents and waited for the storm to abate. And we waited and waited. It rained for hours. The storm the night before had put about 3 inches of water in our cooking pots and when this one finally ended at suppertime we had 5 more inches in the pails. It was so wet that we resorted to using white gas to get the fire going. Now we were really cold and wet and had wet sleeping bags too. We put together a pretty good supper all things considered and even baked a cake. The kids climbed in bed and the grown-ups sat around the fire again telling stories.

Around 10:00 or so, in the middle of some fish tale, everyone went silent as we heard a very loud and deep snarl that rumbled in the woods behind our tents. Ben quickly checked the tents thinking that the kids were trying to scare us but they were all inside with eyes wide open asking "What was that?" Now kittens and tigers are in the same family and they can both hiss and snarl. This sounded like a really big cat and rumbled like it was coming out of a 50 gallon barrel. We quickly all grabbed our flashlights and flooded the woods with light. No one got a full, good view of whatever it was but it was tan colored, big, and yet it made little noise as it ran off into the woods. I know of no other animal that could have made that sound and run off so furtively except a cougar*. I have never seen one in all my years of canoe tripping but I know of a few people that have and I am convinced that is what it was. At any rate, none of us felt like sleeping and our bags were wet anyway so we all got in the biggest tent together and by huddling together stayed a bit warm and got a few hours of shuteye. In the morning it was in the 30s and starting to sleet. We managed to get a fire going and produced a big pot of hot oatmeal. We packed up our gear and headed back to the base where a hot lunch and better yet a sauna* awaited our group. The sleet turned to light snow as we loaded up our gear in the canoe base parking lot and we knew this would be the last trip to the canoe country for this year but the memory of the big loud snarl of the cougar would last to the end of our lives.

24

CANIS LUPIS

The timber wolf has gotten a bad rap. He is feared, but unreasonably so. He is mysterious and a creature of the night. Yet wolves are great parents to their young and do not deserve the bad reputation that everyone seems to believe about them.

When I first started guiding canoe trips in the BWCA* in 1964, to hear a wolf howl was a rare event, and to actually see one was almost unheard of. We occasionally heard one howling far off and once in a while saw tracks and scat* but I never actually saw one until years later. Now their numbers have increased so they have been taken off the endangered species list and seeing and hearing them is quite common.

A few years ago I was installing some handmade signs at the scout base, and had to run to Ely a couple of times that day for supplies. Each time I went or returned on the Fernberg road* I saw a wolf on the highway. I suspect he was working on a road-kill deer or some other creature but I saw him 4 times that day.

In the summer of 2002, several of my friends and I decided to take a weekend long canoe trip to the Curtain Falls area right on the Canadian border. It was one of those spur-of-the moment things so we had only a week or so to prepare. We worried about getting an entry point* permit but found several were available for the Stuart River route. We checked the map and saw why few campers chose to enter on that route, because it had several very long portages*. We had no other options so we secured our permit and got our gear together and set out. We left about 2:00 AM from the Twin Cities and arrived at our starting point on the Echo trail by 9:00 AM. By dark that evening we had made the 14 portages and we were at Curtain Falls. It was definitely a very long day and we were all exhausted. We set up camp, ate a quick supper and sacked out. We were a bit pokey in the morning and quite stiff but after coffee and enjoying the warming morning sun we felt a bit better.

We had an enjoyable day exploring the area and caught several nice fish. Our island campsite had a big rocky point that had a divot in it that had collected quite a bit of rainwater. I thought we should heat up some rocks in the fire and throw them in the collected rain water so we could have a hot bath. It would be like a hot tub without the bubbles but the water was kind of stagnant and full of algae so we used it for a live well for the decent sized northern* that Bruce had caught. Later when some of the others came back from fishing, Bruce took them down to the small pool intent on showing off his fish. On the path down to the pool, Bruce glanced upward and said pointing "Cool . . . look at that eagle, he's got a fish". As it turns out it was Bruce's fish. The eagle had neatly taken off with the stringer and the fish that we had intended to be our shore lunch. That was a first time event for any trip I have ever taken. I've lost lots of fish to snapping turtles but never to an eagle.

After a couple of great days our adventure drew to a close and we decided to go half of the way back so the last day wouldn't be so tough. We paddled and portaged back south toward Stuart Lake and after some searching found a great campsite behind a point in a hidden bay. It had log benches and a great canoe landing with a gigantic flat rock that faded gently into the lake. We had a nice campfire that night and turned in. About 5:30 AM we were awakened by the sound of a pack of wolves howling very loud and very close. The guys literally came rolling out of the tents wide eyed. It was so close and so loud at first we all thought someone was imitating the wolves to scare us but it was real. They carried on for 10 minutes or so and couldn't have been more than 100 yards away just across the small bay. Chuck started howling back at them and they were answering back. Worried that the pack might pay us a visit, Bruce said to Chuck "Shut Up!!!!!!" Now that we were all wide-awake we made breakfast and headed back to the cars we had left on the Echo Trail. Everyone remembers this trip because of the wolves we heard.

Several years earlier I was on a trip near the same area. We were camped at Rebecca Falls less than 15 miles from Stuart Lake. We were lazing in the sun on top of the big rock between the twin falls above the campsite enjoying the scenery. I looked over across the bay at the campsite there, and said "Hey, we've got company." I saw a German Shepard dog walk into the empty campsite and I began looking for the canoes and the campers that had undoubtedly brought him along. It is quite common to see families come up and bring their pets.

But there were no campers and it wasn't a German Shepard. It was a mother wolf and she had a small pup with her. We grabbed the binoculars and watched them for nearly an hour. I watched her patiently teach the pup survival skills. I have never seen this behavior documented before in wolves. She waded out into the shallows until she was in water about a foot deep and just stood there. Suddenly she batted a small fish out of the water, landing it a few feet from the pup. I am not sure that the pup realized it was food right away because he played with the flopping fish for some time before he took a bite. After catching and eating several more fish, the wolves silently slipped away into the woods. We were grateful for the chance to witness their activities.

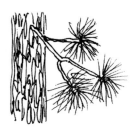

25

THE CATHEDRAL

I had just returned from a 250 mile marathon trip, and found out the Scout base was short on guide staff. I was scheduled to take out another crew without the usual day off. I had made my trip to town to restock my depleted fishing tackle box and had eaten the obligatory steak and lobster meal at Dee's Bar and Restaurant and was organizing my gear for the next crew I was to take out. They were scheduled to arrive shortly after lunch. I decided to take a considerably shorter trip as my body was suffering a bit from the strains of the last trip. Studying my trail map I saw a series of small pot hole lakes (small often unnamed lakes) that lie between Canadian Agnes and Louisa Lakes that I had always wanted to visit. The problem was there were no portages* marked between them. No problem . . . I figured we could bushwack* our own.

The next day I met my new crew. Jack O'Neal was the adviser and the crew was from Salina, Kansas. All together there would be thirteen of us, so we had to take five canoes. That was another good reason for planning a short trip. I asked, "would you guys like to see some lakes no one has gone into for years?" Manipulating crews to plan a trip where you would like them to go is so easy it is almost sinful. "Yeah, lets' go there" they agreed and I added pointing to the lakes on the map, "the fishing could be very interesting cuz very few people ever go there". We packed our gear and food and traced our route on the map that would take us through a lot of uncharted territory. The farthest north we would travel would be to the big arm of Canadian Lake Agnes that angles to the Northeast. Our route included at least a dozen spots where no portages were marked on the map. It would surely be an interesting route, even though the 8 day trip would be only about 50 miles long.

We paddled up to Prairie Portage*and stood in line with about 50 other campers at the ranger station* waiting to register our route and pick up our fishing licenses. We ate lunch there and spent some time searching the sand beach looking for trade beads. The rangers had jars full of beads, arrowheads, clay pipes and musket balls that they had found on their beach. Prairie Portage used to be the site of a fairly large Indian village many years ago and artifacts are still turning up as the waves turn over the sand. We found a few beads but nothing else.

We paddled on to Burke Lake where we camped for the first night. We had time to fish and landed a couple nice lake trout*. The water in Burke is so clear you can see almost 20 feet down. The meat in the trout filets wasn't as pink and oily as I had seen in trout caught in some of the other deep lakes but it was excellent eating. We traveled on through Sunday Lake and took the two Meadows portages leading to Lake Agnes. The portages were long and rocky, as well as muddy from recent rains.

Paddling up Lake Agnes a couple of miles we could hear Louisa Falls. Louisa Lake is nearly 70 feet higher that Lake Agnes, so the falls and rapids drop quite a distance. Below the main 40 foot cataract the pounding of the water has scoured out a chest deep pool that can easily hold a whole crew. We stood in it with the falling water pounding the tops of our heads. The cold rushing water was very refreshing. We moved on after a quick lunch, and paddled up Louisa Lake about half way, where we diverted to the west into a small pot-hole lake. We were surprised to find a faint portage trail to this tiny lake from Louisa. We set up camp and again landed a few trout but nothing worth bragging about. That night we studied the map to try to figure out the best way through the maze of small lakes.

In the morning we cut our first portage to the north into the closest of a series of eight small lakes. To make a portage trail you have to walk through the woods relying on your compass and marking trees with blazes on both sides with your axe. If there is a lot of underbrush or downed timber, or swamp or rock formations, it can be a challenging project. This particular path was quite easy to make. We marveled at the variety and color of all the different kinds of mushrooms and fungi that had sprouted up in the damp duff* after the recent rains. Fungi thrive on organic matter, and the duff on the forest floor consisted of leaves, twigs and lots of compost that mushrooms love. When temperature and moisture levels are just right the spores of the mushrooms grow, sprouting up seemingly overnight. After we crossed our bushwhacked portage to the next lake, we found a campsite there that even had remnants of a wood supply left by the rock fireplace. I guessed that it had been at least 20 years since anyone had used the spot because the firewood supply was almost rotted away and there was a tree about 5 inches in diameter growing in the fireplace. We continued on seeing some country that hadn't been visited in a long time. That night we had to make our own campsite because there weren't any.

The next day we portaged into Fauquier Lake and then headed northwest toward Dettburn Lake. We had to cut two portages to hop into and out of small lakes get there and climb over a ridge that must have been 100 feet tall. The next day we walked more than we canoed but found a few stretches of beaver streams that were dammed that allowed us passage. The last mile or so of stream that led into Lake Agnes was impassible so we just threaded our way down a well-used animal trail on the west bank. As we portaged along in the shade of the forest canopy we noticed that the woods were fairly open and the trail ran along side of the biggest white pine tree that I have ever seen. I had to flip my canoe off and take in the grandeur of it.

It must have been at least six to seven feet in diameter. When the rest of the crew caught up we called a halt to the long portage and ate lunch on the trail under this gigantic monolith. It took six crew members holding hands to encircle it. It had to be well over 120 feet tall. It reminded me of being in a cathedral with the sky for the ceiling and the great tree was one of the pillars. Reluctantly, we loaded our gear and continued down the trail. There were two more gigantic trees on that trail that we thought might have been left by the loggers back in the late 1800's to reseed the woods. I wondered how many hundreds of years old they were and how they had survived the lightning and fires that so often claim these giants of the woods. They were surely here when the Pilgrims landed on Plymouth Rock. It made one feel pretty small and insignificant. The trail along the creek finally opened up to the bay in the arm of Lake Agnes. The trees thinned as we neared the lake and finally we got to the waters edge and a beautiful huge beach. There was a great campsite there that was little used because it was so far off the beaten path. Anyone who ever did paddle up that bay would surely want to come back. The beach was there because the long narrow bay funneled the wind to the northeast shore where centuries of breakers had eroded the rock to form the sand. It was a great spot that we enjoyed for the next two sunny days.

The rest of the trip was on well-traveled lakes. We had only gone 50 miles and I am sure we walked at least 15 of them. The great pines we had seen were surely the most memorable part of the trip. It was good to take a trip that gave us the time to explore nature and recharge our strength.

26

THE BAD CHOICE

Every canoe trip involves multitudes of decisions. Most of the time choices don't involve life or death or risk injury. Most of the time the right choice is made and no problems develop. Once in a while a decision can put a person or a whole crew at great risk. Sometimes a simple wrong choice can lead to a cascade of bigger problems.

On one canoe trip with a crew of scouts we were about two days paddle out from our base on Moose Lake and the crew was doing well. Two canoes were ahead of me and were doing good finding the route and reading the maps. We had come to a portage* and the first two canoes had made good time and were on their way across. I surveyed the small rapids they were portaging around and decided that my bowman and I could easily walk up the stream and avoid the labor of carrying our gear.

We hopped out in the knee-deep water and began walking the canoe up the shallow stream. We soon came to a small falls perhaps three foot tall and I thought we could just pull the canoe up over it. The scout that was my bowman weighed maybe 90 lbs and although wiry was not very strong. As we pulled the canoe up the falls, we both struggled on the slippery bottom and soon found the canoe too tough to handle with its load of gear. Water started to pour in over the gunwales and within seconds the canoe with its load of water became impossible to hold back in the fast current. My bowman lost his footing and went bobbing downstream. I tried to hold on to the canoe that now weighed about 3000 lbs with its load of water but it knocked me down as it swung broadside in the creek. I jumped up, but was now on the downstream side of the swamped canoe trying in vain to hold it back.

The stern soon found a big rock to lodge against and the canoe swung totally broadside catching the bow keel* against a big tree root with my ankle caught in between. The canoe tipped sideways, open to the current and made a perfect dam totally blocking the stream. The water cascaded over the canoe nearly drowning me. The pressure was crushing my ankle and planking started breaking out of the bottom and all the tacks on the port side tore loose letting the canvas rip free from under the gunwale* the whole length of the canoe. The bowman came wading back upstream to help me but couldn't budge the wedged canoe loose and soon was taking another ride down the bumpy creek bottom.

Thankfully the last canoe in our party came to the portage and as they had seen me wade up the stream, they followed suit. They soon came upon the drenched bowman who quickly got them to help in what had become a very serious situation. With three more big scouts wrenching on the canoe it finally came loose and I was free. At first I wasn't sure if I had a broken ankle but it turned out to be only some bad bruising. We went back downstream to the start of the portage and loaded up our gear and then walked the trail around the rapids. At the head of the portage the rest of the crew waited unaware of the problem that we had encountered. When they saw the damage to my canoe they thought the trip was in jeopardy.

We took a closer look at the canoe and thought we could make it seaworthy again. With their pocket-knives the scouts took out all the screws the whole length of the mahogany gunwale and removed it exposing the hundreds of tacks that the canvas had torn loose from. We then carefully pulled all these out and tried to stretch the canvas back to its original position under the gunwale. Using several small round rocks for hammers we re-tacked the canvas into place and replaced the gunwale and all its screws. The repair took about three hours but soon my Old Town canoe was back in working order even though quite a bit of canvas showed through between the ribs where the planking was now missing. I learned from this experience that most of the time portages are there for a reason. Trying to get out of work sometimes ends up causing way more work in the end. The seemingly easy way is not always the best way. Sometimes you just can't do it alone and need help.

27

THE LEVIATHAN

This is a story about a fish . . . . a great big fish . . . . the biggest fish I ever caught. The tale begins with plans for a 12 day canoe trip. It was about 1990. Eight of my friends and co—workers decided in the spring to take a long canoe and fishing trip. We wanted to spend time at Darky Lake fishing top-water for bass* and also a few days at Rebecca Falls fishing for big northerns*. The only entry permit* we could get was for Canadian Lake Agnes so we procured our reservation and began to make plans. Our permit allowed us to go anywhere in the park once we had reached Lake Agnes so we thought we would head straight west after going there and reach our preferred destination several days into our trip.

One weekend before our planned excursion, the members of the crew gathered together to plan the menu and list the things to bring. One of the members planning to go was a fellow worker called Bones. He worked with me at the apartment complex where I was maintenance director. His name was Larry but everyone called him Bones because he barely weighed 120 pounds soaking wet.

Bones had led a hard life and as I queried the crew members about allergies and abilities I found out more about him. His cholesterol was off the charts and I found out he had a really bad heart . . . . so bad that he had died once and they brought him back. He lived each day exuberantly like it might be his last. He loved to fish. Despite my misgivings he said he knew what pace he could handle and that he would be all right on the portages*. He was only 40 years old but his body was in bad shape. He begged to be included. I asked "what would we do if you kacked out on the trip?" He said with a grin "If I die on the trip just sink a big 'ol treble hook in me and tie me on some heavy line and heave me over the side of the canoe. If nothing bites after a half hour or so of trolling just cut the line and let me go." His nonchalance was unnerving but we included him in our group. As it turned out he made the trip in fine shape and taught us a few things about fishing as well. We enjoyed several meals of walleye filets because of his great fishing skills.

Finally the day came for us to start our trip. We made the four and a half hour drive from St Paul to Ely. Soon we were in our canoes and on our way. We wanted to get the most fishing time in we could, so we left a vehicle on the Echo Trail at the Nina Moose River entry point so that we would not have to make a big loop back to Moose Lake*, our starting point. Bones and I were in my canoe and we both left our cigarettes behind intending to try to quit smoking on the trip. We also forgot all of our meat in a cooler in the back end of the truck we had left at Nina Moose. It was really ripe when we came out of the woods 12 days later. We took off from the public landing at Moose Lake and a couple hours later were at the Canadian Customs*at Prairie Portage*. We ate lunch and zipped through customs and the ranger station* picking up our camping permits and fishing licenses.

Several hours later we arrived at Louisa Falls in Lake Agnes. We took a dip in the unique rock bathtub below the falls and spent some time hiking and climbing around the beautiful falls. Intending to get some good pictures, I had brought my new Polaroid camera but as I was trying to get into a good spot to get a picture I slipped and dropped the camera in the water. I retrieved it in an instant hoping that I had not damaged the camera or the film. When I tried to get a picture of the falls it just kept on taking them like a jammed vending machine giving too much change until it ran out of film. None of the pictures turned out so I took the camera apart and set it in the sun to dry. Later it worked but the focus was never right so its trips to the BWCA were over.

Upon exploring the campsite we discovered a big four foot diameter white pine that someone had laboriously chopped down and toppled into the lake. The loss of this great tree was deplorable and renewed my desire to teach campers to travel through this country leaving no trace of their passing.

That evening when we started to make supper, we discovered to our horror that we had forgotten to bring all the perishables in the cooler in the back of the pickup we left at the Nina Moose trailhead. That was going to make for some very unbalanced meals. We put on our thinking caps and reworked the menu replacing all protein with fish that we hoped we would be able to catch. We must have worked it all out because I don't remember the missing food items as being a big problem.

Two days later we were making good time and were in Crooked Lake heading west. On the north shore of the lake sits an old 1918 Buick. Rumor has it that it was used to run liquor from Canada during prohibition and it had been driven out there on the ice. We stopped to take a look but it was only a rusted hulk and any parts of value had been stripped away long ago. At about Thursday Bay in the lake the islands pinch the lake down to a narrows and the current in the lake becomes apparent. For anyone traveling the other way in a high water spring it would require some hard paddling but we were going with the flow and enjoying our time by trying some fishing.

As we drifted with the current I saw what I thought was a birch log with a couple of bracket fungi growing out of it floating in the water. As I looked it rolled over and disappeared. "That's strange" I said and I nudged the canoe closer with a few paddle strokes. "It looks like a fish" Bones speculated and as we neared it we realized it was a fish . . . . a giant northern pike* . . . a leviathan! Bones dropped his paddle overboard in his excitement as he tried to grab it. We had no net and as he lost his grip and the great fish slid along the side of the canoe I knew I might only have one chance. I quickly set my paddle in the canoe and leaned over grabbing the fish behind the gills with both hands. I have big hands but didn't come close to encircling his girth.

With a firm grip I gave a mighty heave and dragged the fish out of the water and over the gunwale* into the canoe bottom and up the other side. He was mostly in the canoe but his tail end still hung over the side in the water. I pulled the rest of him in. He was still alive but exhausted. When we filleted him later we found that he had eaten too big of a fish and had gotten gas and had become bloated and couldn't dive. He was like a submarine that couldn't flood its ballast tanks and was stuck on the surface. We marveled at the size of him and got out our de-liar* and took measurements. He weighed 22 pounds and was 47 inches long and about 20 inches in girth. "Wait till the rest of the crew sees this one" Bones stated with a huge grin as we retrieved his paddle and pulled in our fish lines. We hurried to catch up with the others. When we got to the portage* where they were waiting for us they asked "Did ya have any luck fishing?" Bones answered "Just got one" and he turned around and reached down for the stringer. The reaction from the crew was disbelief. "What lure were you using?" they all wanted to know. "I caught him barehanded" I said and told them how.

Dave got stuck portaging the monster fish and later as we made camp we said it was too bad we couldn't bring him back to get him mounted. We ate the great fish that night and for two more meals before he was consumed. We had to split the fillets in half flat ways because they were two inches thick and would not have cooked through. No one had a knife with a long enough blade to reach through the fillets so we had to cut from both sides. We fastened the fishes' big head on a tree branch and propped his mouth open with a stick. I think you could have almost put a football in his mouth! It makes one think twice about dabbling fingers or toes in the water. I think the great fish would have died because of the size of the fish in his gut. He was not near as tasty as some of the smaller fish we caught later in the trip. Unless I ever get to fish in the ocean I doubt I will ever catch a fish that big again and to have done it bare handed makes it an even better story.

28

HER FIRST TRIP

I met Kathy on a blind date arranged by Jim McKay, an advisor from one of my canoe trips. We really clicked and the following December we tied the knot. I talked my bride into taking her first canoe trip that next summer. I was still working at the Scout canoe base but begged a few days off near the end of June to take Kathy and her six year old son Scott on their first canoe trip.

We were living in a mobile home we had just purchased and I had to commute to the base from Ely where we had parked our trailer. Kathy was eager to find out what was so fascinating about the north woods and why I was so enthralled about it. She was a Nebraska farm girl and living in Ely around all those lakes was like being in a foreign country to her. We planned our trip long in advance and gathered our gear. We also were taking along her son Scott who was about six years old at the time. It would just be the three of us and we waited eagerly for the date we had set. There was only one complication . . . Kathy was pregnant and at the scheduled time for the trip she would be six months along.

Kathy checked with her doctor who advised no boat rides. She didn't tell him about her planned trip and assumed it wouldn't be that tough, thinking that a canoe wasn't like riding in a boat. All she told me was that it was ok to go. I wanted to see some new country so we planned to start our trip on the Echo trail* where it crosses the Nina Moose River and paddle back to the base. It was a fairly ambitious trip and because it was a dry summer it might even be difficult if the river was low.

We asked Digger, one of the guides, to drop us off at the Nina Moose River trailhead and told him we would see him back at the base in three to four days. We took off up the river and Kathy was soon entranced by the forests and the wildlife that surrounded her. She saw her first eagle and managed to make it over the portages* carrying a light pack. We soon discovered that the river was low and we were pulling over numerous logs and rocks that were lying exposed by the low water. Progress was slow and the portages shown on our map were tough to find or nonexistent. Within a few hours we crossed under the loop of the road that runs south of the Echo trail and found ourselves truly in the wilderness. Late that night we finally made it to Serenade, a small lake along side the river. She was tired and I cooked up a supper and did some baking after the tent was up. We slept like logs.

The next morning we were off again but the river became even more difficult to navigate. We had hoped to make it to Crab Lake that night but the travel in the river was slowing us down so much with all the pulling over logs that we finally gave up trying to paddle it. We could make better time walking along the bank carrying our gear so that is what we did for several miles. Later, I finally left Kathy and Scott behind to rest and took the axe and compass and blazed a trail straight through the woods to the next lake. I came back for them and found that she had started a small fire and even though I had left them alone in the middle of the woods she didn't seem too concerned that I might have gotten lost. We had a late lunch and continued on finally making it as far as Cummings on the second night. Kathy was really tired and being pregnant was adding to her discomfort. Scott was having the adventure of his life but he too was exhausted and we all slept hard that night again.

The next day we were free of the difficulties of river travel but now had to contend with a number of portages to get back to civilization. By the time we made it to Burntside Lake Kathy was very uncomfortable and we both were getting worried that she might go into labor so we decided to end our adventure. We paddled across the lake to the nearest resort and made a phone call to the Scout base to arrange to be picked up. Kathy had a great time but really got chewed out by her doctor when he found out what she had done. I never knew there was a problem until she started having labor pains the third day and didn't tell me until after the trip. Little Matthew waited to be born until September and was carried full term. I like to think that the canoe trip we took while Kathy was pregnant is the reason he is such an avid camper and canoeist today.

29

OVERCONFIDENT

It was June of '67 or '68 and I was assigned to lead one of the guide training trips that year. We chose an all Minnesota trip for our group that included some paddling on the Isabella River. We planned to do some bushwhacking* through the woods because a lot of our trip was on small creeks that might not be open and a number of small lakes that lie off the usual canoe routes. As guides we were always on the lookout for new routes that took us away from the usual tourist haunts.

One of the guides in our group had a pet crow named Heronimus that he took with him. He kept the crow on a leather tether to keep it from getting itself in trouble. I think he also had one wing clipped so it couldn't fly away. On one of our lunch breaks early in the trip we were eating our usual fare of P B and J sandwiches and red eye punch and we heard a croak from the direction of the canoes. He had tied up the crow on a branch down by the water. Upon investigating the noise we found that Heronimus was no more. There was only his tether and a few feathers. We don't think he escaped but rather was snatched by a sly fox or sharp eyed eagle. The guide that lost him felt pretty down hearted the rest of the trip.

Later in the trip we became confused in an area that had been logged and ended up hitching a ride with a couple of loggers on their pickup camper and spent the night at their logging camp trading stories. We were back on schedule for our trip and the next morning we started our trek downstream on the Isabella River. It was a high water spring because of the heavy snow that year and the rapid melt in May. The river was unusually high and we found we made excellent time because of the current. Many of the small portages* were flooded out and no portage was necessary as the rocks and rapids were under water. We just paddled right through them. Back in the 60s most of the portages were marked with signs showing the length of the trails in rods. We saw one sign that was entirely underwater and the portage again was unnecessary. After not having to portage about 6 times we began to think it was great.

One canoe of guides was ahead of me and we were approaching a spot on the river that was marked as a 79 rod portage on my map. Owen, Bubba and Pete were in the lead canoe. I stood up in the stern of my canoe to get a look at what was ahead and I yelled a warning to them that they had better pull over and look the river over before proceeding because I didn't like what little I could see in front of them. Without a thought they shouted back that they could make it. As the current pulled us closer I knew they were getting into big trouble even if they couldn't see it coming.

I waved the two canoes behind me over to the left shore and angled my canoe to a safe spot. Owen, Pete and Bubba disappeared from our sight as they rode their canoe down a big smooth slide of water. The river funneled down the slide which dropped about four feet. The slide was about 100 feet wide and about the same length. My concern wasn't the slide but what came after. The river parted and split around an island. Below the slide were about a quarter mile of Volkswagen sized boulders and a number of small waterfalls that no kayak let alone a canoe could negotiate. The roar of the rapids was so loud it sounded like a train and you had to shout to make yourself heard.

I scanned the area below the slide for a sign of their canoe and saw nothing. They had simply vanished. With my heart pounding and knowing that seconds could mean the difference between life and death, I vaulted over my bowman and ran the length of the portage constantly scanning the rapids to my right looking for a sign of them. The rapids were so loud and violent I was expecting to see a broken up canoe and gear crashing down the churning cauldron. Nothing! At the bottom of the portage a couple of minutes later I still saw no sign of them and I had the sinking feeling that I was going to be looking for bodies and they would show up downstream somewhere drowned. I again determined to look harder for them hoping they had been able to grab onto rocks and save themselves. I started back up stream crashing through the alder and underbrush right at the edge of the river looking vainly for a sign of my three friends. As I reached the top of the portage where the rest of the crew had pulled in I still had not seen them or heard any cries for help. Someone in the crew pointed to the island and thank God there they were. They had realized too late that they were in a world of hurt and had paddled hard to land at the island before they got sucked into the maelstrom below. The current was so strong that they had tipped over trying to get stopped as they raced alongside the island. They had managed to save all the gear and were now pulled up on the small island. Now the problem was that they were trapped by the swift current on their island refuge. We had only a small amount of rope . . . not near enough to be of any help to them. I could barely make myself heard over the roar of the water. I knew that we could not help them and their only chance to get to safety was to paddle against the current back up the slide of water and cross over to where the rest of the crew was gathered. It took a bit of doing but by shouting over the roar of the water they got the idea of what I thought they needed to do to extricate themselves.

They reloaded their canoe and got it pointed the right way and began paddling hard. It seemed like they got about half way up the slide and just hung there making no progress even though they were paddling as hard as they could and were kicking up rooster tails with their frantic stroking. The middle man began paddling too and slowly they made progress up the slide. The stern man struggled to keep the canoe in line with the current and finally they pulled away from the top of the dangerous chute. When I saw they had reached safe water, I sent the crew down the portage and waited at the beginning of the trail for my three friends. I'm a pretty laid back guy but I was prepared to ream them a new one if they bragged about what they had just gone through. As their leader I was close to panic throughout their ordeal. As they approached I could see by their pale expressions that there would be no bragging. "Did you learn anything" I asked. They all nodded. "'Nuff said," I stated.

30

THE STORM

As beautiful as it is the canoe country up north is not very forgiving. Mistakes made can turn deadly in a hurry and help is not usually close at hand. High water and dangerous rapids are one particular peril. Another can be getting lost. Accidents such as burns or cuts or broken bones can happen easily if you are careless. Storms are a danger that in the outdoor camping environment are difficult to avoid.

One particular trip I was paddling south on Kashapiwi Lake. Looking down the lake I saw a storm cloud advancing towards my crew. It looked like a wall cloud in front of a violent prairie thunder storm. It was a dangerous looking cloud and looked like it might catch us in the middle of the lake so I hollered to everyone to paddle hard, and three man it*, to an island ahead of us for shelter. The island offered little to shelter us but put us out of the worst of the wind. We got to the island in the nick of time and pulled up all the canoes and turned them over. We quickly lashed them to the nearest trees with the painters* and we all crawled under them as the storm hit. It had looked like a wall cloud and I expected hard wind but instead it started to hail. The hail went on for nearly a half hour and when the storm passed we started talking about how to make ice cream out of the three inches of ice that had accumulated on the ground. We had to talk quite loudly as

the drumming of the hail on the bottoms of the aluminum Grumman*
canoes had made us nearly deaf.

On another trip we were paddling south from U. S. point in Basswood
Lake in very calm and glassy water when the sky started to darken. The
humidity was so thick that we were dripping with sweat in the afternoon
heat. As the sky turned greenish-black I began to get nervous and started
to angle our route closer to shore. Then the lightning started and I knew
we needed to get off the lake in a hurry. The rumble of thunder carries a
long ways in the north woods and we could hear it getting closer. Sound
travels about 1000 feet per second so if the time between the flash and
the boom is five seconds it is about a mile away. We were still a good two
miles from the shore and our counting of seconds put the lightning less
than a half mile away. I then noticed a buzzing in my ears and my beard
began to tingle. A jolt of fear went through me when I saw my bowman's
hair was sticking straight out from his head. I knew we were building up
an electrical charge and could be struck by lightning at any time. The
lightning bolts don't just come out of the sky, they also rise up off the
ground from any highly charged surface. We both crouched down in
the canoe and paddled as hard as we could to the nearest land. I think
if either of us had licked his finger and extended an arm we would have
been toast. Burnt toast! We made it safely to land and weathered a couple
hours of heavy downpour under the hastily erected dining fly. We were
thankful that we were safe.

Sometimes you can do little to avoid heavy weather. One of my
crews had made it to Canadian Lake Agnes the first night and we made
camp on a small two acre island about a third of the way up the lake.
Directly to the north and to the south of our small island lay two
other much bigger islands. The night was clear with no threat of bad
weather. We went to bed with dishes out and a lot of clothes on the
line expecting only dew in the morning. About four in the morning I
heard the wind start to come up and thunder rumbled in the distance.
Soon it became apparent we were in for a serious storm as the wind
really increased to a roar and the tent began to belly in on the side. The
two bigger islands were funneling the wind into our campsite like a
giant wind tunnel. The wind was straight out of the west. Within a few
minutes the roar of the wind became even louder and we began to hear

trees crashing down and the clanging of dishes and camping gear being scattered into the woods by the gale. I crawled out of my collapsed tent and ran around to the scouts trying to keep them calm and telling them to hug the ground as they huddled inside their collapsed tents. In the dim light of dawn I looked out at the lake and the waves approaching the island were four feet high but were being torn off by the wind. The wind was so strong I could hardly stand up. The power of the storm was awesome! I was being pelted by water that the wind was picking up from the lake as well as sand, twigs, and equipment that the wind was sweeping off our small campsite.

Suddenly, I remembered the canoes. We had pulled them up and tied them to trees but I knew they were exposed to the worst of the wind on the west side of our little island. I ran down to the spot where we had beached them and to my horror they were all gone. I ran to the other side of the island squinting in the pelting rain to see if they could be spotted downwind but saw no sign of them. I heard a banging along the rocks where a spit of land sticks out of the island and spotted the 2 Grumman's, swamped. I waded out in the knee deep water and grabbed onto one of them. I couldn't empty the water out for fear of turning into a kite so I just pulled the canoe into the reeds where it was somewhat sheltered from the blast of the wind and went back for the second one. I tied them up as best I could and then went searching for my old town. I found it 20 feet in the air impaled on a branch of a big white pine.

As the storm abated the crew crawled out of their downed tents and surveyed the wreckage of our camp. A number of trees had gone down and the big pine my tent was tied to was partially uprooted. We retrieved my canoe and spent the morning patching it and gathering our scattered gear. On a stump near where the canoes had been tied sat one of the crew members straw hats, unmoved by the wind. As we headed out from camp later in the day we felt fortunate to have survived. We saw bent up canoes and a couple of flares from campers that had their canoes blown away. We later heard at Prairie Portage* that the winds had topped 90 miles per hour. In hindsight we could have anchored our canoes better and if we had known what was coming we would have camped in a less exposed spot. We were in the wrong place at the wrong time and we thanked God that no one was injured.

31

CRACK FISH

There was a time early in my guiding career when I refused to let the scouts in my crew go fishing until we made camp for the night. My thinking was that fish bite best in the early morning or at dusk and we needed to get our traveling miles out of the way before we dug out the fishing poles. We could get to camp earlier that way and then have time for doing the more fun things. The problem was that often I had complaints that we were passing up great fishing spots and that morning and evening fishing might be better for walleyes* but bass* and northern pike* bit all day long. Near the end of my second year of guiding, I relented and began to troll a lure out the back of my canoe everywhere I went. I let the scouts fish too as long as they didn't get too far behind the rest of the crew. Often we had to portage fish and we sometimes got into camp a bit later but I just couldn't pass up those good fishing spots anymore. Indeed, the three biggest northern pike I have ever seen were caught mid-day.

After fishing on so many trips, in so many different places, and at different times of day, one becomes very adept at pulling in lots of fish. You read the weather, sunlight, lake structure and develop a real feel for what lure will work, when it will work and what you are likely to catch. You start to have a lot of fun with predictions. I would be trolling a lure, perhaps a red and white daredevil* or maybe a river runt* plug and I would say to my scout bowman, "Do ya see that weed bed up ahead off the point?" He would answer "Yeah, so what about it?" I would reply, "When our canoe gets about 50 feet past the point I'm going to have a strike and pull in a four-pound northern for supper." To this statement his typical retort would be, "Oh yeah . . . right!" Then the big fish would strike and I would haul him in and the scout would turn around and gawk at me in awe, as if I had supernatural cognitive powers. The word would get around and the scouts would treat me like a God.

Often I took one of the scouts who hadn't had much luck out fishing with me, and I might say, "Drop that black hula popper* just to the left of that bunch of lily pads. "That's right. Now let it sit until the ripples expand out to about ten feet. Okay, now twitch your rod tip and you will have a bass before you get four pops in." Splash and the fish would strike. Again I would get the look. Nothing like a surface strike to get your heart rate up and make your eyes pop out of your head!

Often I would loan out my lures to the scouts to insure that they would catch something. Sometimes I would loan out my rod too if they had never fished before. On one trip to March Lake I took pity on the crew cook who hadn't gotten much of a chance to fish. He took the bow position in my canoe while the rest of the crew worked on supper and we set out to see what we could catch. We both trolled spoons on opposite sides of the canoe and soon found ourselves in the middle of a big school of walleyes. We kept getting strikes often both having a fish on at the same time. They were all in the three to four pound good eating size. In less than 45 minutes we were back at camp with 17 nice walleyes that made plenty of fillets for the next two meals. I don't mean to brag about my fishing skills . . . It's just that we fished so much that we couldn't help but know what was going to happen a good share of the time. You can still be surprised however no matter how skillful you are.

On this particular trip, I remember camping in Ogiskemuncie or some other small lake nearby on the USA side of the border. We had started early, paddled hard and were looking for a campsite where we could relax and dry out our gear from the rain the previous day. We found a spot that didn't have a very good canoe landing but the ledge above looked good from the water. I hopped out and gave the site a once over to see if it would be suitable for our crew. "This is home for tonight" I hollered. The campsite was a giant flat ledge with plenty of tent sites and a kitchen area that would make Julia Childs drool. We pulled up the canoes, unloaded the gear and set up camp. Tent stakes didn't work because the big flat ledge was solid smooth rock so we weighted the corners of the tents with boulders. It would be a hard bed but smooth with no twigs to poke you through the tent floor.

The homemade fireplace was built against a Volkswagen sized boulder that would serve well to reflect the heat of the fire. Around the cooking fire were several large square boulders with flat tops just the height of kitchen cabinets. I had to admire the layout. It was a pleasure to mix the cake batter on the ready-made counters without having to bend over. We set up the fire and got the reflector oven* going with the cake mix in the pan. We soaped* the outside and bottoms of the pots so the soot would wash off easily, heated water and got coffee going and a big kettle of water for doing the dishes later. I got out ingredients for a stew and for desert, rice and raisins with brown sugar that I call spotted dog. Soon supper was ready and the crew dug into the food with a relish. The aroma of the fresh cake baked in the reflector oven wafted through the pines.

We had made it to camp early enough that the boys had dug out all their wet clothes and sleeping bags and had them scattered all over the campsite to dry them in the late afternoon sun. Most had dumped their packs contents and were drying them too. What a mixed up mess the camp was. Gear was all over laying on the rocks and hanging on every bush and branch. I wondered if they would be able to sort out who belonged to which in the morning.

If this great campsite had one glaring fault it was the big deep split or open crack in the rock ledge that extended about 50 feet into the campsite coming within ten feet of the fireplace. It was narrow but just wide enough for your foot to drop into it if you weren't paying attention to where you were walking. It was a real danger and I said "Be very careful where you walk or you might end the trip with a broken leg!" They heeded my words and no one barked a shin or worse broke a leg or an ankle. That would have been a trip ender for the whole crew.

After dark we made popcorn in the biggest kettle for the boys, and the whole crew sat around the campfire winding down after a good day and a great meal. The scout leaders and I topped off our coffee cups and were having a great time telling stories. The scouts were eating up all the tall tales being told as well as all the popcorn.

During a lull between stories I heard a rattling sound just behind me and I turned to see what it was. "What the heck is that" I thought. There are very few snakes in the BWCAW* or the Quetico Provincial Park* and a rattler would be very rare especially at night. I saw a fishing pole laying just behind me with its tip near the crack in the rock. The end of the pole was twitching wildly. The fish line threaded down into the crack where the weight of the attached lure had pulled it. Without any help from anyone but the Almighty, the rod, reel, and lure had hooked a fish that had been hiding in the water at the bottom of the crack about ten feet below. The crack was wider down below and deep enough that the water connected to the lake. The rod was twitching away so I grabbed it and turned the crank hoisting up a small eight-inch perch. I swung it around into the firelight so they could all see what had caught my attention. "Hey, hey . . . I got me one I exclaimed"! Within a few seconds the scouts' flashlights came out, along with more fishing poles, and the crack was explored with beams of light and fish lines with lures were soon probing the depths. Now the circle of scouts around the fire, became a line of scouts along the crack, all armed with fishing poles having a great fun hauling in many more small perch. They were too small to keep and all were returned to the lake but the boys sure had fun for a couple of hours. The perch were probably hiding from predators or taking shelter from the heat of the day. I learned one more thing about fishing that night. You can catch fish sitting around the campfire in the middle of your campsite in the dark.

The scouts called them "crackfish".

32

FERGUSON

Most canoe trips have a lake that is a destination point half way into the trip. Often upon reaching that goal, the crew enjoys taking a layover day*. Sometimes the lake is remote or small and unvisited. Sometimes it is a lake that is larger and just tweaks ones imagination. In most cases it is the planned highpoint of the trip.

Ferguson is such a lake. I think it is named for one of the many explorers who came to the North Country hundreds of years ago. I had never been to the lake and on many maps it looks inaccessible because many maps do not show all the portages* that are there. Ferguson can be reached either from the Cache River or the creek that connects it to McKenzie Lake. This crew chose to enter from the lake and exit out the river. Because the lake is quite a ways from the Scout base on Moose Lake* the crew chose to go up Lake Agnes to get there quickly so that we could have a layover day at the Lake and do some fishing. After all the usual preparations and packing our crew got underway in good time the following morning. We had hoped to get to Agnes the first night but due to some needed coaching on canoe handling and a pretty stiff breeze we had to settle on camping in Sunday Lake. The crew was a little green and I hoped that they would be able to pull their weight so that we could make our planned trip.

ROY CERNY
The next day dawned and we got an early start. We got through the two Meadows portages in good time and set our canoes into Lake Agnes by late morning. A stiff southerly breeze had come up which was definitely to our advantage as we were traveling nearly due north. We found a couple of saplings and some odds and ends of rope and tied all the canoes together. With a couple more poles we tied the dining fly up for a big sail and away we went! We were cruising up the lake so fast that we surfed down the big rollers that the wind had built up. The shape of the canoes pinches the waves and lots of water was splashing in so everyone that wasn't involved in holding on to the sail or steering had to bail frantically to keep us from swamping. We were making such good time that I had the cook make sandwiches to go as we sailed along. We prayed the wilderness grace and passed the sandwiches around and kept going. By early afternoon we were at the top of Lake Agnes and we had to dismantle our tri-hull sailing catamaran* and go back to paddling through Murdock Lake. Soon we were in Kawanipi Lake and still had a tailwind. The bowmen broke out their raincoats and draped them over their paddle blades and held them vertical with their feet, and spread the raincoats with their arms and we were again helped along by the stiff wind. Soon we were in McKenzie and looking for a campsite. We had covered over three times the distance of the day before because of the tailwind and we felt more rested because we hadn't had to paddle much all day.

We set up camp and did chores and as it was late June the sun wasn't going to set until about 9:30. We had plenty of daylight for a couple hours of fishing. We knew the lake was swarming with northerns because of the great habitat lining the shore for miles. The vast majority of the shoreline of this big bay has six foot high reed beds extending out into the water several hundred feet. The lake bottom is mostly sand. The northerns* must have been starving because they were biting on anything that was thrown out there. My tackle box was a bit depleted so I was resorting to using all those weird lures that you carry along but never use because you know that they won't work. I caught northerns on an old tablespoon with a treble hook in the bottom. An old sparkplug with a hook in the bottom worked well too. We just kept landing fish. I think even a small chunk of aluminum

121

foil would have worked as a lure. Soon we had to stop for fear with all the fish in our canoes we might not be able to eat them all. We headed back to camp and hailed the others to come in as well. 57 northerns lay in a pile on the shore when we all unloaded. We ate fish until we were nearly bursting and had the leftovers the next morning.

The next morning we found the creek that leads into Ferguson. We were excited to be getting to the goal of our trip. We paddled into the lake and found a great campsite with a nice picnic table and benches around the fireplace. On a number of the white pine trees in the site there were the skeleton heads of giant northern pike tacked up on them. Another feature of the site was a number of jars nailed to trees through their lids. In the jars were notes left by previous campers that told where they were from and when they had camped at this spot. Many told of fish that had been caught in the lake. We had an interesting stay at the site as we read of the tales the campers told. Many of the notes were over 20 years old. A number of the notes were from Charlie crews from the Scout base that had camped at the spot. On our layover day the weather turned drizzly and the fishing was not as good as on McKenzie Lake. Judging from the size of the fish skulls on the trees however, one probably would be wise to keep fingers, toes and other appendages out of the water when the fish were biting. It is probably not a lake I would want to skinny dip in.

We returned to the base through Williams, Hurlburt and Kashapiwi Lakes during the next few days hoping that some time we would be able to return to Ferguson and try again for the big lunkers that we knew were lurking there.

33

THE BEAR CAPER

The first two summers that I worked at the Scout base I arrived in early June driving a 1950 Ford. It wasn't much of a car but it ran and there were no payments on it as I had purchased it from a friend for $50. It had a voracious appetite for oil which I replenished every 50 miles or so with a half gallon milk carton full of used free oil from a five gallon can that I kept in the trunk. It smoked so bad people often pulled off on the shoulder as I passed by, waiting so they could see where they were going. But the car ran and was reasonably dependable. It had holes in some of the pistons and had so little compression that when you shut it off the engine would continue turning over for a while as it coasted to a stop. It would get us to town and back and I often served as the designated driver for our nights on the town in Ely. While I was on canoe trips the car sat in the parking lot just waiting to be cranked up again.

When you are out on the trail time seems to stand still. A lot can happen in eight days when you are out of touch. Upon returning from one trip I was asked by one of the guides on base if I had heard that Israel was at war. "No" I responded to which he replied "they won". It was the six day war. After guide training week, you often never saw any other guides that would be tripping on other shifts* unless you ran into them by accident out in the woods. The eight or so guides that went out on trips the same day you did, became the buddies that you hung around with for the rest of the summer.

Later that summer I returned from an eight day trip to find every one glancing at me strangely. It seemed that they were all curious about something. I even looked at myself in the mirror to see if there was something about me that was causing the stares. I checked my fly and it was zipped up. I went about my business but couldn't help but feel that everyone was dieing to ask me "does he know?" I finally asked a few people what was going on but could get no satisfactory answer. Eventually someone came up and asked "Did you know there is a bear in your car?" I looked at him like he had lost his marbles and didn't believe him. When asked the same question later from someone else I thought maybe there was something to this. I took a hike to the parking lot and cast a quick, inconspicuous glance in the window of my car. I saw nothing and figured they were playing a joke on me. When I heard it a third time I went back for a more thorough inspection of my vehicle and spotted a large pile of blueberry tinged feces on the front seat. Shading my eyes I spotted a small bear cub sleeping down by the gas pedal. "What the heck . . . how did he get in there" I wondered.

It seems a certain guide named Voldi was in town one night with a bunch of guides from his shift. While visiting the Yugoslav home or one of the other local establishments, over pitchers of beer, they were discussing commercial outfitters and the lengths they go to in order to attract customers. One particular outfitter, who shall remain unnamed, had caught a small bear cub and kept him caged in front of his store to draw in the tourists. "It's a shame" they said, "to treat a wild creature like that" "We should do something about it" they opined. Voldi agreed and with his confidence fueled by sufficient Fitgers, developed a plan. Later that night they sprung the bear loose. They thought they should take it out to the base to release it. They stuffed the wailing cub in a number two Duluth pack* getting only mildly scratched in the process and Voldi shouldered the pack, jumped on his motorcycle and brought him out to the base. The cold air on the ride cleared up his thinking and by the time he got to the base he realized they might get in big trouble for what they had done so he thought it best not to release the bear until he could figure out what to do. The only obvious place to keep the stolen bear was locked in my car.

Thus the strange looks that I was getting the next afternoon when I came off the trail. But now what should I do? Not planning any car trips that evening, I thought I would play dumb and sleep on it until I could find out who had put together this ill conceived plan. The next morning I snuck by my car to check on the bear and found he had escaped. The driver side window was one that if you bumped the door hard enough, the window rolled down by itself. The bear had accidentally freed himself. I cleaned off the deposit he left on the seat but was still in the dark about who had done it.

The base had a lot of problems with bears getting into the garbage from the dining hall. A trap had been set the night before. It was made of two 50 gallon barrels welded together with a spring-loaded door that would drop shut when the bait left inside was disturbed by an animal. Voldi heard that they had captured a bear overnight and went to check to see if it was the AWOL cub. As he lifted the door to look inside he was met with the head of an angry big old sow bear that let out a loud snarl. "Wrong Bear" he croaked as he slammed the door shut and beat a hasty retreat. I never found out who his accomplices were and the outfitter still does not know who sprang his tourist attraction.

34

THE CRASH

In the early years before all the regulations were put on the canoe country, the use of the wilderness was much different. On Basswood Lake there were a number of large resorts. As the designation of wilderness became defined by law, they were all dismantled, closed or moved. On Basswood and many other large lakes there were motor—boats with unlimited horsepower. For a time there were a number of houseboats that plied the waterways. I was once stopped by a 75 horsepower speed boat on Basswood. I had watched as he zoomed around the lake as if he was looking for something and he finally pulled up to my crew. "Where am I on this map" he asked as he handed me a Minnesota highway map. I told him he probably needed a different map in order to find his way and gave him one of my Fisher map* sections, pointing out the bay on Basswood that he was looking for. He expressed his gratitude and resumed zooming around the lake. I guessed that I should also have given him lessons on the use of the compass and how to orient a map but thought he would eventually figure it out if he didn't run out of gas first.

On Moose Lake* it almost became hazardous to canoe as the large outfitters all ran towing service up to Prairie Portage.* The faster they could go the more tows they could complete in a day and the more money they could make. Thus the boats and barges got bigger and bigger and the horsepower wars went into overdrive. They would race to the portage with people and canoes loaded aboard and give little thought to the giant wakes their monster boats were producing. One had to point his canoe into the wake to keep from capsizing. Eventually the 25 horsepower rule put the damper on things and put all the outfitters on equal footing.

Airplane flights over the park now have to be made at high altitude and everything in the BWCA* and the Quetico* are off limits to landings. Only the forest service is allowed low altitude flights to check for fire. Lac La Croix is outside the park and can still have takeoffs and landings. On one trip across the lake my crew popped out from behind a group of islands and was almost run over by a small floatplane trying to take off. He gave us a salute with his social finger for interrupting his takeoff and veered off in a different direction. If he hadn't seen us it could have been catastrophic.

Prairie Portage and Bottle Portage at one time had jeeps that could be hired to pull boats across into the larger lakes. Now that no motors are allowed in those lakes the jeep drivers went out of business. Dawson portage is four miles long and crosses from Sand Point Lake to Lac La Croix. It is operated by Hamburg's resort and can be taken by scheduling them for pickup. We once took the portage and were met on the beach by our driver. He loaded our canoes on a trailer and us into his old bus. The bus was beat to pieces and the door hung precariously by one hinge. I commented that the road looked a bit rough and he smiled and said "you ain't seen nuthin' yet". We careened down the bulldozed path and climbed boulders so big the bus bottomed out several times. We were tossed about like marbles in a can as he headed into a swamp knocking down trees as he tried to avoid hitting a bus going the other way with another load of passengers. It was like an amusement ride at Valley Fair Park in Minnesota. It was worth the $10 just for the thrill.

One afternoon working at the base we heard a plane trying to take off from Moose Lake. It was one of Pat McGee's pilots taking a group of people to one of the fishing lakes at the perimeter of the park. The plane made several attempts to take off without success. It was too heavily loaded. The pilot dropped the passengers off at the dock at Canadian Border outfitters intending to fly back to Ely to get the larger twin engine Beechcraft to be able to take the people to their destination with one trip. The pilot was a bit of a hot dog and took off successfully without his load. Instead of flying over the lake until he had some altitude he stood the plane on its side and winged to the south over the trees heading for the water airport at Ely. Then we heard his engine sputter, stall and restart. It sputtered again but didn't restart. Within a few seconds we heard a crash a couple miles away and saw a column of smoke. We rang the alarm at the base and loaded a bunch of guys in the base fire truck with some Indian backpack pumps and a bunch of extinguishers. Sandy, the base director had gotten to the scene first and had everything under control. The plane had run out of gas due to a faulty gauge and the pilot had put the plane down in a thicket of poplar trees. The plane nosed in and caught fire burning the plane to a crisp except for one float. The pilot had escaped with only singed eyelashes. He lost his job but at least he didn't lose his life and the passengers were safe. It was an exciting afternoon but we were disappointed that we didn't get to help put out the fire that consumed about an acre of forest.

35

MOTO-SKI

Most of my stories involve summertime activities. The other nine months of the year are equally interesting. When I started working at the Scout base on Moose Lake, I was a Junior in college. I continued working there as I finished at South Dakota State University and for the next two years after when I was teaching at a small high school in Delmont, South Dakota. I loved the north so much that I began looking for a teaching position closer to the boundary waters. In 1968 I signed a contract to teach the sciences at Mountain Iron High School. It was only an hour's drive from Ely! For the next three years I was able to hunt and fish right in the place I loved best. I soon discovered that when the snow begins to fall and the thermometer plummets one can develop cabin fever quite rapidly. Living that far north I found that the shortest days of winter really are short. The sun would rise after I was already teaching classes and it would be setting when school let out. I had never gotten into ice fishing so I looked for something else that would be exciting to take up the winter evenings.

I discovered snowmobiling. On a trip out to the base I got to ride my first sled, an old Polaris that belonged to Sandy Bridges, the base director. I was immediately hooked on riding. I started looking for a sled and found that the new Moto-ski was just what I wanted. Soon I was the proud owner of a Zephyr model that sported a 19 horsepower, one cylinder engine and a long seat that could hold three people. It was a narrow track machine and it took a lot of body English to keep it upright. It would do 55 mph! I rode it everywhere, even to teach school in the mornings. In Mountain Iron the snowmobile was almost a necessity and many of the students rode them to school when the roads were bad. One of my chemistry students, Tom Hardy, shared my enthusiasm and often went sledding with me on his Arctic Cat. We would ride until bedtime some nights and nearly ran out of gas a few times. I was not kind to my snowmobile. I blew up the clutch and put a hole in the hood and windshield. All the bogie wheels broke off at one time or another and had to be re-welded. Once I cranked it wide open to see what it would do and the dogs on the pull start cable locked up, seizing the engine and I rolled it several times breaking off the windshield and the handlebars. I drove it home using a pair of vice grips to steer. On one stop at the brink of one of the open pit mines Tom and I got off the sleds to empty our bladders and look over the scenery. The lip of snow we parked on broke off and dumped both of us and our machines into the pit. We fell about 40 ft landing in five feet of soft snow. Again we damaged our sleds and took nearly three hours to find our way out of the mine.

That first year snowmobiling was tough because there was too much snow. It just wouldn't quit. By late January it was 60 inches deep on the ground and it stayed that way for nearly two months. When you got off the beaten trails you felt like a mole because the machine would sink about two feet into the fluff as you drove along. We got stuck many times and it was very hard on drive belts. The snow was so deep that trails got made in places they shouldn't. All familiar landmarks and many dangerous spots were simply buried. I sank my machine in three feet of water once not realizing I was on thin ice under the snow. As the snow melted and the trails compacted dangers started becoming apparent. Going about 30 mph one night I was following a well used trail. It ran right over a woven wire fence that now had the top rung of wire exposed. I planted both skis solidly into the wire and my machine did a cartwheel throwing me about 30 feet. I had my snowmobile suit unzipped and I filled up with snow as I slid along. Soon I looked like the Pillsbury doughboy except I had a scratch on my cheek and one of my lower eyelids got pushed under my eyeball. I lucked out because I stopped sliding just short of a large pine tree. Several of the students lost their lives that winter through drowning and decapitations from wires. One ran into the back of a snow covered car at high speed. It was dangerous.

When I had first gotten my new sled I invited Tom to go with me up to the canoe base to try it out. We could only haul one sled so we thought we could both ride on mine. I had never heard of the notion that in deep snow you could go farther on a sled in five minutes than you could walk in five hours, Nor the idea that you should always sled with others on sleds in case of trouble. We were woefully unprepared. We had no food or water, no spare drive belts or even tools and no snowshoes. We thought we would take a quick spin across Moose Lake* over to Wind Lake. Then we were going to run up to Prairie Portage* and back down the Moose Chain to the base. It was a total distance of maybe 25 miles.

The snow was about three feet deep and the going was a bit rough but soon we found ourselves on Wind Bay of Basswood cruising along at a nice clip. I began smelling burning rubber and soon there was a loud bang. We stopped and opened the hood discovering a disintegrating drive belt that had flipped over. It wasn't broken yet but we obviously couldn't go on. We turned the machine around and tried to nurse it slowly back the way we had come, a distance of about five miles. Tom walked along side offering encouragement as I nursed the machine along slowly. Soon the drive belt broke out in the middle of the bay and we were both afoot. As we waded through the deep snow we discovered several patches of slush we had gone through and got ourselves good and wet. It started to snow and visibility was dropping. It was already dark but we plugged along thankful that we were familiar with the lake and could still make out the skyline. I hated to leave my new sled out on the lake but we had no choice.

Exhausted and thirsty we made it to Moose Lake and could see the light from Wilderness Outfitters a mile or two away. A bunch of snowmobiles came by and we thought we could hitch a ride but they never heard us yelling above the roar of their machines and we were too slow to run out in front of their headlights. About 10 o'clock we stumbled into Wilderness Outfitters restaurant and the 50 or so people that were drinking and partying fell silent as they stared at us as we entered. I guess we looked like death warmed over. We were covered with frost and our clothes were frozen solid from the waist down. We downed several bottles of pop before our thirst was quenched and ate five or so polish sausages before we got our strength back. We explained what had happened and one of the patrons said he would take me out to the sled the next day to fix the belt and bring it back. We never made it out to the sled and he bogged down in slush before we even got off Moose Lake. I resigned myself to coming back the next weekend with Tom and his Arctic Cat to try to get it back and we headed home so I could teach school the next morning.

It snowed another two feet during the week. Tom and I left for the base Friday night. The forecast was for clear skies but bitter cold. We were armed with supplies, tools, food, a new belt, and snowshoes. We left for Wind Bay on Tom's machine about nine in the morning telling Sandy Bridges at the Boy Scout base we would be back by five in the late afternoon. The going was slow in the five foot deep snow and we got stuck several times. We decided to leave Tom's sled at the end of the first Wind portage and continued on snowshoes. It was getting dark when we finally got to the second portage and we stopped to build a fire and have a bite to eat. I told Tom to keep the fire going and I would go out on foot to get my snowmobile.

I couldn't find it! I thought sure someone had found it and stolen it. Finally, in the moonlight, I saw a glint of chrome sticking out of the snow a few inches and felt relieved. It was getting bitter cold and I was thankful there was no wind. It was so cold the ice was contracting with resounding booms that scared me out of my wits. I heard a couple of trees crack open as well. I had never put on a drive belt and by the time I figured out how to pry the centrifugal clutch plates apart I had frostbite on three fingers. The machine, now repaired, started reluctantly on the third pull. I jumped on eager to get back to the fire and promptly got badly stuck. 20 minutes later I was racing over the drifts, determined to keep my speed up so I wouldn't bog down again.

In the shadows of the moonlight I couldn't determine exactly where the portage began but knew I didn't dare slow down for fear of getting stuck in the slush near shore. I missed the trail by about 30 feet and got stuck again. Tom came and helped me get out.

Back at the warm fire we assessed our situation. It was 10 o'clock at night and bitter cold. We decided to sit by the fire until daybreak and then head back to the base when we would be able to see better. We had an ax and a saw and cut a number of whole trees down keeping the fire roaring. Years later I could still find that spot on the trail where there was a bed of coals 10 ft across and about a dozen trees cut off about seven feet off the ground as we stood on the five foot deep snow. The saw blade shattered in the cold and the ax chipped its edge. During the night I rolled into the fire burning a hole in the leg of my snowmobile suit.

When morning came we were down in the mud at the bottom of a five foot deep crater 30 ft across. The fire had melted the snow all around us. Tom headed across the lake on his snowshoes and I put out the fire and tidied up our makeshift campsite. It was cold! I loaded the gear on the sled and pulled the starter rope. It pulled hard and the grease and oil were so stiff that I didn't think I could turn it over fast enough to start it. I had to hand feed the rope back in as the rewind spring could barely pull it. Finally it started and I jumped on. I goosed it, killed the engine and jumped back off. "What the heck" I thought. "Why wouldn't it go?" I tipped the machine on its side and saw the reason. The track was encased in frozen slush from the night before. An hour later after beating all the ice out with a log I tried to start it again without success. I had to pull the fouled plug and use ether but finally it was running. I met Tom coming back on snowshoes to see what was taking me so long. He jumped on the back of my machine and we quickly crossed Wind Lake to the portage into Moose Lake.

Back at his machine he explained that he wasn't able to get it started because of the cold. With some of my ether we finally got both sleds running and we headed across the trail toward Moose Lake. We pulled up to Sandy's cabin about 2:00 in the afternoon. We heard the drone of an airplane out over the lake as we entered. Nobody was home. We started a fire to warm up and immediately fell asleep exhausted. An hour or so later Sandy arrived. He was irate that we hadn't come back the previous day and had Pat McGee out flying around looking for us. He was relieved we were all right. We asked "Why were you so worried . . . we're both eagle scouts and can take care of ourselves." He said "Go look at the thermometer". It was standing up between the storm window and the inside window in the front of the cabin. In the cold it wasn't very accurate because it read higher than it really was outside because of the heat from the cabin. It said -42 F.

36

UP WILDGOOSE CREEK WITH A PADDLE

The crew arrived packed in a single van. There were eight in the group and they were exhausted. Not only were they packed in the van but their gear left little room for them to sit so at least three of them had to ride horizontal laying atop their packsacks and duffel bags. They had driven from Tjunga, California and had been on the road for days. They were excited and eager for their adventure to begin in spite of being cooped up in the van for so long.

The advisors name was Warren and his son Scott was also in the group of explorers. We ran through the required preparations for the trip, packing the food and equipment and getting issued our life jackets and paddles. We sat down as a group and planned an ambitious trip, entering the Quetico through Basswood Lake and traveling north through Sark, Kawanipi and Sturgeon Lakes and then angling east through Jean Lake and a series of small potholes to our destination . . . . Wildgoose Lake. On the map the lake is small, perhaps a mile across but it promised to be off the beaten track and might hold some good fish. We would return through Wildgoose Creek and then travel the border lakes for a sprint back to base the last two days of the trip. The small crew eagerly agreed to the plans and we headed to the lodge for a campfire. I explained the guides would put on the program that would further educate them about the wilderness.

One of the guide staff members going out that shift explained about fishing, another about leaving no trace of your presence in the woods. Someone else talked about cooking and the gear in the kettle pack. Then my friend Don Helms carried in a Duluth A-3 pack and set it on the table. He talked briefly about what gear to bring and what to leave behind. He then unbuckled the pack saying he would show them how to get three scouts gear jammed into one pack. When he opened the pack, out popped Charlie Smith, the smallest guide on the staff that year. He might have gone 100 pounds but it was all muscle and he could portage a canoe with the best of us. He jumped down and got a second pack that he proceeded to empty showing the group of eight crews going out how to pack the gear for comfort, accessibility and the best use of space in the pack. My tired crew headed for tent city for a good nights sleep after the campfire with much anticipation of what the next day would bring.

We got off to a good start the next morning and by late afternoon were settling in to a campsite on North Bay of Basswood Lake. The scouts were amazed by the lake country having nothing remotely like it back in their home state of California. On night two we camped in Sark Lake and by the third day we had made it to Kawanipi Forks. We moved on the next day through the big lake Sturgeon. It has a distinctive beach on a point about halfway down the lake on the south side where we set up camp and enjoyed a good swim after a long hard day. Night five was spent in Jean Lake where we cleaned up a very messy campsite.

The next day our goal was to reach Wildgoose Lake and we got an early start paddling. Soon however our route through Pelee Lake burned up all our daylight as we used up nearly five hours just getting across one very difficult portage*. We doggedly kept paddling through Badwater and Your Lakes. As the sun set we crossed a short portage in the creek leading to Wildgoose . . . . almost there! I had been holding the carrot in front of the donkey so to speak, by telling the crew we would have a good campsite and have the lake all to ourselves and that the fishing would be fabulous because no one in their right mind would go through all the portages we took to get there. As we rounded the last turn in the creek and glided quietly into the lake our mouths dropped open.

We counted eight campfires burning around the shoreline. Now Wildgoose is a small lake and I knew there weren't that many campsites and yet each fire represented someone camping. So much for solitude, and having the lake to ourselves. I paddled over to the one campsite that I knew about to see what was up. I suspected that it was an Outward Bound group that was doing their solo, and I was right.

Outward Bound School* is an organization that works with teens, teaching them cooperation and self confidence. They have a great program and are based on the Kawishiwi River south of Ely. Part of their program involves taking the teens out on difficult canoe trips where they teach them survival and self reliance by requiring them to camp solo for three nights. A number of former guides from the canoe base have gone to work for the Outward Bound program.

As I approached the campsite I heard the leader shout "Holry"* I answered with "Redeye*." This is a secret code that Sommers Canoe Base staff has used for years to identify that they are from the base. Holry is a type of rye cracker that we packed for lunches and snacks and redeye refers to the punch base we carried for drinks. As I paddled up I recognized Barry Bain standing in the light of the campfire. Barry was a former guide at the Scout base. I explained our predicament and that we were on our last legs and needed to make camp and get some supper. He immediately offered his campsite because nearly all his crew was out doing their solo. "You don't even need to set up tents. Ours are empty and the fire is built and the wood is gathered. Make yourselves at home. "Here, try some of our Turtle Stew" he offered. It was an offer we couldn't turn down. The crew quickly took over his campsite and grabbed their mess kits, helping themselves to some tasty snapping turtle stew. Barry showed me the shell of the giant turtle they had caught trying to rob fish from their stringer. "Its HUGE . . . must have gone 50 lbs" I exclaimed!

In the morning we caught a few fish but couldn't stay long because we had only two more nights to camp and we were a long ways from getting back to the base. After breakfast we packed up and headed out thanking Barry profusely for his hospitality and wishing them a great trip. The paddle through Wildgoose Creek to Lac La Croix Lake took nearly seven hours. We paddled on another eight miles and set up camp near Curtain Falls in Iron Lake. We had not covered near enough distance and I hoped for good weather for the next couple of days' long paddle. We struggled to get an early start but the tired crew couldn't be speeded up so we left Iron Lake at 10:30 AM. We paddled hard for 12 straight hours and covered over 30 miles that day. We camped on US point on a small beach that night. A quick supper of canned beef on rice topped off our long day and snoring was heard within minutes of the crew climbing in their sleeping bags after eating.

The next day we got a good start and made it across big Basswood Lake before the wind came up to turn it to whitecaps. We crossed Wind Lake taking the last two portages easily as the vision of showers, saunas and soda pop came into our heads. The crew had a great time even though they had taken a long and difficult trip. They had seen country not often visited even by experienced canoeists and had crammed a lifetime of memories into eight and a half days.

37

JASPER LAKE DUCKS

Besides fishing, hunting is one of my favorite activities. I owned a trusty old Belgian made browning shotgun in 16 gauge. When I moved up to Mountain Iron Minnesota from South Dakota in the fall of 1968 I looked forward to hunting ducks on all that water in the boundary waters. I came to know Bob Cary when I dated his daughter Barb. Bob was an avid outdoorsman and loved to hunt and fish as well. That fall he invited my friend, Tom Hardy and I to do some duck hunting with him and one of his guides, Harry Lambirth. Bob owned and operated Canadian Border Outfitters on Moose Lake just down the road from the Boy Scout base where I worked during the summers as a guide for scout groups going out on the trail.

That fall when the leaves were turning their crimson and gold colors my anticipation of the upcoming hunting season grew. I had acquired a set of old decoys from a former advisor from one of my canoe trips. His home was in Kearney Nebraska and his decoys had floated and bobbed in the Platte River bringing in thousands of ducks over the years. He had upgraded to the newer plastic decoys and his old set had sat unused for several years in his basement. He took me out hunting several times on the Platte River.

I had never hunted over decoys before, never having the wherewithal to purchase any. While in college our hunting consisted of using chest waders in the abundant wetlands of eastern South Dakota and simply jump shooting any ducks we scared up. I was amazed at the power the decoys had to pull in the flocks of ducks. Hunting the Platte was tough work and the small patches of open water you found within the myriad small channels didn't seem large enough to be able to pull in flocks but I found out how wrong that thinking was. The first time my crew advisor Jim McKay took me out we had 17 flocks fly into our decoys in 3 hours of hunting. They literally dropped in, fluttering between the towering cottonwood trees like leaves falling in the wind. When the first flock arrived we heard the whistling of the wind on their wings before we ever saw them. I was so dumbfounded at how close they were I never got my gun up. Jim got two and my friend Don got one out of the first flock. I soon adapted to this unfamiliar way of hunting and as we came close to limiting out we took turns shooting and choosing which ones to go after. What a blast! When he saw how much I enjoyed decoy hunting he passed his old ones on to me. I fixed the broken bills with Popsicle sticks and tape and gave them a new coat of paint and fresh anchors and cords and took them with me when I moved north.

The day of the hunt came and Tom and I met Bob and Harry at their Lodge on Moose Lake. Bob, the most experienced hunter, suggested that he and Harry should paddle from the lodge down Moose Lake and up Jasper creek to see if they could kick any ducks out and send them to Tom and Me. Tom and I were to take the Moose Lake road back to the Fernberg Road and drive to where Jasper Lake lies along the road. We were to find a good spot and set out our decoys to try to intercept any ducks that Bob and Harry kicked up.

Tom and I set out and were soon putting our canoe in the icy water. We loaded our decoys and guns and paddled out skirting the shore. The map showed a big island and we headed that way thinking the east end would be good for setting up because ducks like to land into the wind and the wind was out of the west. Another small island lay off the end of the large one. It looked like a good spot. Up to this time we hadn't seen a single duck. As we approached the small island about 300 ducks got up off the water behind the island and they all headed west behind the larger island. They were all out of range but we anticipated some shooting would soon be happening.

We quickly set up the decoys in two clumps of about a dozen each with about 50 feet between them. Then we set out the best looking mallard pair from our decoy bag in the space between. It's called the dumbbell setup because the layout represents that shape. Ducks that come in will invariably land between the two flocks with the pair because it represents the safest spot and it has room for them to maneuver. We hunkered down in the rocks and loaded up our shotguns. We watched and listened and tried to stay low out of the reach of the strong northwesterly wind that had a lot of bite in it. After 2 hours we hadn't seen a single duck or Bob and Harry. Soon though, we caught sight of them coming across the lake. As they pulled up they said the going in the creek had been tough because of low water. "Nice setup" they opined. "Did ya see any yet?" they asked. "About 300 got up out of range and headed behind the big island" I explained. "Nuthin since" "We'll go check it out back there" Bob said and he and Harry back paddled their canoe out of the lee side of our island and then turned and began heading around the corner where they could get a view behind the big island.

They had only gotten about 60 yards away from us when Bob yelled "Here they come". And come they did. For the next 10 or 15 minutes all those ducks got up in small bunches and took off into the wind. Their takeoff was toward Bob and Harry so as they gained altitude they flared away from them and flew directly over Tom and I down in the rocks of our small island. Some of them took a look at our decoys and wondered why those ducks hadn't bolted yet. At any rate, Tom and I exhausted our ammo supply in short order. We reloaded as fast as we could, sometimes getting only one shell in the gun before the next batch of ducks came by. My gun got almost too hot to hold. We had no chance to recover the ducks we knocked down because more kept coming. It sounded like a war zone. We had to roll over on our backs and shoot at the ducks going away so we didn't spray Bob and Harry with shot. They ducked down in their Grumman and yelled "shoot 'em as they flare," but I didn't want to chance it. Finally the swarms of ducks thinned out and the shoot was over. Tom and I had gotten to do all the shooting and had each shot a whole box of shells. We weren't sure how many ducks were down but we spent the next half hour trying to find them all. Tom and I thought we had knocked down 20. We found 18. There were four or five different species. In all my duck hunting trips I have never had all the conditions right to provide such a long streak of shooting. I have never had my gun barrel get that hot. Later, Bob took my acrylic paint set and painted a picture of Tom and I on our little island in Jasper Lake blasting away at all those flocks of ducks. He gave it to me and I still have that painting today.

38

THE BIG FIGHT

My third summer of guiding trips for the Sommers Canoe Base I finally landed a 15 day trip. It was every guides dream. A couple of times every summer crews that had been to the base before would come up again and often would schedule a longer trip so they could see more of the Boundary Waters. My crew was from Kearney Nebraska and they also had a sister crew. Mike McMahon was chosen for the sister crew guide. The plans for the trip were for each crew to circle Hunters Island* . . . one from the east and one going west. The crews were to head north halfway through their trips and meet in the town of Atikokan, Ontario Canada on the Kings Highway for a two day layover and then return following each others' routes back to Moose Lake.

The logistics of a 15 day trip gets a bit complicated because of the volume of food that needs to be carried. For a crew of 12 we packed five food packs. There would be no resupply half way through the trip. That meant that several crew members had to double pack on the portages until enough food was eaten to eliminate a couple of the packs. We also carried two reflector ovens, extra cake pans and extra flour and baking powder to enable us to bake bannock or trail bread each night for lunch the next day. By doing the baking we didn't need to take the huge number of loaves of bread it would have taken to make sandwiches for everyone at lunch time each day. It also meant that cooking time would increase because of all the baking we would have to do each night to supply the bread for the next days' lunch. Even though the trip would be 250 miles with 15 days to do it the hours of paddling each day would not be excessive.

Jim McKay was my crews advisor and the sister crew was led by a priest, Father Kristosek and his brother Ed. Spirits were high as we made preparations for a morning departure. The boys were mostly older and quite experienced in canoeing. My crew won the coin toss and elected to go east through Knife Lake and down the falls chain to Kawanipi Lake. Our route would then take us through Russell, Upper Sturgeon, Dore', Pickerel, Batchewaung, and Nym Lakes and then up across the Kings highway to Plateau and the Atikokan River which would take us right into the town.

The trip started out great and we made good time, getting a chance to stop off at Knife Lake Dorothy's for a cold home made root beer. We camped on Knife the first night and I was pleased at the experience the crew had in canoe camping. It was August and the nights were getting longer and cooler as the summer waned. Camping on Russell the fourth night the crew spent time exploring and fishing around Chatterton Falls. The boys were in heaven. The lake country was so different from the Nebraska flatland that they were accustomed to and they couldn't believe you could actually drink the water right out of the lakes. They explained, "In Nebraska almost all of our lakes are reservoirs, formed by damming the streams."

We got a little behind schedule the fifth and sixth days due to rainy and windy weather. As we neared the Kings Highway the seventh morning we could hear the roar of semi trucks hauling logs. We came around a point and saw the highway as well as an all night diner. We hadn't had a home cooked meal for a while so we parked the canoes and trooped in dripping water behind us. We took up three booths and the waitress came by with menus. I ordered about half the stuff on the menu and she started to walk to the next booth thinking I had ordered for all four of us. Jim said "miss . . . I'll have the same but make the eggs over easy and the coffee black". She gave me a disbelieving look but dutifully took each persons' order. We all cleaned our plates.

We were to be in Atikokan the afternoon of the Seventh day. Because of our huge breakfast we found ourselves four or five hours behind. By the time we got to the Atikokan River it was becoming dark and getting quite cold. We huddled below the railroad bridge and talked over what to do. We were still eight miles from town and about to head down a river we were unfamiliar with that had several portages in it around falls and rapids. We elected to stow our canoes under the bridge and hike the tracks into town and come back for the canoes the next day. As I stood under the bridge shivering, Jim said to the crew "Look . . . he's human". I guess my guiding skills had impressed them and they thought I was something beyond an ordinary person. They could see I was sharing in their misery on that cold rainy night. We hiked the distance to town and went looking for the other crew. We found them in the provincial police station talking to the officers and asking if they had seen another crew of scouts come into town. No sooner had they asked the question and we walked in the door. They were relieved to see us and invited us to set up camp with them 100 yards away in the city park. They helped us put up our tents and get set for the night.

The next day, refreshed from a good night sleep and a big breakfast in a local restaurant, we hiked out to our canoes that we had left under the bridge and brought them back. Eight miles is a long way to carry a canoe on your shoulders. It took all morning and we were pretty tired when we returned. We walked around the town taking in the sights and using the local laundromat to clean up our duds. A couple of the crew members were heckled by some older boys driving up and down the main drag. They figured it was because they had their scout uniforms on. They shrugged it off.

The second evening in town about 1:00 in the morning, I was awakened by someone beating on the side of my tent. He knocked it down, and yelled, "come out and fight." I crawled out groggily to confront the prankster. I asked "What is your problem?" In reply I got sworn at and threatened by a young man wielding a big stick. There were five of the young toughs and they figured they could take on our small group of scouts. They had counted the four wall tents belonging to both crews and figured there weren't enough of us to give them any trouble. They didn't realize we pack em in pretty tight and that there were 24 of us in those four tents. The argument was going nowhere and as more and more of the scouts and leaders awakened the bullies realized they were vastly outnumbered. Don Helms, a six foot tall crewmember, came out of his tent swinging a paddle like a giant machete and yelled "Lets git em!" He took off after the perpetrator and chased him up to the top of a big pile of firewood. The rest of the young hoods fled and the one on the woodpile ran too. We heard car doors slam and they sped away. We found out they had beat up a couple of our scouts who were in the restroom. One had a bloody nose and the other a black eye and split lip. The talk of revenge was in the air, so the advisor Jim gathered up every scouts' knives and said there would be no fighting, but rather he would go over to the nearby police station and report the incident. The police took our report and gave first aid to the injured scouts. They sent out a patrol to see what they could find. In a town as small as Atikokan anyone driving around that late at night is easily spotted. In 20 minutes the patrol was back with the bullies all in the squad car. The scouts that had been beaten up had gotten the best look at them and they identified the young hoodlums as the guilty party. The police locked up the 'perps' in the clink for the night. It turned out they were from Fort Francis and were out cruising around looking for trouble. We did not press charges as we were leaving the next morning to continue our trip and would not be available to testify before the magistrate about the incident. The big fight was an exciting but scary diversion to an already noteworthy trip.

Mike, the guide for the sister crew had a flare up of his ulcers and the scout base had to fly Ron Miles, one of the other guides up as a replacement. Mike spent some time in the hospital in Ely upon his return. My crew continued the trip getting a truck ride from town to start at Bewag Lake a few miles down the highway. We completed the trip without further incident. I think my crew matured a lot in the 15 days in the woods. Three of them came back the next summer and worked on staff. One of them, Don Helms, guided for the next three years. Several of his crew members also came back to work at the base. I guess that makes me at least a great grand guide in the whole scheme of things.

I became great friends with my advisor Jim McKay and drove down to Nebraska from my home in South Dakota many times the next few years to hunt and fish with him. Jim set me up on a blind date with Kathy, who a year later became my wife. We were together for 26 years before she passed away from breast cancer in 1996. Now my son Matt and his kids Zachary and Rebecca have all taken canoe trips and have fallen in love with the 'north country' as well. I hope I have taught them well.

39

THE MOUSE
THAT POURED

The second summer I guided I had a crew come in from the Pony Express Council*. I don't remember what state that crew was from but from their slow drawl I am guessing Missouri. We planned a trip to a few lakes that would be new to me and provide hopefully, some good fishing for the crew. There were 13 of us in total as this was before the limits of nine on crew size that are imposed today. We had five canoes in our group that made for tougher portaging because of the additional load to haul.

The first night we camped on a small lake called Meadows on the Canadian side. I had never camped in Meadows before, only passing through on the way to Canadian Lake Agnes. I had heard it had one campsite at the south end of the lake that we found easily. After setting up camp and grabbing a bite to eat we launched the canoes to try fishing. I had seen a lot of good structure for bass* as we paddled to our camp and I suspected we might have some decent luck. Top water lures pulled a few strikes but not many fish. Those that we caught were a bit on the small size. Changing tactics, I pulled out my fly rod and put on a wet fly. Using it like a bamboo pole I hung the fly over the side and let it sink toward the shallow bottom. The lake was very clear and bass came out of the woodwork to fight over the fly. In plain sight we watched dozens of them attack the bug. There wasn't much left of the wet fly after hauling in plenty of foot long smallies* for a pan fish breakfast. We tired of the fun and went back to camp with about 30 on the stringer that weighed about a pound apiece. I suspected the fish were stunted from over population because no other predator fish were caught. The population had no controls other than fishing to thin their numbers.

The second night we camped on Dack Lake to the east of the top of Lake Agnes. Night Three was on McKenzie Lake where we again experienced great fishing in the reed beds lining most of the shoreline on the north end of the lake. It mattered little what lure was thrown out . . . northerns* attacked them all in a feeding frenzy resembling sharks attacking a bloody victim. We piled up about 50 northerns on shore that night that kept the crew eating fish for the next 3 meals.

Night four was in Cache Lake after a long portage* of one and a half miles. One of the crew members wore one of those funny fishing hats with a bunch of lures hooked into it. Tiring out half way across with the canoe, he tried to roll it off his shoulders and a hook snagged the yoke* pad. Unfortunately another hook snagged his earlobe as the canoe pulled his hat off his head. He was forced to bend over following the canoe to the ground because he was well hooked to the canoe and could not see to extricate himself. I came along, paused, reached for my small pliers, cut the barb off and told him "you might want to pack those lures in your packsack". I added "an earring might look cool on you".

On that long portage I thought I was going to lose my advisor to heart problems. Jack felt dizzy from the exertion of hauling gear all that way and we took a lunch stop on the trail to give him a break to recover his breath. Jack was about 60 and of an age where overexertion might be a problem. He bounced back quickly but I wouldn't let him carry anything the rest of the day and told him to take it easy and enjoy being pampered.

That next morning Jack got up early at about five AM as he usually did. He had said he couldn't sleep any later than that from the habit of rising early for work for many years. I consider myself a morning person but to me five is the middle of the night. As he had done every morning of the trip, he got up and started the fire. He refilled the coffee pot and threw in some more grounds and waited for the brew to warm up. He had sat alone by the fire every morning performing this ritual and I felt bad that he had no one to keep him company, so I reluctantly crawled out of my sleeping bag and joined him on the log in front of the fire. Pleased that I had joined him, he got up and found my coffee mug and poured me a cup and added the usual four spoons of sugar that I liked in my coffee. The rancid, noxious brew tasted particularly bad that morning and I commented "What the heck did you do to the coffee"? "Why, what's wrong with it?" he questioned as he took a sip. "It tastes terrible" I reiterated. "I just added water and grounds to the pot, put the lid on and reboiled it . . . . tastes great" he suggested but I noticed he said it hesitantly. I got up and checked the pot. When I took the lid off, I noticed an unfortunate mouse, now dead, who had sampled the wares the night before and drowned in the pot. "What are you doing?" he questioned when I dumped the pot. When he saw the reason he nearly threw up. We made a fresh pot and it tasted a lot better. The crew had a good laugh about the mouse that poured.

We were able to spend a couple days in a small lake called Jenny or on some maps LeMay Lake and again got in some great fishing. The crew was exhausted from the trek down the Cache River and they slept in. Jack and I went out and caught a 30 inch northern on the first cast with a cheap imitation daredevil called a gypsy king. We paddled back to camp to try to get the rest of the crew interested in going out. Upon seeing the fish most of the boys got up, dug out their poles, and went out landing a few more northerns and walleyes for breakfast. Jack and I had another cup of coffee being very careful to inspect the pot for floating critters first and then headed back out to fish again. We went back to the same spot we had caught the first good sized northern and cast the scratched up fake daredevil out again. On the first cast we got a solid strike and hauled in another much bigger one. It measured 42 inches long and weighed 18 lbs. We got back to camp and as we unloaded the canoe the boys in camp yelled down "Did you get any?" Just One" Jack answered. "We didn't need any more" he said. Their enthusiasm for fishing rose dramatically when he hauled the fish up into camp. We stayed in LeMay Lake for another day but no other fish that big were landed.

After we ate the big northern I had the notion to bring the head and tail back with us and have each of them mounted on boards and use them for bookends or maybe putting a big slinky spring between them and hanging it on the wall with a plaque saying . . . stretch your imagination. But after dragging the head and tail along on a stringer for a couple of days I forgot them at one of our campsites and discovered it too late to go back for them. I still think it would have been a cool idea.

Back at the base, a few days later, we took saunas and cleaned up. At the traditional campfire that night the crew presented Jack with a small ladder that they had lashed together out of twigs and string. "It's to put into the coffee pot at night so the mice can get out and don't drown" they explained. I don't think Jack will ever live down the story of the mouse that poured.

40

BACK ACHES AND
THE BROWN TROUT

I had been working on my good friend Bob Shelton to take a trip to the Boundary Waters for a couple of years. His boy Dan had been on several canoe trips already and both father and son were avid fishermen. Bob had not done a lot of camping. Finally with a lot of apprehension he agreed to take a ten day trip with our motley group of friends, family and church members. Of course he worried, that because he had a desk job and didn't get a lot of exercise, he wouldn't be in shape to handle taking the tough portages* that we were planning. I told him that if I could do it with my bad back and knees that he surely could. He also worried about what we would eat as his wife Pat was a great Italian cook. Craig, another good friend who was also going along, assured him saying "Don't worry Bob, Roys' cooking is just as good as Pats but it's on a different level." That did little to allay his fears and he continued to fret over trip details.

The big day to leave finally arrived and all the members of the group assembled at my house late in the evening. We loaded the canoes on the vehicles that would make the trek to Ely. Then we packed up all the food, getting rid of as much weight as we could and double bagging everything to make sure the dry goods didn't leak out in the packs.

When everything was ready we tried to get a few hours of shuteye but the excitement of the upcoming trip made it hard to sleep. About 2:00 AM we took off and made it up to Hinkley, Minnesota on 35 E in short order where we made the obligatory stop for coffee and sticky buns at Tobies' restaurant. The rest of the trip up went like clockwork and we kept up CB chatter between the vehicles to keep each other awake and the vehicles going between the lines.

At Ely we ate a hearty breakfast at Vertines restaurant and stopped at a few of the outfitters for last minute purchases of maps, lures and bug dope. Soon we had driven the last few miles out to the Echo trail and the Nina Moose River launch point. That night we camped in American Lake Agnes. Fishing there was a disappointment and I promised better fishing the next couple of days in Darkey Lake where we would camp for a couple of nights. The next day we paddled through Argo Lake where the water is clearer than in any lake in the Quetico* Park. We trolled valiantly through the lake with every sort of spoon and deep running plugs trying to catch an elusive lake trout* without success. That night we made it to Darkey Lake and camped on the big rocky point at the north end of the lake. My back was getting sore after I had wrenched it on the Argo-Darkey portage. I tried my usual stretching exercises to loosen it up but had to settle for a couple aspirin to ease the pain. We set out fishing top water in the lily pads where the Darkey River runs into the lake and also fished the lake arm that connects to Brent Lake. The bass fishing was mediocre but enough were caught for a couple good fish fries.

Bob had an attraction for water. It seemed each time he got near it he would slip or fall or slide in and he was constantly getting wet. We joked about it and he took it good naturedly but was disgusted that he couldn't seem to stay dry. We set out trying to get a lake trout in the deep parts of the lake but the trout again eluded us. As we were trolling, a speedy Sawyer canoe overtook us and the two guys in it stopped to chat. We immediately recognized them as Canadians because of their accent. We soon found out that they were rangers patrolling the park. They asked if we had all the proper permits and licenses and we said we did but they didn't ask to see them. It was a good thing because all our paperwork was back at the campsite. They asked if we knew of anyone else camping on the lake and we pointed to the campsite on the southeast shore of the lake where we had seen the light of a campfire the previous night. Off they sped after wishing us good luck with our fishing. They carried very little gear, traveling light to cover a lot of ground in the park. One of the rangers in a swimsuit sported a severe case of sunburn and poison ivy rash. It didn't look like too enjoyable a job to us.

The next morning we were due to move on to Rebecca Falls on McAree Lake. When we got up my back was so stiff I could hardly move and I knew the others would be carrying the canoes. It was quite windy as we headed out toward Wicksteed Lake. Bob and Dan had brought along a depth finder and had not used it as of yet. As we paddled along trolling our lines I asked, "How deep does it say it is here?" "27 feet" Bob answered shortly after turning it on. "Can you see fish too?" I asked. "Yep and there's a big one at 25 feet right below us" he exclaimed excitedly. Just then Dan grabbed the rod and lure he had been trolling and set the hook on a nice strike. About 10 minutes later he landed a dark colored somewhat ugly fish with big teeth that I had never seen before in all my years of fishing in the North country. It weighed five pounds on the de-liar* and we put it on the stringer to show the others. Later we found out that it was a brown trout. It was the first I had ever seen. It was good eating that night.

I limped over the Wicksteed portage and the next couple portages carrying only the kettle pack and having to have help getting it on and off. My back was getting worse instead of better. Gulping more aspirin, I made it to Rebecca Falls where we discovered our favorite island campsite was already taken by a group that comes up to that spot every year. We settled for camping below the falls on a nice spot that is covered by big pines. Some of the crew went fishing and others opted to take baths. Bob cleaned up and got dressed in fresh dry clothes. Having no sooner done that, he made the mistake of getting too close to the edge of the lake and reaching for a dropped paddle in the water. The branch he was hanging onto for balance slowly bent and he slowly slid down the rock face as he was reaching for the paddle. The branch gently bent as he continued to slide in until he was up to his waist. I heard him swear for the first time that trip as he knew he would again have to dry out his clothes.

Our lures just weren't producing many fish and we were getting discouraged because the group across from us were going out twice a day and hauling in dozens of walleyes*, throwing them all back and taking pictures of the ones that were over eight pounds.

They even hooked into a giant fish that took them a half hour to land. During the fight that we watched with our binoculars, the man was almost bitten in the arm by a giant northern that leaped out of the water, jaws snapping, right next to their canoe. When he had landed the big fish we hollered "Bring it over so we can see it!" He paddled over showing us a 54 inch sturgeon he had brought in. I said "I thought you had a big northern on that nearly bit you in the arm." He said "I don't know where that one came from . . . must have struck at the movement he saw . . . nearly bit my elbow"!

We inquired as to the reason for their phenomenal fishing success. He stated that he comes to Rebecca Falls every year and brings leeches and night crawlers for bait. He suggested "try dragonfly Larvae . . . they are in full hatch right now." And they were . . . every rock along the shore was covered with them. We busied ourselves gathering the bait and Bones, another crew member went out and landed about a dozen two pound walleyes that made our best fish meal yet. The walleyes were perfect eating size.

I was too sore to fish and Ed was working on my back tapping pressure points with a rock and a stick and giving me a massage. I was living on aspirin. Bob, Craig and I looked pretty ratty with our grizzled gray beards and gray ratty hair sitting on shore drinking our coffee wearing only our dirty gray long johns. Too soon it came time to head back home and we packed up paddling south into a stiff wind.

When we got to Lake Agnes the waves were big three foot rollers and progress was slow. Bob was my bowman and he kept looking at the shore seeing the same big boulder that we just couldn't put behind us. "Can't keep this up much longer" he groaned as we both struggled to make headway in the heavy wind. "Keep paddlin' Bob" I encouraged and after a long time we began to move ahead. As we reached the south end of the lake we were more protected and we made much better speed. Back at the vehicles a couple hours later Bob said "I sure didn't think we were going to make it." After a tough trip, simple things like a good hot shower, an ice cold can of mountain dew and a comfortable chair are so very appreciated. Also my trip to Marty Chiropractic.

A few years later Bob had a severe bout of Pancreatitis and was hospitalized for a long time. He lost a lot of weight and looked pretty tough. The folks at church made up a poster sized get well card and passed it around for everyone to sign and to put encouraging words on. I pondered what to put on the card and settled for a quick sketch of the outline of a canoe with the words "keep on paddlin' Bob" written inside the outline. I didn't need to sign it because I knew he would know immediately who had put it on the card. He said he was greatly encouraged by my words as he thought about the trip and the perseverance it took to complete. He slowly got over his illness that also took a lot of perseverance and positive attitude to overcome.

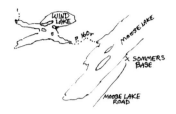

41

FASCINATED BY MAPS

I am intrigued by maps . . . especially those of the hundreds of square miles of the Boundary Waters area. Fisher* and MacKenzie* are the chief suppliers of maps for canoeists looking to ply their crafts in the lake country. Indeed, unless one spends his lifetime in the woods, a map is a necessity to find your way around the myriad lakes, islands and bays abundant in this area scoured by glaciers and left pristine by God for us to explore.

When you first glance at maps of the region you will notice the pattern of the lakes that lay almost like wood grain from the north to the south. The advancing glaciers thousands of years ago scoured the land clean and dug trenches down to bedrock in a pattern parallel to their movement to the south. In this area known as the Canadian Shield some lakes have been scraped hundreds of feet deep while others less so. In the last millennia some have been filled back in by erosion and by eutrification.* Some lakes have floating bogs composed of roots and rotting vegetation of plants, bushes and small trees that have grown out from their perimeters to cover over the shallow areas. Beavers, forest fires and erosion and weather have further altered the landscape as well as man with logging and mining operations in the past before the area was designated wilderness.

Lakes were named for many things. Some were named for their shape such as Knife, Spoon, Angleworm, Crooked, Square, Ladyboot or Cross; some for their location such as North, South, or Western; some for their discoverers like McKenzie, Thomas or McEwen; some for their features such as Gunflint, Magnetic, Silence, or Clear; many for animals, fish or birds like Moose, Trout, Birch, Beaver, Bentpine, or Beaverhouse. The French voyageurs named some like Lac La Croix. Many sport Indian names such as Gabimichigami, Ogishkemuncie, Kekekabic, and Windigoostigwan. For some lakes such as; This Man, That Man, No Man and Other Man or Lake l, Lake 2, Lake 3 and Lake 4 or Bays Wednesday, Thursday, Friday, Saturday and Sunday in Crooked Lake you have to wonder what the people who did the naming were thinking. Each lake is as different as snowflakes and each has its own personality and unique features.

Having traveled many different routes covering over 8000 miles through both the Quetico* and BWCA* sides of the border I have been fortunate to have been an observer and a camper in many of them. Just looking at a map can set me off on hours of storytelling if I am not told to shut up.

When I worked at the Sommers Canoe Base* with the BSA, (Boy Scouts of America), we posted a large map of the wilderness area and the guides would mark portages*, campsites and features they had seen on their trips on the master map. Eventually it contained so much information that even the local outfitters would visit the base gleaning information on campsite locations and portage difficulties as well as what kinds of fish could be caught in which lakes. The map was valuable for incoming crews in trip planning. The old map has disappeared and a new one is posted that doesn't contain nearly as much information.

The old enemy, time, has robbed me of many memories of former trips. I used to be able to almost see shoreline features go by as a moving mental picture when someone would describe a route they had taken but now I too have to rely on maps to help me remember routes when I go on extended trips.

In general the north and eastern part of the boundary waters wilderness contains the most weedy and shallow lakes as well as meandering rivers like the Wawiag and Cache. The south and western part of the park contains more exposed rocky shorelines. There are exceptions to this description but it is generally true. The climax forest* of the area is red and white pine as well as jack pine, balsam and spruce. Almost all virgin forest has been cut many years ago and many areas have been logged a second time for pulp wood. The trees that come back first are poplar or aspen and birch. In a few areas of the park some hardwood trees like elm and ash can be found but conifers birch and poplar are more the rule. These short lived trees are replaced eventually by the longer lived pines and other conifers. If left alone for thousands of years the conifers would be dominated by the white and red pines.

The loggers in the late 1800s and early 1900s built many wooden sluiceways and coffer dams to change water levels in the lakes to make it easier to gather the logs into the larger lakes such as Basswood. There the railheads would receive the rafts of logs and transport them to the mills. Many remnants of the old logging days such as barges, rail beds and old logging camps can still be found in the woods. They thought they would never run out of trees but within a few short years the whole boundary waters area was logged off. Mining made less of an impact in the boundary lake area, but remains of several old cabins and old mines are still there. One cabin I found on the man lake chain contained hundreds of core samples from test drilling. Other less obvious signs of man include old Indian encampments and petro glyphs*, trapper cabins, and portages made by Indians and Voyageurs. More recent changes to the wilderness include campsites, latrines and trail improvements. Years ago, during the depression, portage rests, trail signs and docks were built on many of the trails but they have since been removed. The wilderness was being overrun by resorts, houseboats and unlimited horsepower speedboats and snowmobiles until it was designated a wilderness area. Now canoeing and hiking is the only way to see this magnificent area.

I hope each of you that read these stories has the opportunity to see and sense what I have experienced in my lifetime of canoe tripping. It will change you and give you a new appreciation of Gods creativity.

42

KASHAPIWI

The name Kashapiwi is Indian in origin but I don't know what it means. I have traveled through or camped in this lake perhaps 10 times over the years. It conjures up memories of great times in the boundary waters. The lake is about eight miles long and is oriented North and South on the map. It is a popular lake and gets quite a bit of canoe traffic. It has about 10 campsites in it and also a ranger cabin next to a fire tower that is no longer manned. It can be entered or exited in eight different places with varying degrees of difficulty. The tough portage from Yum Yum Lake I have described in a previous story. Kashapiwi is known for its great lake trout* fishing because of its great depth. Trout like to stay in water that is about 42 degrees so most lakes that aren't at least 75 feet deep don't have them. In the warmest part of the summer trout go very deep to stay at their 42 degree comfort zone and Kashapiwi has the depth and structure they love.

On my first trip through the lake we watched a man on a campsite pull in a couple of fish as we were passing by looking for a spot to camp. We dropped in on him as he was baiting another hook and paddled up to chat and find out what he was using for bait. "Chicken guts" he explained are the best bait. "Smellier the better!" He loaded up a glob of them on a treble hook weighted with a big sinker and tossed the line out a few feet and let it roll down the steep rock face into the depths. Within a minute he had another one on and hauled it up to add to the nice batch he had already on the stringer. "I've got my supper caught. You better find a campsite and get busy catching yours" he exclaimed proudly. We went looking for a site but not knowing the lake well at the time we settled for a bare rock ledge just big enough for our crew. We had to paddle down the lakeshore for firewood as no trees were growing where we were camped. We made the best of the site and decided it could use a little camp furniture. We erected a picnic table but ran out of logs for the top. I noticed that the frost had fractured off a big flat section of our ledge so I enlisted the help of the whole crew and we carried the 600 pound slab over and set it on our framework. The boys were so proud of their table they carved their crew number and my name in the frame and it is still standing today nearly 40 years later the last time I was there. We did catch some trout but not having any chicken parts did so with silver KB spoons for lures.

On another trip through the lake we got caught by a bad hailstorm. Luckily we had made it to shore and took shelter under our canoes until it was over. We still hadn't found a campsite so I thought I would look for the hidden campsite I had heard about. I knew only that it was on the east side of the lake and that it was on top of a high cliff. We paddled along the shore until we came to a small notch in the shoreline where a big clump of cedars hung their boughs right down to the water. Above the cedars was a cliff about 50 feet high. I spotted the tell tale pile of rocks making up the fireplace on the top of the cliff. The crew, very puzzled, must have thought I was daft as I paddled right into the cedars. In the shade under the branches the crew was surprised to find a nice landing with logs set up to rack the canoes onto. We unloaded our gear and racked the canoes in a nice neat row. "Load up for one last portage*" I said over their groans and moans. We trekked up a narrow trail to find a nice campsite at the top of the cliff. Behind the campsite lay another small lake that supplied our drinking water. "No skeeters up here in this nice breeze" the advisor stated. It was the coolest campsite we had found the whole trip.

Years later I returned to the lake with my son Matt and several friends. We came into the lake from the south. I wanted to avoid Yum Yum so we came up through the Isabella beaver stream. My son was ahead of Harlan and I and he had the map . . . we had the compass. He took the stream but we took the portage. The stream and the portage don't go to the same lake. A couple lakes later we hadn't caught up to them and went back to look for them. About 4 hours later we finally got back together and vowed to stay in sight of each other from then on. We camped in Kashapiwi that night and went trout fishing. Only Harlan caught a trout but it went eight pounds and was big enough to feed all six of us a nice supper that night. Our trip continued through Joyce, Marj, Paulette, and Brent Lakes. Trolling through Brent Lake yielded a big clump of weeds dragging our lures down but when we stopped to clear them Harlan's boy found a five and one half pound bass* on his lure inside the clump of weeds. I guess it was so tangled up in them it couldn't give much of a fight. Another nice supper!

I had been suffering from a bit of flu and fever and was feeling pretty punky for a couple of days. No fun being sick in the woods. I seemed to have no strength. The next night, camped in Darkey Lake the fever broke and I woke up to a soaked sleeping bag and drenched underwear. I must have sweated a gallon! When I got up I felt weak but I knew I was on the mend. I unzipped my down bag and set it in the sun to dry and gathered clean clothes and a bar of soap. I took a long leisurely bath in the shallows of the lake and washed all my clothes. Lying in the sun drying off felt like heaven.

Near dusk I felt good enough to go out top-water bass fishing in the Darkey River that entered near our campsite. What great fun! Even if we hadn't caught any it was a blast seeing how close we could cast our black hula poppers to the lily pads and stumps. I overshot my mark near a downed cedar and dropped my lure over a log about four feet out from shore. The log was about three feet above the water and my lure wound around it a couple of times before it stopped, swinging about a foot above the water. A nice three pound bronze back bass leaped up and impaled himself, his tail just touching the water but not giving him any purchase to shake the lure! "Whoa . . . did you see that!" I shouted. We put him on the stringer for tomorrows breakfast and fished on, catching several more nice ones before the mosquitoes drove us back to the campfire.

Earlier, in the excitement of fishing I had lost my grip on my rod when I set the hook on a nice one and it went over the side. "Dang it! I can't believe I did that" I groaned. A few minutes later my black hula popper* bobbed to the surface. The big bass had spit the lure. We paddled over and grabbed the lure that was still attached to my rod at the bottom of the lake. Carefully pulling in the line we had recovered everything. I can truthfully say there is a God and He watches over us very closely.

Two days later we had made it back to the Scout base that we had departed from 10 days earlier. While relaxing in the hot sauna after our trip Harlan said "With all the great fish we caught I'm bringing my video camera next time." But that's in another story.

43

LEPIDOPTERA

Lepidoptera is the Latin name for butterflies and moths in the category of living things grouped under the larger heading of insects. They fascinate me. As a youth I had a picture—framed collection that was a prized possession. I had a butterfly net and spent a lot of time in the summer collecting and searching for unusual specimens. Today I would be looked at as being a bit odd, but back then I was so enthralled by all sorts of living things in nature that I didn't care if people stared at me as I ran after butterflies with my net. I even raised monarch butterfly larvae in small homemade cages, collecting milkweed leaves for them to eat. When I discovered caterpillars on the carrot tops in our garden I added them to my miniature insect zoo, continuing to feed them carrot tops to see what they would turn into. Several months later and in the middle of winter the pupae they had formed hatched and I had zebra swallowtail butterflies for my collection as well.

On my very first trip to the boundary waters among the many things that fascinated me were the butterflies and moths. I saw a cloud of banded purples fluttering over a mud hole on one of the portages*. They have a dark purplish-black iridescent wing with a bright white, very predominant stripe across the top of each wing. They are only medium sized but in clusters are very eye catching. I thought it strange that I had never seen them before back on the South Dakota prairie where I was from.

Moths are even more fascinating. They can be much more colorful than butterflies and quite a bit bigger. You can tell them apart from butterflies easily two ways. First look at the antennae . . . Moths have antennae that look like small feathers. Butterflies antennae look like a small hair with a knob on the end. Butterflies have thin bodies but moths have fat hairy bodies.

One warm humid night at the scout base where I worked, I headed up to the Sauna* building to enjoy a relaxing sweat bath. As I entered the bathroom I noticed many moths on the screen near the outside light. One that really caught my eye was a big chartreuse green moth with a band of purple on the leading edge of each wing. It had tails about five inches long and its wingspan was just as wide. I had never seen one before and was spellbound by its size and color. Maybe you think I'm some kind of kook for being interested in thing as mundane as butterflies. I guess to me it's just a part of stopping to smell the roses. I am interested in all of nature. With my education in science, all things found in nature, rocks, trees, flowers, birds, animals, fish and so on tweak my interest. I see how all things in nature work together to make up a well-balanced environment as long as man doesn't interfere too much. There are so many unusual things to see in the aquatic and forest environment of the north woods that I don't think I will ever tire of exploring it.

When I was canoeing on my very first trip I was even fascinated by the clarity of the water in the lakes, and the fact that you could drink right from them without worrying about pollution. I was from South Dakota where most lakes were a muddy brown and visibility was limited to a few inches. In the BWCAW* there are lakes that the bottom can be clearly seen 30 feet down in calm water and bright sunlight. You can see the weed beds and the fish that live in them. Often you can see the fish take your lure when you are fishing. I've seen giant six-inch striped leeches swimming through the water.

The trees and how they can cling to the rocks and withstand the wind is curious. The color of the lichens growing on the rocks catches my eye every time I see them. When we have a wet spell up north all of a sudden, seemingly overnight, dozens of different kinds of brightly colored fungi sprout up from the forest floor. It is neat to see how tall and thin the trunks of the aspen and birch become as they slowly race each other upward to reach for the sunlight. I love the downy soft look of a big white pine viewed from a distance. The Canadian Jays are fun to watch as they steal food from the camp kitchen. The too loud hammering of a distant Pileated woodpecker demands your attention. The lack of fear of the doe that wanders into camp and sees humans for the first time is priceless. The hand of the creator is all around if you just take the time to look.

Have you ever seen a sundew? They have their own little nitch in the nitrate poor soils of the north-country. They are tiny . . . only one quarter to one half inch tall. I first saw one growing on an old deadhead log semi-submerged in the creek leading out of Wind Lake. The rotting wood it was growing on provides little nitrogen so the plant exudes a sweet sticky fluid on the hairs growing out from the ball perched on its short stem. Ants, gnats and other small insects are attracted to the sweet syrup and become stuck to it like flies to flypaper and then the plant releases enzymes to digest them and claim the nitrogen in their bodies. The pitcher plant, also found in boggy areas does the same thing by providing a one-way hair lined passage for insects into the core of its folded leaves where a small pool of digestive enzymes drowns and digests the unwary guests, extracting needed nutrients.

Traveling by canoe, your pace is slow enough that the marvels of Gods creation reveal themselves in a never-ending panorama. Using all your senses to take in the wonder and beauty greatly enriches the human spirit and helps us from assuming too prideful a position of our place on this planet earth.

44

FAST CARS
AND HOT WOMEN

Catchy title eh? I have a lot more experience with the fast cars than with the hot women so this tale will center on the cars. In the summer of 1964 when I first made the trek to Sommers Canoe Base* for my summer job I was driving a 1950, blue ford sedan. Not much of a car but I was in college and it was wheels and it was bought for only $50. It did sport brand new snow tires but didn't have much else to brag about. It guzzled oil in prodigious quantities . . . . so much so that I fed it used oil from a five gallon container I kept in the trunk. It took a half gallon, from a milk carton every 50 miles. The oil blew out the exhaust pipe in a stinking blue cloud and also sprayed out of several leaks as well as from the filler spout. The spray of oil under the hood would gather on the firewall and the wind stream would cause it to migrate out at the back of the hood where it would creep up the windshield and onto the roof. The car had holes in several of its eight pistons and had next to no compression but it kept running and got me up to the base for two summers in a row. I gave rides back to South Dakota for a couple of the guides after the season was over. Returning home after the second summer I gave John Thurston a ride and we ran out of gas late at night and had to spend the night in the car until early morning when we hitched to a station for a refill. That year at school I traded the car for a sweater and a pair of moccasins and looked for another.

A friends' brother worked at a savings and loan and he had a car for sale. It was a sports car . . . an Austin Healy 3000J. "$900 eh? Don't know if I can afford it?" I replied. "Sure you can. I can write the loan right now." I had forgotten that he worked at a savings and loan. My first sports car . . . "WOW!" And I wish I still had it because it would be worth about $15,000 today. Now I traveled up to the base in style. The next summer my brother Paul rode with me, having landed the job of Maintenance Director for the summer at the base. The car was a blast to drive on all the curvy roads around Ely and I would drive all over on my days off just for the fun of it. It was a bit of a babe magnet but I took out a full schedule of trips that summer including one 15 day trip and my days off to get dates were pretty limited. I drove it up to inspiration point a few times on dates where we would sit and watch the northern lights from the high cliff but other than that it just served as stylish transportation. Paul and I rigged up a rack for the top of it at the end of the summer and we brought home a used old town canoe that I had bought from the base. The car had a hydraulic clutch that had gone out so we drove all the way back to South Dakota by power shifting. I'm sure we rounded off all the gears with all the grinding. That fall I fell asleep at the wheel returning from visiting friends in Nebraska and I rolled the car, totaling it. I am here today because I had my seatbelt on.

My next car was a 1965 VW bug that I drove through the winter, but dreams of another sports car ran in my head. I had seen a bright red Jaguar XKE a few times when I had traveled to Mitchell, South Dakota for sports events. I was now teaching at a small high school in Delmont, South Dakota. On one trip to Mitchell I saw it again and it had a for sale sign in the back window! I called the phone number and we dickered over the price. I had to sell the VW to come up with any money at all and I was having trouble doing it. We finally settled on $3000 and he would take my VW and sell it in Mitchell. I talked to my banker and returned to Mitchell to pick up the car. He gave me a ride in it taking it up to 125MPH and scaring me to death. He showed me how everything worked and we shook hands on the deal. I drove it home with both hands held tightly on the wheel. It ran like a dream and was strange to drive. My butt was only about six inches from the pavement and about a foot in front of the rear wheels. Getting in and out was an art form and I had to relearn how to steer from behind so long a hood. I studied the manual and learned that in England the hood is the bonnet and the trunk is the boot. I had a 3.8 Litre, dual overhead cam, 6 cylinder, 265 horsepower engine at my command. It could do 165 MPH and lay rubber in any gear at any speed! I learned that the yellow no passing lines on the highway had to be extended a lot longer for a car so low to the ground. I couldn't see very far down the road from my hunkered down position and others couldn't see me either. That summer at the base I was the envy of many of the guides and gave a lot of them rides to town. I made it the 22 miles to Ely in 16 minutes. It might still be a record. The road then had way more curves and three miles of it was gravel. The St Louis county sheriff caught up to me after one of my trips to town and congratulated me saying "Quite a piece of driving but hold it down a bit." I think he knew I worked out at the base because he didn't write me a citation. The car was indeed a babe magnet but too small inside to allow for any shenanigans. With the convertible top down I spent many pleasant hours driving the back roads. I nearly hit a moose one night and did roll a bear in the ditch after he lost a race with my fender. I drove the car for two summers all around Ely.

The second summer on a trip to town I noticed the acceleration was not up to snuff. When I got to Ely and stopped at the first light I smelled burning brakes. Glancing in the mirror I saw smoke and realized it was coming from beneath the Jag. I jumped out and looked underneath. Both rear discs glowed cherry red and burning grease was dripping from the rear end. I ran to the nearest house and grabbed a garden hose jerking the hose rack off the wall in my haste. I yelled to the man who came to the door "My car is on fire." And he came out to help. The hose cooled the discs and the brakes let go. The car had duel master cylinders that worked in tandem but one had jammed. I had to disconnect the brakes and leave the car in town until I got back from my next canoe trip. Owen Gibbs volunteered to ride along with me two weeks later and help me get the car to Duluth where the nearest dealer was located. We drove to Duluth carefully using the emergency brake to stop but it was soon pegged out and we had no brakes at all. We came into town on central entrance which is highway 53. It comes out on top of the hill but the address of the dealer was on Superior Street down by the lake 900 feet below. I put the car in low to get it rolling and then quickly shifted into reverse and slipped the clutch to stop at each intersection. It was pretty tense and a quick glance over at Owen showed me he was scared stiff. He was pastey white and crossing himself like mad. If he could have gotten out of the car, I think he would have genuflected and kissed the ground as well. We soon made it to the dealer and he said, "It's gunna take a week to fix the car 'cause I gotta order the parts outa Chicago". It took about half of what I made that summer to fix the brakes. I still wish I had that car.

I landed a teaching job in Mt. Iron, Minnesota and thought that the Jaguar convertible would not be the best kind of vehicle for the cold winters up on the iron range. I traded the Jaguar convertible for another XKE that was brand new but it was a coupe. The car cost $6600 new. Today that car in mint condition could bring nearly $100,000! The old convertible in mint shape even more. The new Jag had a 4.2 litre 6 cylinder engine and even had air conditioning. It didn't have quite the zip of the convertible however. That summer a couple other guides had bought sports cars as well and the parking lot at the base was looking good. Jim Telford showed up at the beginning of the summer driving a red Alfa Romeo. Ron miles had been the only other guide driving a sports car up to that time with his Little four cylinder Triumph.

I drive more sensible vehicles now but I've never quite gotten over the sports car bug. In my driveway under the carport sits a 1968 Jaguar XKE coupe that needs a new clutch. I picked it up for a mere $6600, and one of these days when I get some time I'll get it running. Its got only 55,000 miles on the engine . . . barely broke in. Some day I hope to be driving it down the road. I wonder if it will still be a babe magnet?

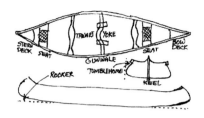

45

OLD TOWN

The name Old Town* to canoeists is like saying Rolls Royce to car buffs. It is the epitome or the state of the art in canoe design.

Canoes have been around for hundreds of years. Early man made his first forays into bodies of water on logs and then discovered if they were hollowed out he could take passengers and goods. They weren't great to portage because of their weight however. With ingenuity the Indians discovered ways to make a similar craft and shed the weight, thus the birth of the birchbark canoe. Using native materials such as lightweight but strong cedar for slats, planking and ribs, and wrapping it with birchbark stitched together with fir roots and sealed with pitch the canoe took shape. The craft was given its shape with gunwales and thwarts and became a much lighter and more maneuverable craft that could haul a great deal of weight. The Eskimos came up with similar narrow craft called a kayak and wrapped them with animal hide except they covered most of the tops as well because of the use in cold, windy ocean waters.

In 1959 when I took my first canoe trip the base had three kinds of canoes: Old Town cedar and canvas canoes, Grumman* aluminum canoes, and Seliga* wood and canvas or wood and fiberglass canoes. Back then a brand new Old Town cost $250. The company was located in Old Town, Maine and made one of the nicest handling canoes you could buy at the time. Today the base has a few museum piece birchbark canoes on display but the ones that go on the trail are still for the most part Grumman and Alumicraft* aluminum canoes. When I started taking trips in 1964, as a guide, all the guides used wood-canvas or wood-fiberglass Seligas or Old Towns. The scouts all used the aluminum canoes. The base had a pile of about 300 of them. Today most of the Seligas that are left are museum pieces and many of the guides use the aluminum canoes. Scouts are being offered, at a small extra charge, the use of Wenonah Kevlar canoes which have become very popular because of their extremely light weight.

One canoe that can never be replaced is the Seliga. I personally met Joe Seliga when I was guiding for the Boy Scouts. Joe lived in Ely his whole life and built over 750 canoes by hand in his garage. All of his canoes can be identified by their distinctive bow and stern plate and have a serial number stamped on the inside bow keel that numbers the canoe and gives the date of its manufacture. The canoes Joe and his wife assembled were of equal quality to the Old Towns, but had a distinctive shape. The more blunt bow and stern gave Joe's canoes a larger carrying capacity and they rode through big waves without shipping much water. For a number of years the scout base bought five canoes from Joe each spring. Guides that used them treasured them and treated them like a mistress. Pampered to the max.

Joe and his wife are gone now, and if you own a Seliga, consider yourself in possession of a treasure. My 1955 model is displayed proudly on the wall in my family room that is built to look like a log cabin you would find in the north woods. Before he passed away, Joe willed his handmade canoe molds to Camp Widjiwagan near Ely, Minnesota. This YMCA camp has a state of the art canoe work shop and may someday reproduce Joe's canoe, but it won't have his touch.

The typical canoe can vary in length from 10 to 36 feet. The best size for the types of trips taken by the scouts is a 17 foot model and indeed is the most popular size sold today because of the ease of portaging and for the large load carrying capacity. Canoes can vary in width from 30 inches to six feet for the big canoe de norde that the voyageurs used on Lake Superior. Most canoes used for tripping in the boundary waters are 34 to 38 inches wide. Many of the trails are so narrow that anything bigger becomes a hassle to portage. For portaging, a canoe must have a padded yoke* centered on the canoe body so that it can be comfortably balanced and carried by one person. Most aluminum canoes that are in the 17 foot range weigh about 75-80 pounds. With life jackets, fishing equipment and a couple paddles jammed in the weight to be portaged can climb to about 90 pounds. These canoes felt light to the guides back in the 60s because our wood canvas canoes would start the trip at about the same weight as the aluminum ones but would soak up water and often would end up close to 100 pounds after a few hours of paddling. Add the extra gear and the guides would be carrying upwards of 110 pounds along with their personal packs that often weighed 30 pounds or more. The new Kevlar canoes weigh in at about 57 pounds and are a dream to portage. Some of the latest carbon fiber canoes weigh only 36 pounds. Most canoes used in the BWCA* have a depth of 12-14 inches.

When looking to purchase a canoe some things to consider are how it is to be used? How much portaging will it see? What does the weight capacity need to be? Will it be used for white water? Will it be used in big lakes with big waves? These questions will often help determine the style and design of the canoe best suited for ones use. A shallow sharply pointed canoe will go fast but do poorly in hauling big loads and will ship a lot of water in waves due to its shallow draft and inability to bob up when waves are ridden over. A canoe with a defined keel steers a straight course but would be a poor choice for white water because it can't be turned quickly enough. A flat bottom canoe is stable but doesn't track a straight course as well as one with a bit of rocker* bow to stern and some tumble home* side to side. A sawyer racing canoe can be as shallow as 10 inches and very sharp bowed but would be a poor choice for an eight day trip into the woods. The light weight kevlars portage easily but must be anchored to a tree at night because they are so light even a little breeze can steal them away from your campsite at night as they act like big kites. I find on a windy day they are blown about much more than heavier canoes especially if they are lightly loaded. A canoe with a high bow and stern will be affected by wind a great deal more than one with a lower profile. The choice of canoe boils down to compromises that will give you the best craft for most of the ways the canoe swill be used.

New canoes cannot be bought for $250 anymore. Prices vary from $600 to over $3000 depending on what a person is looking for. Old town is still the largest canoe company and has been around for a long time. Today canoes are stamped out mass production style with probably less than two or three man hours spent in their manufacture. Canoes are made of fiberglass, royalex, Kevlar, and carbon fiber. Old town still builds about 100 wood canvas canoes a year the old fashioned way but the cost exceeds $3000 per copy due to the high amount of hand labor involved. They sell over 20,000 fiberglass canoes a year. Grumman no longer makes canoes but the company has been bought by its employees and makes the same canoe under the Marathon name. Other new companies are Bell, Sawyer, Mad River, Quachita, and Wenonah. Some old standbys that made wood canvas canoes were Chestnut and Peterborough but I do not know if they are still in business.

A canoe to me is still a magic craft that can take you most anywhere there are a few inches of water and can do it silently without disturbing nature. In my opinion they are the only way to travel easily in the BWCA*. I fish out of them, sail in them and have eaten many a lunch out of them on the open water. I think I have seven of them now up in the rafters of my carport. Two of them are Old Towns. They are still my first choice if I take a trip to the 'Bound*".

46

DIAMOND WILLOW

I saw my first diamond willow walking stick when I was 15 years old at a scout camporee*. It was an awesome piece of work . . . sanded nice and smooth with all those red diamonds showing through multiple coats of varnish. The scoutmaster who owned it said he had found it on one of his hikes and brought it home. He said he had spent quite a bit of time finishing it. I thought it was pretty cool and I wanted one but he had failed to share what diamond willow looks like in the wild so I never knew what to look for.

Years later several of the guides at Sommers canoe base had sticks of willow as well and by quizzing them I finally knew what to look for. Butch Dieslin took me aside and showed me a stand of willow as well as several attractive pieces he had harvested. I began looking for willow stands and finally found a few pieces that were highly figured and made myself a nice staff.

After the big blowdown in 1999 when so many trees went down in a single storm that the fire danger became critical, the scout base worried that their property was at great risk. They hired a couple of D-9 cat drivers to cut a firebreak around the base property. 25,000,000 trees had gone down in the fourth of July storm in a few minutes. The base property was at the leading edge of the blowdown that extended for nearly 100 miles in a 20 mile wide swath. The base buildings suffered only minor damage but the threat of a major fire was real and with all that fuel lying on the ground cutting a firebreak seemed like a good idea.

The cat drivers showed up and began following the orange tape markers that the staff had started laying out. They worked with such speed that they overtook the guys that were marking out the property perimeter. The tumbled trees were so impenetrable that the staff couldn't stay ahead of the drivers so they began working from behind using their compasses to steer the cats in the right direction. In two days time the drivers had a 100 foot wide path around the perimeter of the base property clear out to Flash Lake and back. They said they had worked slower than usual because they didn't want to throw a cleat so far back in the woods.

I share this story because I salvaged several clumps of willow that they dozed down and brought it home turning it into a queen sized head and footboard for my bed. I thought if the walking stick looked so cool a whole bed made of it would look even better. It turned out to be quite striking. This led me to make a seven piece dining room set, an entertainment center, dozens of picture frames, a map frame and a hat rack. A friend of mine, Bruce Bauer, began helping me and we decided this hobby might be able to make some money. Soon we formed a company and began turning out rocking chairs, plant stands, tables of all kinds and dozens of other useful and attractive pieces of furniture. My two renters, (at the time), Parker West and Jeff Smith got in on the act and set up a web site at bcrustics.com. Jesse Krech, another friend who works for me occasionally, added his expertise at computing and soon we had a top notch web site as well as business cards and a nice brochure. Mark McCoy who had just been benched by a bad motorcycle accident came over every day for months and peeled and sanded the willow we had gathered. We cut willow at Bruce's brothers' deer hunting land as well as property owned by Butch Dieslin. A lot of willow was found along the Fernberg Road near Ely as well as on the Canoe Base property. We have sold several thousand dollars worth of furniture but have been hurt badly by a couple of consignment stores that didn't pay us. I still hope that the hobby can pay off and am still making furniture when I have time aside from my regular jobs.

Willow likes to grow best near swamps where it can get ample moisture. I have read that there are five different species of diamond willow. Typically it grows in clumps like a big shrub. If pieces are cut off it will grow back from the roots. One to three inch diameters are the common sizes found but we have found several that have grown into trees six to eight inches in diameter as well as one ancient willlow that was nearly two feet thick. The willow has narrow leaves and a clump will also sport many dead and dying branches. If its source of water dries up the plant will let part of itself die off, to preserve a remnant that will flourish again when moisture returns. It is tenacious. The live parts will be white with red diamonds growing around stubs of twigs or damage on the trunk. I think the diamonds are actually scar tissue where the plant it trying to close off or grow over breaks in the bark. Insects bore holes in it and the color varies from white on the live parts to brown, tan, grey light blue or red on the older dead wood. By looking at ripples on the bark you can find pieces that have the greatest chance of being figured but you won't know for sure until the bark is peeled off and the sticks are sanded.

Making furniture out of willow is labor intensive and that is putting it mildly. First the willow has to be found and cut and transported to the workshop. Peeling takes about fifteen minutes for a six foot stick. Then the peeled sticks are set aside to dry for a few weeks so they can be sanded easily. We use a random orbit sander to smooth and shape the pieces. After many hours of work enough pieces are prepped to give you the raw materials to start making a piece of furniture. The items made are works of art because every one is different. Willow varies so much in size, color and shape that it does not lend itself to any mass production process. Sometimes the piece of wood itself will give us ideas of what to make out of it. Through trial and error we have learned how to make the rockers for a chair and what size and height a seat must be to be comfortable. We have combined willow with pine, maple, redwood and cedar on seats and arms of chairs and the tops of tables. Willow is not a large enough species to make into lumber for the flat parts of furniture such as table tops. The color of pine is similar enough to willow to look quite good in furniture.

We have accumulated in the last few years a number of tools that make the work go faster. We have several large drills we use along with some aggressive drill bits from Milwalkee Co. that we use to bore holes. The ends of the legs and rungs are doweled by turning them down with cutters that fit in the drills. It works like an oversized pencil sharpener that turns the end of a log into a dowel instead of a point. All connections are glued. The piece has its legs trimmed so it will sit level and then gets a final sanding before getting three coats of polyurethane with several more sandings between coats before completion.

Even though making this furniture is time consuming we have gotten such rave reviews that we continue on. It is still a hobby and it is still fun so I guess that is why we still do it. We haven't made much money at it yet but that may change as the word gets out about our products and we attend a few more craft and trade shows. The pieces we have made have made our creative juices flow and have given us a lot of satisfaction. Everybody should have a hobby that can be an enjoyable outlet for ideas. What'yours?

47

RANDY

During the summer of '67 or '68 early in the season we got a call from the Canadian rangers saying that one of our Sommers Base crews had a lost scout. One of the three Ogle brothers, Tom, Ted, and Terry who were all guides that summer had taken a crew up to Kashapiwi Lake. They had then traveled up to Keefer and Sark Lakes where they had decided to trek into a lake off the beaten trail. Their goal was to get to Pierna Lake where few had ever traveled hoping for good fishing and solitude.

Much of the trek into the lake involved walking along a nearly dry creek that connected the lake to Sark. When they arrived at the lake and counted noses they came up one short. Randy, one of their scouts, hadn't made it across the portage*. They went back looking and spent several hours calling. As darkness fell they built several bonfires that they hoped he would see and find his way out but without success. In the morning the decision was made and the guide took a couple strong paddlers and set out for the ranger station* giving them the message which was then relayed by radio to Sommers Canoe Base*.

It was early in the season, and many of the guides and base staff were awaiting crews that would be coming in over the next week and a half. It was decided in short order to send a number of staff to assist in the search. 27 people could be spared for a few days. Time off was cancelled and trips to town were postponed as the orders were given. We had two hours to get ready. Basic food stuff was packed, tents were rolled, canoes were readied and each of us chosen to go hurried to gather our personal gear.

The trek to the lake started at dusk. Six canoes were tied three each to two sport boats that were powered by five horse Johnson "kickers*". As one of the more experienced guides, I was chosen to run one of the sport boats that were nothing more than wide bodied canoes. The gear was all loaded and we were off. Within the hour we were at Prairie Portage, where each train of canoes was untied for the portage. It was dark enough that we walked the trail with small flashlites stuck in our mouths so we could see where we were going. Many of the guides had night paddled on big lakes before but few of them had ever portaged in the dark.

Spurred on by the thoughts of the lost scout, we traveled non stop through Basswood, Burke, North Bay and the Isabella Beaver stream arriving in the big lake Kashapiwi before sunrise. A couple of hours later we got to Sark Lake and made our way to Pierna Lake where we met with Sandy Bridges the base director who had arrived before us by float plane. He laid out a map and a plan to grid off all the area on both sides of the portage where we would concentrate our search. We ate a quick breakfast of oatmeal and gulped down some coffee in the makeshift headquarters campsite. We were all exhausted from the 13 hours of nonstop travel just completed, but were eager to assist in the search and rescue effort. Sandy was pleased that we had all gotten there so fast and explained how we would lay out the grids with blazes* on the trees marking the area to be searched. He didn't want anyone else getting lost which was a real possibility in the dense forests surrounding the campsite.

We set out with maps, compasses and hatchets for blazing the trees and soon the name "Randy" was being hollered everywhere echoing constantly through the trees. We knew he had a personal pack that contained extra clothes, a rain poncho and his mess gear so at least he had some equipment that he could use to protect himself from the elements. By the time we started looking it was the morning of the third day that he had been missing. Our real fear was that he had panicked when he had lost sight of his crew on the faint trail to the lake and had run off and perhaps fallen and broken a leg or gotten a concussion and couldn't get up or holler at us even if we came close to him in our search. We tried to stay close enough to each other to stay in sight but it was hard in the thick underbrush. At noon after about five hours of searching we were instructed to report back to the camp for lunch and a progress report. We grabbed several glasses of koolaid and a handful of raisins along with our two peanut butter and jelly sandwiches as Sandy marked off on the map with a highlighter the areas that had been searched. Soon we were back in new areas of the woods continuing our search. We were getting bug bitten, scratched and hoarse from hollering as the afternoon passed by. A chopper from the Duluth airbase had joined the search and the pilots made passes over the area all afternoon. At about dusk we trekked back to camp.

As supper was being prepared the chopper flew over dropping a plastic bottle with a message inside. Randy had been found and picked up by the chopper! He was OK and unhurt except for lots of mosquito bites. He was being flown back to the base and his parents were arriving in two days to pick him up. It was good news. We changed our supper menu to something more appealing and even baked several apple pies. That night we slept like we were dead. We got up late, ate a leisurely breakfast and broke camp. All that day we raced our two strings of canoes. The other Johnson motor had a few more RPMs than mine so he would slowly take the lead but he had a big dent in his gas tank so I would pass him again because he had to refuel more often. We stayed about even. On the last mile or so before arriving at the canoe base, the guys in my canoe train started to horse around steering their canoes in big swerves that made it hard to pull them. Finally I had enough and held up my hunting knife for them to see. When they realized what I was going to do they started shaking their heads no, but it was too late and also too tempting . . . I reached back and cut the rope setting them free to paddle back to the base on their own. My sport boat raced ahead free of its load. At the dock a few minutes later I grabbed my gear and raced to the showers. I didn't want to get caught by the staff that I had forced to paddle in to the base.

Later we looked for Randy to see how he was doing and to ask how he became lost. We found out that he had gone to Ely to a dance! We couldn't believe it. Through questioning we learned he had built a shelter but hadn't signaled the chopper right away. He had a red sweatshirt and the shiny mess kit could have been used for a mirror to flash the searchers. What it boiled down to was that he was looking for attention, and thought getting lost was a good way to get it. If I ever have another child the name Randy definitely will be near the bottom of the list of possible names.

48

COLD, WET SUMMER

The weather that summer started out OK. The ice had gone out late, so when the staff practiced canoe swamping in the lake, during training week, it was a bit of an ordeal. The guide staff knew the water was still in the upper 40s for temperature, so we fired the sauna* several hours early. We wore long johns and parkas as we paddled the canoes out 50 yards from shore and then deliberately tipped them over. Cliff Hanson, the base director was "old school", and insisted that every staff member down to the assistant cooks participate in the canoe swamping exercise during staff training week early in June. The water was so cold it took your breath away, and it felt like we had been dipped in liquid fire. It was nearly impossible to do anything but gasp as each of us slithered over the gunwales* and paddled the canoe full of water back to the shore as quick as we could. When we reached the shore we threw our paddles to the side, ditched our life jackets and sprinted for the hot sauna. It took about 15 minutes for your body to realize the temperature change and begin to break a sweat. I believe a human could only survive 10 or 15 minutes submersed in water at that temperature before succumbing to hypothermia. I believe that summer was when three fishermen's bodies, clad in life jackets, washed ashore in Basswood Lake about the time we did our swamping test. They hadn't drowned but died of the cold. They had been out fishing for trout and simply tipped over and didn't know the proper procedures to get to shore or else they were too far out in the middle to get in before hypothermia set in.

The rest of June and July the temperature was a bit below normal and the lakes never did warm up enough to make swimming comfortable. By late July the sky clouded over every day and it stayed unseasonably cold. A weather system moved in and then never left. Every day it rained or drizzled for 17 days in a row. We saw the sun for two hours one day for the whole month of August. Each day it would cool a bit more until the morning of the twelfth of August, when my crew woke up on a campsite on Crooked Lake to find half an inch of ice on the bottoms of our overturned canoes. The crew was in shock at how cold it had become as was I. Later that morning as we paddled back toward the base we dodged snow squalls on Crooked Lake and as we passed Table Rock we saw that the snow had begun accumulating on the grassy areas. You just couldn't put on enough clothes to stay warm in the wind and the damp air.

At lunch, seeing how chilled the crew was, I ordered us to a vacant campsite where we built a fire to try to warm up around. I promised hot soup and hot cocoa for lunch but the crew huddling around the fire nearly cut off its air supply and it took a while for the pots to come to a boil. When a pair of dirty grey wet socks was hung over the soup pot on a stick to dry I had to draw the line. I told the crew to start a second warming fire so the food would not be ruined by an unwashed day old gray sock falling in the pot.

The horrible weather had not only dampened the spirits of the crews traveling out from the Scout base but killed the enthusiasm of the guides as well. Usually eager to head out on a trip, the guides became reluctant to plan anything but the easiest of routes. The cold wet windy weather caused an excessive number of injuries that summer as well. Donnan Christianson broke his leg severely as the wind twisted his canoe as he was flipping it up on his shoulders. He had to be taken to his home in Duluth where his dad, a physician, set and pinned his leg. He was out for the summer. Another Guide, Joel Pickens, was picked up bodily by the wind as he flipped his canoe. He was thrown into rocks, tearing muscles in his back. Mike McMahon had his ulcers act up and he spent some time in the hospital as well. Jim Bachman got blood poisoning from blisters he got trying to walk back to the base from Ely. Bill Quinn suffered shoulder separation because of his slight build and had to take it easy the rest of the summer. I got a case of atheletes foot or jungle rot that was so severe I was leaving bloody footprints and had to be sidelined for a couple weeks until I healed up. A car crash that summer sidelined a couple more staff. All together 12 of the 60 guides spent time in the hospital that year. It was a summer most of the staff wanted to forget because of the misery they went through.

Nearly every trip even in a good weather summer has a day of rain or wind. Conquering adversity strengthens the spirit. A trip made difficult by the weather is still a memorable trip for the scouts so the staff tried successfully for the most part to make the excursions into the woods full of unforgettable experiences for the scouts. Fish were still caught, wildlife observed, meals cooked over campfires, and routes were traveled. Stories were told around the campfires at night and the hardships and difficulties became part of the tales to be told by the scouts to their friends and families back home. Ah . . . the memories.

49

THE GIGANTIC FISH

My son, Matt, seventeen, was enjoying a ten-day canoe trip with me and a bunch of his teen-age friends. He loved to hunt and fish. I had enjoyed teaching him all the skills I had learned by experience over the years. He had grown into a big strapping boy, and had become strong enough to carry a canoe. I have forgotten who the other crew members were on this particular trip, since we have taken so many to the boundary waters, but I'll never forget the day Matt hooked into "the gigantic fish." We were camping at Rebecca Falls on the Canadian side of the Boundary Waters in the Quetico* Provincial Park. The 30 foot high falls is about two easy paddling miles north of the Canadian border where Iron Lake spills its water north into McKree Lake. It is, in my opinion, the most beautiful spot in the whole park. The Canadian Quetico/ Park wilderness covers over 1000 square miles. Canoeing is the only means of transportation among the myriad interconnected lakes and streams in the summertime.

Dividing the falls into two separate cascading torrents is an island of perhaps five acres. We had pitched our voyageur tents* at the base of the falls. The campsite is not a four star rated spot but commands an awesome view and boasts of great off shore fishing. At night, we were lulled to sleep by the roar of the water that went by just outside our tent door. The larger falls on the right side of the island has some excellent bass fishing in the fast water flowing about 100 yards out from the bottom of the falls. Sometimes all you bring in is the head of a fish on your line because you didn't crank in the fish quickly enough to prevent a large northern pike* from biting it off. If you cast a lure into the current below the falls, the circular movement of the water will work your lure for you in a big loop. More than once, I have caught a bass* and a northern* together on the same lure, as the bigger predator fish hooked himself going after the already hooked bass. Right at the very base of the falls is a big flat rock where the water swirls past on its way into McKree Lake. We call this swirling eddy "the black hole." If you stand on the rock as you bring in a fish, or your lure, and pause for a couple of seconds before you lift your lure or fish out of the water, often a northern pike of Olympic size will come up out of the swirling, dark depths. Right at your feet, it will make a lunge or a flashing 3-foot leap out of the water as it goes after your lure or hooked bass, so you have to be ready.

On this particular warm, sunny morning however, we had no luck at the large falls so we walked about a hundred feet over to the left side of the island and were casting out into the fast water below the smaller falls. We were using ultra-light gear to make it more exciting. This falls is only about 15 feet wide, but the water smashes against pillars of rock called Ely greenstone as it tumbles down the 30-foot drop to the lower lake. The falls could be more aptly described as a roaring cascade, as it has no single drop. It certainly would be a disaster to fall in or have your canoe sucked into the current at the top. At the very base of the falls, below an imposing, overhanging cliff is a small spot of flat, calm water beneath some overlooking cedar branches. Standing on the slanting rock above me, Matt thought he would try to skip a small shad rap* into the spot of calm water, although that would not have been my lure of choice for that small spot. I was fishing with a black and white jointed rapala*, standing on a rock shelf about 50 feet further down the rocky ledge. Matt heaved a mighty cast over the fast water aiming for the calm spot. He overshot his mark and his orange bellied, perch look alike, shad rap bounced off the rock cliff behind his target, but his lure fell just right into the calm spot. He waited a few seconds and just as he was about to twitch his rod tip to bring the lure to life, there was a big swirl as a fish gulped down his lure and disappeared. It made a mad dash for the boiling cauldron of foaming water below his ledge and headed for the bottom.

"I got one!" he yelled to me and I glanced up to look. His rod was bent over double and it wasn't twitching. "You're snagged," I shouted back at him above the roar of the falls. "Not either" he said. "I saw a fish take it!" "If you know for sure it's a fish," I told him, "you gotta gently horse it out of the fast water and get it down in the calmer water by me, or you will never get him landed". He carefully adjusted his clutch* on the reel and eased the fish off the bottom. His reel began to scream as the fish made a run out into the lake, and soon he was scrambling down the rocky ledge to me yelling "Outta my way", trying not to run out of line and hoping to keep up with the fish. Cranking in as fast as I could, I scampered out of his way and tossed my rod to the side. I lit up a smoke and prepared to enjoy watching the action.

It was apparent that this fish was going to be huge as Matt had very little control over what the fish wanted to do or where it wanted to go. Matt nearly ran out of line several times, as the fish fought with the line, making long runs to the bottom. Slowly it tired, as Matt continued to carefully horse it off the bottom, where it seemed to want to sit, and let it run several more times. His lightweight line was only six pound test so he kept his reel clutch adjusted loose to prevent the line from snapping. After about ten minutes, we glimpsed a big flash of white as the bright sun reflected off the side of the fish when it briefly surfaced about 50 feet away. Wide eyed, with mouths agape we both exclaimed, "Wow did you see that!!!"

After a 20 minute battle fighting the fish and with arms tiring, Matt shouted "Dang it!" "He must have broken the line" Matt moaned, as he dejectedly began reeling in. The line had gone limp and he cranked in hoping the fish had only spit out the lure so at least he could get it back. As the line came in we were both shocked to see that it had gone limp because the fish was swimming right up to us. Two inches of leader was sticking out of a giant northern pikes mouth. We both were elated because the monster looked like he had hooked himself good. "Hope he doesn't chomp through the 20-pound steel leader with his razor sharp teeth" I worried. We had no good plan on how to land him.

This monster northern pike was nearly five feet long and about five or six inches between his eyes. His body girth had to be at least 24 inches. "Was he on steroids?" I wondered. I would guess his weight at 35-40 lbs. He was a leviathon . . . strong, with sharp teeth and dangerous to handle. We had no net, no club, no gaff or a gun. A second passed as we debated whether to jump in and alligator wrestle him on to the bank. I cast a quick glance around but saw no big logs close by on the bare rocks to club and subdue him.

The fish made the decision for us. He opened his mouth, vomiting out a three pound bass that had originally gulped down Matts lure. The unfortunate Bass, still alive, was well hooked with the lure entirely engulfed in his mouth and the hooks safely out of the giant northern pikes way. "Oh no . . . take it-take it-take it!!!" Matt whispered hoarsely as he tried to stretch out his pole to urge the northern to grab the bass again. The gigantic fish cooperated and proceeded to rip the bass apart with a feeding frenzy that made us wonder if he was akin to a shark, and that maybe we were fishing in the ocean. "I swear I'll never skinny dip in this lake again." I gulped, vowing never to risk the loss of fingers or toes or worse, my family jewels to instant amputation by hungry fish.

But alas, the fish heard or saw us up on the bank from his underwater lair. He suddenly stopped his feeding and literally backed up a foot or so to get a better look at us. We saw his big, silver dollar sized eyes roll upward as he scrutinized us. He evidently didn't like what he saw, so he gave a flick of his tail and silently submerged like a big submarine and he was gone. I won't print the words Matt used as he threw his rod down in despair and burst into tears. I said, "This is one fish story you can tell over and over again." And thus, I have shared it with you, the reader, and if you ask me about this tale "I will swear that I have not stretched the truth one bit!"

50

THE BULGUR BRIGADE

The summer of 2000, seven of my friends and I embarked on a 12 day trip into the boundary waters that has come to be known as the bulgur brigade. The idea for the trip was proposed by an old friend from my guiding days, Johnny Oosterhuis. We had become reacquainted, after over forty years apart at the guides reunion, an event held every other year in Ely, at the Northern Tier High Adventure Boy Scout Camp*. He had been going on trips with Butch Dieslin and his friends each year and said we should plan a trip as well. "Would you come along?" I asked. "Absolutely" he responded. I thought it would be a great time to get reacquainted with John and would also be a great time for my son Matt to go and see some of the rest of the Quetico* that he had only heard about through my stories. After all I wasn't a spring chicken anymore and who knew how long I would be in good enough health to make a trip that ambitious again.

Plans were made. Permits were secured. Preparations began. John is a decorated and retired Viet Nam veteran. His plan was to pack his gear and arrive on his motorcycle at my house a day early to help with the final preparations. Matt and I had a busy summer in our construction business and as the day of departure neared we found ourselves with a lot to do in a short time. We had decided to drive up in my big white van but it needed brakes badly. We tore off the front tires and had parts laying all over as we frantically searched for a new set of front discs. We had dug out a lot of our gear but hadn't yet purchased the food. The canoes were still on the rack up in my carport . . . We weren't ready by any means.

John showed up at my house in South St. Paul after a ride up from Bettendorf, Iowa. He parked his big cruiser motorcycle and tried to enter the gate to the side of my house where he came face to face with my Cane Corso Mastiff. Rocco was as scared of John as John was of him and Rocco nearly blew him out of his shoes barking at him. Soon they were great friends as John saw through his bluff. John was a bit disconcerted as he surveyed the state of our preparations. As a military man John was used to things being very organized and everything in its place. I told John to be cool and not to worry and that everything would work out. We finished the brakes with daylight to spare. We made a quick trip to REI* to pick up the last few items of equipment. Then it was off to the grocery store to buy the food for the trip. Back at home later, we packed the food in plastic bags and got everything labeled. We took down the canoes and tied them on the vehicles. After a short nap we jumped in the trucks and headed north in the wee hours of the morning eager for our adventure to begin. Five hours later we were eating breakfast at Vertines' Cafe in Ely. An hour later we were at the Moose Lake* landing, off loading all our gear. We stowed our vehicles at the Scout base just up the road.

Finally on the water, we relished wetting our paddles and were soon at Prairie portage* to pick up our fishing licenses and camping permits. All of our crew members were fairly experienced paddlers and by late afternoon we reached Singing Brook Portage between Burke and Sunday Lakes. We opted to stop because of the threatening weather. We had hoped to get to Louisa Falls on Canadian Lake Agnes but made it there early the next day. John got to swim in the bathtub below the falls but the rest of the crew were reluctant because of the cold water as it was only mid June. I don't believe John had ever gotten to swim in it when he guided and wasn't going to miss the opportunity. We portaged up the steep falls and paddled away to the north in Louisa Lake stopping for the night in Farquier Lake. The pots got badly coated with soot because of the resinous pine we were burning. John had brought his gas stove and used it to make coffee each time we camped but we preferred using wood for fuel because of its abundance and the speed at which we could cook. A wood fire warms one up as well and we spent many a night telling tales around the campfire.

The guys didn't know what to make of John for a while. They never knew when he was serious or kidding. John and I played to each other often and had the guys guessing a lot of the time. We fished the whole trip, trolling a lure out of each canoe almost all the time. John couldn't get over our giant tackle boxes and big lures but he went with the flow. We kidded him about his little ultralight rod and tiny lures that he had brought but he caught fish too and his were better eating size.

As both John and I were returning to our old stomping grounds that we hadn't seen in 35 years we were amazed at how much of the forest on Kawanipi Lake had burned. It must have been the big fire in 1991. We saw that the big log jam that had been in place since 1900 had washed out of Chatterton Falls on Russell Lake. We loved the campsite on Sturgeon a few days later. It is a sand beach nearly a quarter mile long. This part of Canada known as the Canadian Shield* is mostly rock, water and trees. Beaches are a rare sight.

John had never been down the Maligne River that was the next segment of our trip. After the river we gathered to eat lunch and after looking at the map, I suggested we take the short cut portage from Tanner Lake to the Darkey River rather than paddle the six miles it would take to get to the same spot without taking the portage. We wondered why the portage was labeled Eat-Em-Up on the map. A hundred yards into the portage I remembered taking the portage years before and knew how bad the trail was but we were committed to taking it. An hour or so later we were scraping the mud off ourselves and laughing about the swamp but I don't think any of us would want to ever take the trail again. We were soon camping on the big point in Darkey Lake and fishing for bass* with top water lures. We caught a few but didn't have the great luck that I remembered from years past.

We moved on through Argo and Roland Lakes marveling at the clear water. We were held up by big, close, roller waves at the end of the Darkey-Argo Lake portage and had to wait for the wind to abate. The waves were so high and so close together we shipped a lot of water before we got across. We finally arrived at our favorite spot . . . Rebecca Falls. We set up camp and the fishing lines came out.

During the trip we saw a bear and a moose and several deer as we traveled. We saw bald and golden eagles and turkey buzzards feeding on a carcass. We caught a number of big fish but I think Parker West had the biggest with a northern weighing in at about 16 lbs. Our trip took us to most of the major waterfalls in the park notably those of the falls chain and the Basswood River. The crew faced adversity with a smile and took the cold weather and muddy portages all in stride. John was impressed. We learned much from him . . . new tent styles and camping equipment, clothing and different ways of camping. I believe he learned from us as well that the old tried and true ways of camping still work well. I was impressed that in spite of his organized military background that he allowed us to lead and to do most of the trip the old fashioned way, and that he was able to fit in with our loose and disorganized style of camping that still worked out well in the end. If I would give John a call and say we were going again he would say "Sign me up!"

In addition to our long trip, I took two short week-end trips that summer. The next summer I had planned to go to the Ukraine on a short term mission trip. Upon taking a routine physical, longstanding problems with my heart were found that necessitated triple bypass surgery. I didn't get to go to the 'north country' that next summer but have made several trips since. I have to say that I never knew I had problems that serious and the symptoms had accumulated so slowly that they were unnoticed. I am glad that I didn't drop dead that summer on the very strenuous trip that we took.

51

THE GRANDKIDS GREAT ADVENTURE

Memorial Day weekend of 2005 was when our canoe trip turned into a great adventure for my two grandchildren, Zach and Becca and my son Matt's fiancée Michelle and her boy Gene.

We were able to procure the last permit available for the Moose Lake area for the Friday before Memorial Day, so we loaded up our gear and cleared out the cupboards for food for the trip we planned. All the kids had been on a trip to Wind Lake the year before so they had a pretty good idea of what it would be like this time.

Zack was well into puberty and was growing like a weed. He must have grown six inches the last year and lost a lot of his baby fat. Matt and I were hoping he would be able to portage a man-sized load this time. The portage into Wind Lake from Moose Lake is a half mile and has a pretty good climb to it right at the beginning. Becca was still a skinny little mouse of a girl that might tip the scale at 60 pounds but she was bright and cheery and wanted to help a lot with the cooking. Gene was the same age as Zack but didn't have the size to portage too heavy a load yet. He planned to be the chief firewood gatherer for our weekend outing. We made the trek to Ely on Friday morning with the obligatory stop at Tobies restaurant for hot cocoa, coffee and caramel pecan rolls on the way. Upon arriving at Ely we ate again at Vertin's restaurant, and then picked up a few last minute items and gassed up Matts Tahoe. Matt roared down the Fernberg road for the last 22 miles of driving out to the public landing at Moose Lake*.

The day looked a bit threatening, and we had some patchy showers on the way up but as we loaded our gear and headed across Moose Lake, the wind was nearly calm and it was cloudy and cool. We made our way to the Wind Lake portage where Matt and I shouldered canoes after we had loaded up the three kids and Michelle, with packs, fishing tackle, life jackets and paddles. Matt and I had to make one trip back across the portage to get the last two packs but in 45 minutes we were on our way up Wind Lake. The day was looking better and better and the kids and Michelle had done great on the portage. We broke out the fishing gear and trolled our way up the lake hoping that the point campsite would be open. Wind Lake is shaped like a three tentacled octopus and the point campsite we wanted was right where the arms joined the head. It would give us easy access to all parts of the lake. Michelle hooked into a four pound northern* with a funny girly looking pink lure. "Beginners Luck" I said but I cast a glance into my tackle box knowing that I had nothing that color available. Shoot! I settled for a blaze yellow Cyclops spoon.

Our desired campsite was available but was covered by five to six big birch trees that the beavers had dropped across the campfire area. We popped up the tents, laid out the sleeping bags, hung the dining tarp and gathered firewood for the next few days supply. The kids wanted a fire right away but we ate sandwiches and headed out fishing instead. Michelle soon caught a beauty of a smallmouth*that weighed four pounds, I landed a seven pound northern and her son Gene caught a three pound largemouth bass*. Matt and Zach also scored hits on northerns. A couple hours later we gathered at the campsite and cleaned the fish for supper. Knowing we couldn't eat them all we released all but one northern and the two bass. We remembered to take pictures first. The boys dissected the fish's stomachs to see what they had been eating and then proceeded to figure out what all the other internal organs were. It had been a good day and Becca had done a good job cooking the fish for an 11 year old. Zacks job was to make chocolate pudding for desert and Gene kept the fire burning. We turned in shortly after dark and as soon as we crawled into our tents it began to rain and kept up for several hours. We were lulled to sleep by the rain drops.

In the morning, it was foggy but promised to clear up and the wind was calm. After a hearty breakfast, we hit the lake again landing another batch of fish to eat. Becca had never caught a northern before and she was the only one who was skunked. Tiring of fishing and with the sun beaming down we took a long leisurely nap in the afternoon. Later on the glassy lake we tried all our top water baits but had no luck. I think the water was still too cold.

On Sunday we fished our way down the first arm of the lake and into Wind Creek. I thought it would be fun for the kids to explore the old logging camp on wind bay at the other end of the second wind lake portage. On the way up the creek we spotted some small insect eating plants on some of the old submerged logs stuck in the creek. The logs were from the logging that had taken place around 1890. The plants we saw were called sundews, and were very tiny and looked like a small sunburst. The rays of the sunburst are covered by a sticky sweet juice that attracts gnats and no see ums, which get stuck to the plant. The plant then digests the bugs to get nutrients that it is lacking because of where it grows.

In the middle of the trail, wind creek doubles back and you have to ford it. I just splashed through not worrying about getting wet but all the others shed their shoes and socks trying to stay dry. We spotted a beautiful bald eagle sitting in a tree close to the trail and found several osprey feathers. At the far end of the portage, I led our group into the dense underbrush and showed them the remains of foundations of several old buildings from the old camp. One was the remnants of an old horse barn nearly 80 ft long. The kids found pieces of a few old hand-blown, cork stoppered whiskey bottles and the door of an old cook stove. I remembered seeing a bucket of double bitted axe heads that I had discovered on a previous trip but the brush was so thick it was difficult to remember where. We gave up the search and hiked back to the canoes. On the second fording of the creek, Matt slipped and fell in getting his backside wet. We arrived at the canoes and fished our way back to camp. Becca landed two nice northerns on the way back.

They weighed three and four pounds respectively and now everybody had caught fish. Another fun day was almost over.

Back at the camp, the ravens that had a nest right over our tents were shooing away an inquisitive eagle. The nest was about three feet across and the birds were interesting to watch. On the downside, they made it difficult to sleep past daybreak as their little one would start in complaining loudly about being hungry. Back in camp, I watched over the kids while Matt and Michelle made one last attempt at catching fish. It began to rain quite hard but soon we had a beautiful rainbow to look at. Becca and I baked a spice pecan cake on the reflector oven* and it turned out great. When Matt and Michelle came back wet and empty handed, they were consoled with cups of steaming gourmet coffee.

On Monday morning, we ate up as much of the leftover food that we could and we had a five-course breakfast. We broke camp and everyone helped out, making short work of rolling the tents and packing. We talked about coming back later in the summer or for sure next year and taking a real trip where we would move every day and paddle to see new lakes and new places to fish. I think we are all up to it.

52

THE SECOND FIRST TRIP
BUT NOT THE LAST

Kathy had passed away from breast cancer the spring of 1996. I did not actively seek a new mate for many years but really missed female companionship. Midge came into my life after my son and daughter in law insisted I meet her and had Midge email me to introduce herself. Midge had lost her husband Tom a few years before so we were in the same boat so to speak. We settled on meeting at the VFW where she liked to go every week to sing Karaoke. We seemed to hit it off right away and made plans to get together again. Soon we had a weekly date night at my house where we played a lot of scrabble with friends. I brought Midge along on a couple of trips to visit our bible camp and the Scout canoe base that were such big parts of my life. Soon she was coming to church with me every week and I got to meet her two boys and the granddaughters. We grew closer and decided to plan on a May wedding.

The wedding was a fun affair with shotguns and camo being the attire and colors marking the event. My brother in Law Dale who is a pastor, as well as Bruce my regular pastor officiated at the event that was held in my house. Dale wore biker leather and Bruce wore a hunting vest and a sidearm. The bride and groom wore camouflage colored outfits. We waited a couple of weeks to go on our honeymoon so we could help my brother move to Montana. Our 6000 mile honeymoon started there and we saw a lot of beautiful scenery out west in the mountains.

Midge had one quite large concern when we planned to join our lives in marriage. It involved all the canoes stored under the roof of my carport. She knew how to swim but was terrified of riding in canoes because as a girl scout she had a bad experience, tipping over in one and not knowing how to swim. I assured her that we would remedy that problem and soon we brought a canoe up to her camper trailer located on a friends' farm near several small lakes. We brought a canoe to a close-by lake and spent some time gliding around the shore catching a few small bass*. Gradually Midge became more comfortable riding on a canoe. I had to remind her to ride on a canoe . . . not in it, letting the canoe roll under you, but keeping your body vertical to keep the canoe balanced. Her confidence improved and we planned for a more ambitious several day excursion to Wind Lake in the Boundary Waters. This would involve planning menus, packing food and equipment to bring, and taking a half mile portage as well as cooking over an open campfire.

We set the date to go and obtained our permit. We brought along my grandson Zachery and a neighbor kid named Carl to help with the portaging. Carl had never been to the boundary waters before and was pretty excited about the prospect of catching some lunkers. Zach had been on many trips and knew just what to do. We brought the boys for a couple of reasons not the least of which was they really wanted to go along. But another reason was that I had jimmied up my knee and I wasn't sure how well I would do on the portage*. The morning of the day we were leaving Midge had a doctor appointment to check cholesterol, blood pressure and ask about her wrist that had been sore for several weeks from a fall she had taken. About two hours before departure she returned telling us the doctor had xrayed her wrist and told her it was broken. He wanted to put a cast on it but Midge said "no . . . I'll just keep wearing my leather wrist brace because we were headed off for a canoe trip and she didn't want to ruin it for us. I'm sure the doc smacked himself in the forehead when he heard that! Whatta gal! So after loading up my jeep with the food and gear and tying on two canoes on the roof we set out for Ely.

We had a pleasant drive north and were soon in Ely doing some last minute shopping. We launched our canoes at the public landing and a few minutes later arrived at the Wind Lake portage. We were both badly out of shape and were glad we had brought the boys along to do the heavy lifting. Midge and I limped and wheezed our way across the half mile portage while the boys' dog trotted the canoes and most of the heavy gear over to the Wind Lake side of the trail, making a couple of trips each. We paddled to the back of the big bay and pitched our tents at the sand beach campsite. We gathered the wood, built the fire and cooked up a great supper. I wanted to impress Midge with what you could make out on the trail so we broiled up venison backstrap steaks for supper and had baked potatoes. A cake made in the reflector oven topped off the good supper.

In the morning we had bacon, eggs and pancakes and brewed up a pot of coffee. Soon we were back on the water wetting our lines and trolling around the shore hoping for some good strikes from the big northerns I knew lay somewhere beneath the surface. Carl and Zack headed to the other side of the bay. Midge and I caught a mix of large and smallmouth bass* and northerns. Midge was mostly a hook and bobber fisherman and I had to convert her to using lures and leaders. She soon had some nice strikes and was running ahead of me in total number of fish caught. Back at the site for lunch we feasted on peanut butter and jelly sandwiches and leftover cake. After lunch we were back to fishing. The boys thought they had a great spot on the opposite side of the bay. Soon we heard shouts and racket from their side of the lake and later met them out in the middle. They looked a little damp. They had hooked a big one and Carl had leaned over too far to try to grab it and they had upset the canoe. They managed to save their poles and the lures that floated but lost a lot of the lures that were divers and sinkers. Even though the water was only six foot deep where they dumped they drifted away from the spot and couldn't relocate where they had lost their gear. We shared from my tackle box so they could continue fishing.

That day had been cloudy but I could see by late afternoon that the cloud bank would pass and I mentioned to Midge that we would see a great sunset. As the sun eased down below the retreating cloud deck the reflection appeared in the glassy lake surface and the whole underside of the cloud bank turned bright red, orange and yellow. We scrambled about with our cameras taking dozens of pictures and ten minutes later the sun was down and it was over. Later in the clear sky that night Midge marveled at seeing the Milky Way galaxy and at how bright the stars were. I had hoped to be able to have her see the aurora borealis too but it did not appear.

We had come in early enough to catch some zees that afternoon and again cook up a great supper. We had fresh fish that Midge liked a lot even though fish is not her favorite meat. We also made a pecan pie with a lattice woven top crust that was fantastic. In the morning we made up a batch of dough that we rolled out on the canoe bottom. We then cut it up with a cup and the top of the bug spray can into raw donuts. After deep fat frying them and rolling them in sugar, cinnamon and nutmeg Midge and the boys pronounced them excellent.

Our luck was holding in the good weather department and we continued a relaxed pace of fishing, sleeping, cooking and enjoying the scenery. Later the next day Midge hooked into a nice fat northern that weighed about eight pounds . . . the biggest she had ever caught. As I held it up over the canoe trying to unhook her rapala* the fish got frisky and I lost my grip. As the fish fell to the bottom of the canoe creating a big ruckus, the rapala hooked the thick part of my left thumb and buried the hook. Then the other end of the lure hooked into my pants in the crotch. Luckily about that time, the fish unhooked himself but left my thumb impaled to my crotch. As Midge turned around in response to my yelp, I was dropping the big fish over the side and reaching for my filleting knife to cut the lure out of my pants. "What are you doing? She screeched, but then gasped when she saw the lure buried in my hand. I cut out the hook from my trousers leaving about a one inch hole by the fly. I couldn't squeeze my pliers hard enough to cut off the barb so I could back out the hook. We opted to paddle carefully back to the campsite so I could work on it on shore with the first aid kit close by. On the way, we came upon a Sommers crew camping near the point and we paddled over asking for some first aid help. They had a big kit and a large side cutter but still couldn't snip off the barb of the hook. Rapala quality! Instead they crunched the barb down flat and I was able to back out the hook tearing only a little more flesh out of the puncture wound. They bound up my hand to the point where I had to say stop. I think it would have been in a cast in a sling if I had let them keep on with the first aid. We thanked them profusely and headed back to our beach.

The next day an old guide buddy of mine from over 40 years ago dropped in to our camp to visit. We traded some of our food stuff to him since he had lost a lot of his to a bear a few nights before. He spotted my bandaged hand and said I should change the bandage to keep it clean. He had some new fangled bandage that would work well for this he said. It did but he neglected to mention it shrinks when it gets wet so that was the next problem we faced. Finally I opted for just a band-aid that would have been enough from the start.

Soon it was time to head back to home in the Twin Cities. We longed for hot showers and fresh clothes and cold sodas. The boys did the hard work again on the portage and soon we were on the road for home. We all want to go again. For next summer we have been putting the pressure on Midges' son Dave and daughter in law Cassi to go with the two granddaughters Haley and Mandy. My renter Skip wants to go too and bring his daughter Raynee. Skip is 6'6" and over 200 pounds so I think between he and Dave the hard work of the portaging will be taken care of and Midge and I, the old geezers, will be able to again limp and wheeze our way over the trail and again have a great time in the woods. I think I will look for some chain mail gloves for handling fish for the next trip. Perhaps a cod piece as well.

GLOSSARY

Alumicraft

A canoe company that makes a popular, very serviceable aluminum canoe.

Aurora Borealis

Colored bands of light appearing in the northern sky at night caused by ionization of the atmosphere.

Bannock

Trail made bread with no definite recipe much like coffee cake with flour and baking powder being the chief ingredients.

Bass

Two varieties of fish found in the boundary waters known for their fighting ability. Largemouth are native, smallmouth were introduced in the 1930s

Blazes

Slash marks made by an axe or hatchet in trees to mark a portage trail path

Bound

This is a slang term referring to the Boundary Waters

Bourgeois

This is a merchant who was in charge of a group of voyageurs heading out on the trail to trade goods with the Indians.

Brush Crash

When plowing through the woods without a definite trail using a compass and axe to mark a trail to the next lake.

BSA

Boy Scouts of America.

Bulgur

This is a cracked wheat cereal commonly used for a hot breakfast. It expands greatly, takes a long time to cook and is filling.

Bushwhack

See brush crash . . . making a portage through the woods

BWCA

Boundary Waters Canoe Area.

BWCAW

Boundary Waters Canoe Area Wilderness.

Camporee

A fun filled weekend camp out by many scout troops.

Canadian Customs

This is the border crossing entry point into Canada. There are two points of entry. Crane Lake and Saganaga. Other entry points must be made with a remote entry permit.

Canadian Shield

A descriptive term referring to a large area of Canada that was scraped down to bedrock during the last period of glaciers.

Catamaran

This is a two or three hulled sailing vessel. Tying two or three canoes together creates one.

Climax Forest

The dominant species of trees that will replace all others if a forest is left unattended for many years.

Clutch

This is a device on an open faced reel that will allow the line to slip if a fish pulls too hard on the line.

Coffer Dam

A temporary usually wooden dam created to raise the water level to make rafts of logs easier to float to another location in a logging operation.

Council

A small sub division of one of the twelve regions of the Boy Scouts of America.

Crappie Flop

This is a slang term referring to the death throes of a creature as it lies dying.

Cyclops

A brightly colored metal spoon lure with a distinctive shape and action.

Daredevil

An old standby spoon lure usually colored red and white but also in black and white and many metal colors and finishes.

Deliar

A small spring loaded scale for weighing fish and eliminating tall tales of fishing prowess.

Duff

The organic matter that piles up on the ground of the forest made up of leaves, twigs and debris that forms humus and eventually soil. It can burn and care must be taken around fireplaces in campsites.

Dutch oven

A covered cooking utensil made of Iron or Aluminum that is used for baking in the coals of a campfire

Echo Trail

A main road leading west out of Ely, Minnesota that threads 40 miles through the border lakes and on to Crane Lake.

Entry Point

A lake or river designated as an official place where the boundary waters can be entered to begin or end a canoe trip

Eutrification

This is the process of erosion where a pond or lake gets filled in or grows over with vegetation over a period of thousands of years.

Fernberg Road

A main road leading northeast out of Ely that runs over 20 miles leading to Moose Lake, Snowbank Lake and Lake one entry points.

Fisher Maps

An American company that provides canoeists with maps of the Boundary Waters area.

Flatfish

A plug lure similar to a Lazy Ike that has a distinctive wobble and is effective on a number of species of fish.

Garbage

This is the middle position in a three person canoe. This rider is responsible for balance, bailing and paddling in emergencies.

Grumman
A very sturdy brand of aluminum canoe that the Scout Base has used for over 50 years

Guide Trip
The boot camp like canoe trip that the guides take in early June to get in shape for the summer canoeing season and to train in the new Swampers (guides in training)

Gunwales
The wood strips inside and outside the sides of a wood canoe, usually made of mahogany.

Hammer Handle
This is an immature northern pike with a big head and a skinny body that has little meat. They are too small to keep for eating.

Holry
A rye cracker used by the Scouts years ago as a trail snack. Now used as a code to holler out to an unknown canoe group. "Holry" If the group is from the scout base they holler back "Redeye"

Hunters Island
This is an area of land roughly tracing the perimeter of Quetico Provincial Park and the border lakes. This perimeter is over 250 miles.

Interpreters
This is essentially, the same as a guide. This persons' responsibility is to lead the scout group into the wilderness and teach them how to camp and canoe properly and safely and to teach them the history and makeup of this unique place of the world

Keel
These are the strips of wood on the underside of a canoe marking the centerline of the bottom side. A prominent keel aids in steering a straight course.

Kettle Pack

These are the packsack that contains all the cooking pots and pans, reflector oven, dining fly, axe, saw, shovel and all kitchen gear. Usually a Duluth A-2 pack was used.

Kickers

This is a slang term referring to outboard motors.

Knife Lake Dorothy

A sweet elderly gal that lived for many years on Knife lake on the Canadian border. She was a registered nurse and sold homemade root beer and candy to passing campers from her cabin on Isle of the pines in Knife Lake.

Large Mouth Bass

A native species of bass. It can be identified by the size and position of the mouth.

Layover Day

This is a day of no traveling or moving of campsites. A time to rest, relax and fish and cook and enjoy the woods.

Lederhosen

Leather shorts held up by suspenders commonly worn in alpine regions of Europe but also popular as sturdy camp wear in the canoe country.

Loon

This is the Minnesota state bird common in the boundary waters that has a haunting, distinctive call. They are black and white with red eyes and weigh about nine pounds and are very beautiful.

Lures

These are inanimate artificial fishing bait that may be wood, metal or plastic replicas of things fish like to eat.

MacKenzie Maps

A Canadian company that provides canoeists with maps of the Boundary Waters

Moose

These are the largest creature in the north woods. An adult bull may weigh over 1200 pounds and have an antler spread up to six feet across.

Moose Lake

This is the name of the lake where the Boy Scout Base is located and the starting point for most of the scout canoe trips. It is six miles from the Canadian border and is about 3 miles long.

Muskeg

Floating bog found in shallow areas of ponds lakes and rivers. Bouncy to walk on, difficult to portage over and slow to form eventually will fill in a lake or pond and turn it into a meadow.

Northern

This is a long, snaky, predatory fish commonly known as a northern pike. They have sharp teeth, do not school up and can weigh up to 40 pounds and grow to five feet long. Probably the most commonly caught fish in the North Country.

Northern Tier High Adventure Base

This is the new name of the Charles L. Sommers Canoe Base when the responsibility for its operation passed from region 10 of the BSA to the National High Adventure program of the BSA.

Old Town

A brand of canoe made by an old established company in Maine. It is one of the oldest and most reliable canoe companies around today.

Orient

The act of placing your compass on your map and turning your map so that north on the map points north like the compass so you can find your way in the wilderness.

Outward Bound School

This is a canoe camping program for teenagers with a program stressing teamwork and self worth and reliance. Its headquarters is located just south of Ely, Minnesota.

Pack Sack Stew

This is a typical last meal on a canoe trip where the cook tries to use up all the leftover food stuffs in one big pot of stew. The recipe color and flavor is different every time.

Painter

The short length of rope tied onto the bow or stern of a canoe used to lash it down at night, or tie it up to a tree on shore.

Petro Glyphs

Ancient Indian paintings found on rock cliffs in dozens of locations in the Boundary Waters. They are believed to be hundreds of years old. The paint used was made with iron oxide and fish oil.

Pike

A category of fish most commonly applied to the northern pike, but also the walleye pike

Portage

This is the trail or path between bodies of water that allow you to travel through the boundary waters. Some are hundreds of years old having been used by Native Americans.

Portage Signs

These are the signs marking the trails and their length. All have been removed to try to let the area return to the wilderness it once was.

Prairie Portage

This is a heavily used trail linking the US and Canada at the end of the Moose Lake chain.

Primus Gas Stove

A small portable one burner stove using white gas as a fuel often used when a fire ban is in place because of dry weather.

Quetico

The Quetico Provincial Park is the Canadian counterpart to the BWCAW.

Ranger Station

A manned cabin where one can purchase Canadian fishing licenses and camping permits. They are located near the main entry points to The Quetico.

Rapala

This is a fishing lure that was originally introduced to resemble a minnow. The original lure was made of balsa wood and came from Finland. The company has expanded, and now makes hundreds of different lures and has captured three quarters of the fishing market. Some are jointed to have a more realistic action.

Redeye

The presweetened beverage mix used by the scout base for years. If you hear another canoeist in the bound yell out Holry, (you can bet it is a scout or former scout from Sommers Canoe Base) so by answering redeye you will identify yourself as a Charlie guide too.

Reflector Oven

A folded up, flat, light weight stainless steel or aluminum contraption that opens into a V shaped oven with a shelf. The oven is used for baking by the reflected heat of a wood fire,

Region 10

This is an old division of the BSA encompassing the Dakotas and Minnesota. The original 12 regions that the US was divided into have been condensed into six today to be more efficient.

REI

Recreational Equipment Incorporated. A store that sells a variety of camping gear.

River Runt

A fat little fishing plug sporting two treble hooks and a metal lip that is no longer made but in its day was a real killer for bass, northerns and walleyes.

Rocker

This is the amount of rise of the keel in the bow and stern of a canoe. A canoe with several inches of rocker turns more easily in white water.

Rod

A unit of measure commonly used on maps to designate the length of a portage. One rod equals 16 ½ feet, or about the length of an average canoe. One mile is 320 rods long.

Rollers

These are tall waves that are tough to paddle through without shipping water. (Water that comes aboard when you don't want it to.)

Ropes Course

An obstacle course set up by the Outward Bound School as a training and confidence building exercise.

Sauna

A steam bath originating in Finland, where the participants sit in a small enclosed building heated by a wood fired stove. Atop the stove are rocks that are doused with water to create steam. The participants switch themselves with birch branches to draw the blood to the surface and open the pores of the skin for cleansing. After working up a good sweat, they would dive into an icy stream or roll in the snow to cool back down.

Scat

The fecal droppings of animals in the woods from which they can often be identified as well as what they have been eating.

Seliga

This is a handmade wooden canoe of highest quality crafted by the hands of Joe Seliga of Ely, Minnesota. Only 750 were made.

Shad Rap

A fishing lure made by the Rapala Company that imitates a small shad.

Shift

A shift at the base consisted of eight or nine crews either coming in from a trip or going out on a trip on the same day.

Sigurd Olson

He was a renowned teacher, naturalist and author who made Ely his home. His great love for the wilderness helped preserve it for future generations.

Sister Crew

When groups came to the base that was too large, they would have to be split into two groups. The other crew was called the sister crew.

Smallie

This is a small mouth bass. Or bronze back.

Soap the Pots

A procedure of coating the exterior of cooking pots, before they are placed over a wood fire, with soap to make the soot easy to wash off. Lathered hand or dish soap, or even shaving cream works well.

Sommers Canoe Base

Charles L. Sommers wilderness canoe base was the original name for the present Northern Tier High Adventure Base that was created for the Boy Scouts of America. The name honors one of the original founders of the base.

Swampers

These are former crew members who have returned to be trained to be guides at the base.

Swamping

This is tipping over your canoe.

Three Man It

This is a situation requiring all three passengers in a canoe to paddle.

Thwarts

The wooden cross members of a canoe between the gunwales that help a canoe hold its shape.

Trout

This is a difficult to catch, deep running species of fish found only in the deepest lakes in the BWCA. It is slow to reproduce. The meat is pink and oily and delicious.

Tumblehome

This is the inward curve of the sides of a canoe.

Voyageur

Frenchmen employed in the transport of goods and furs in trade with the Indians in the 1700's-1800's. They were small and wiry and very strong but seldom lived beyond their thirties due to hernias and syphilis. They wore colorful sashes and hats and plied birchbark canoes through the great lakes and all over Canada and the northern United States.

Voyageur Tents

This is a style of tent like a tall pup tent that could be set up without poles by tying to nearby trees. They were used by the canoe base for a number of years.

Wall Tents

A heavy canvas tent with short side walls use by the canoe base for over 40 years. They weighed nearly 25 pounds.

Widjiwagan

This is a YMCA camp located on Burntside Lake near Ely. They have a very excellent canoe program and a state of the art canoe repair workshop. They only use wood canvas or wood and fiberglass canoes, (no aluminum or Kevlar) some of which are 70 years old. Their canoe campers range as far north as the Arctic Circle.

Wenonah

A modern, Kevlar, canoe favored by campers because of its sleek lines and light weight.

Witched

This is a method of locating water underground, for digging a well. This is done by using a forked stick or bent wire.

Yoke

The center thwart of a canoe that is usually curved and has shoulder pads mounted on it, for comfort while carrying it on a portage.

CPSIA information can be obtained at www.ICGtesting.com
Printed in the USA
LVOW12s1749171213

365746LV00002B/327/P